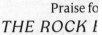

Praise for

THE ROCK EATERS

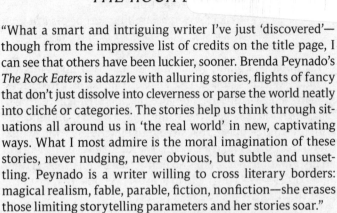

"What a smart and intriguing writer I've just 'discovered'—though from the impressive list of credits on the title page, I can see that others have been luckier, sooner. Brenda Peynado's *The Rock Eaters* is adazzle with alluring stories, flights of fancy that don't just dissolve into cleverness or parse the world neatly into cliché or categories. The stories help us think through situations all around us in 'the real world' in new, captivating ways. What I most admire is the moral imagination of these stories, never nudging, never obvious, but subtle and unsettling. Peynado is a writer willing to cross literary borders: magical realism, fable, parable, fiction, nonfiction—she erases those limiting storytelling parameters and her stories soar."

—Julia Alvarez, author of *In the Time of the Butterflies* and *Afterlife*

"A stunning debut collection comprised of provocative stories that are oddly healing and horizon-expanding. An exciting new voice."

—Jeff VanderMeer, *New York Times* bestselling author of *Annihilation*

"A genre-bending sociopolitical commentary with prose that shines." —*The Washington Post*

"I love Brenda Peynado's big, beautiful imagination and the way her stories open up whole universes of possibility in only a few vivid pages. She is a magical mindbender—in conversation with Karen Russell and Margaret Atwood—who helps us understand the troubling issues of our world through a speculative lens. *The Rock Eaters* will put a spell on you."

—Benjamin Percy, author of *Suicide Woods*, *Thrill Me*, *The Dark Net*, and *Red Moon*

"This book. This beautiful, fierce, tender, aching, and glorious book. *The Rock Eaters* has the range, depth, art, and humanity that is short fiction at its peak. These are stories that demand you sit and breathe after finishing. From rocks that hold sorrow to hands and arms that stretch forever, Peynado's voice is singular. An extraordinary collection."

—Erika Swyler, bestselling author of *Light from Other Stars* and *The Book of Speculation*

"This book is a giant. What staggering reach and ambition Brenda Peynado's stories have: here are aliens, tortured superhumans, angels, sufferings literalized as stones, ritualized drownings, enchanted sleeps, the hauntings of home, all rendered with the kind of power that sweeps us effortlessly from exhilaration to despair and back again. *The Rock Eaters* is the work of an imagination that brooks no limits, that claims, masterfully, all territories as its own. I'm in awe of this book. It's one of the most thrilling debuts I've read in years."

—Clare Beams, author of *The Illness Lesson*

"*The Rock Eaters* is vicious and beautiful, full of characters who will refuse to leave you at peace. Both painfully realistic and mind-bendingly fantastical, these stories capture the sense of displacement that comes with recognizing who we really are. Read it now, and see for yourself."

—Annalee Newitz, author of *The Future of Another Timeline* and *Four Lost Cities*

PENGUIN BOOKS

THE ROCK EATERS

Brenda Peynado's stories have won an O. Henry Prize, a Pushcart Prize, the *Chicago Tribune*'s Nelson Algren Award, selection for *The Best American Science Fiction and Fantasy* and *Best Small Fictions*, a Dana Award, a Fulbright Grant to the Dominican Republic, and other awards. Her fiction appears in *The Georgia Review*, *The Sun*, *The Southern Review*, *The Kenyon Review*, *The Threepenny Review*, *Prairie Schooner*, and over forty other journals. She received her MFA at Florida State University and her PhD at the University of Cincinnati. She currently teaches creative writing at the University of Houston. This is her debut collection.

THE
ROCK
EATERS
STORIES

Brenda Peynado

PENGUIN BOOKS

PENGUIN BOOKS
An imprint of Penguin Random House LLC
penguinrandomhouse.com

"The Stones of Sorrow Lake" in *The Georgia Review*, Spring/Summer 2016. "The Whitest Girl" in *Ecotone*, June 2017, reprinted in *The Pushcart Prize Anthology 2018*. "Yaiza" in *Kenyon Review Online*, May 2017. "The Drownings" in *The Masters Review*, January 2017. "The Great Escape" in *Chicago Tribune Printer's Row*. "The Kite Maker" on Tor.com, August 2018, reprinted in *The Best American Science Fiction and Fantasy 2019*. "What We Lost" in *The Sun*, January 2018. "The Rock Eaters" in *Epoch*, March 2016, reprinted in *Lightspeed*. "True Love Game" in *Ninth Letter*, December 2016. "The Touches" on Tor.com, in November 2019. "The Man I Could Be," in *Hunger Mountain*, May 2017. "Catarina" in *Slice*, October 2018. "The Dreamers" in *The Southern Review*, Spring/Summer 2017. "We Work in Miraculous Cages" in *Quarterly West*, November 2015. "The Radioactives" in *Day One*, September 2017, reprinted as a Kindle Single.

LIBRARY OF CONGRESS CATALOGING-IN-PUBLICATION DATA
Names: Peynado, Brenda, 1985– author.
Title: The rock eaters: stories / Brenda Peynado.
Description: [New York]: Penguin Books, [2021]
Identifiers: LCCN 2020033789 (print) | LCCN 2020033790 (ebook) |
ISBN 9780143135623 (paperback) | ISBN 9780525507277 (ebook)
Subjects: LCGFT: Short stories.
Classification: LCC PS3616.E96 R63 2021 (print) | LCC PS3616.E96 (ebook) |
DDC 813/.6—dc23
LC record available at https://lccn.loc.gov/2020033789
LC ebook record available at https://lccn.loc.gov/2020033790

Printed in the United States of America
1st Printing

Set in Jaquen Regular
Designed by Sabrina Bowers

For Micah,
who brings magic to my story

Contents

THE ROCK EATERS

Thoughts and Prayers

The morning before the school shooting passed like any other, all my neighbors out at dawn performing oblations to the angels on our roofs. Families clustered around the sidewalks, mist from our lawns swirling around our ankles, looking up at the angels' pale humanoid faces and downy bird bodies perched beside our chimneys. Our mothers beat their breasts, performing sorrow for the tragedies that always went on elsewhere in the world. Our parents yelled their usual "Thoughts and prayers! Thoughts and prayers!" toward the angels atop our roofs. As children, we were supposed to kneel in the moist grass and be quiet, in case the angels were ever to speak.

The angels, for the most part, barely noticed. They chewed their cud from the grasses and bugs they scavenged during the night and then shat runny white on our roofs, the shingles looking iced with snow despite the Florida heat. When I was in kindergarten, we'd thrown rocks at them to get their attention, but they'd just turned and resumed their silent watch over the neighborhood.

My parents began the ritual, already dressed in their work clothes, looking as polished as a photograph in front of our freshly painted stucco house. I was obedient in my stiff school clothes—my mother never allowed me to stumble outside in my pajamas like some of the other kids.

There was no greater argument in our house than when my mother thought I had done something unworthy of our angel.

Out of all the angels, ours was considered the most blessed of the neighborhood. When my parents came to this country after college, this house was the first one they looked at, and their immigration papers arrived miraculously within the week. While others searched for homes and jobs for months, my parents sailed into their new life, prayed gratefully to their new rooftop patron. When the economic downturn came and brought with it a plague of layoffs, my mother was able to keep her tech job, and my father flourished in a financial field that boomed in downturns ("Betting on failure," he called it). The hurricane tore apart most roofs in our Florida suburb, but not mine. Every day my mother returned to the house, pulling into our drive, she breathed a great sigh as she saw our angel perched beside our chimney: albino faced, sleek winged, dumb eyes that looked at nothing. At our basketball games the parents cheered for us, but it was known that the real game was played silently among the angels.

Across the street, my best friend Rima Patil's family kneeled in front of their ramshackle house, the embarrassment of the neighborhood: mold blooming on the stucco, brown waves along the roofline where the gutters and wooden fascia had fallen into disrepair, a bright blue tarp over the roof above Rima's room, where a hurricane had downed a tree, just barely missing their angel. The blue tarp rolled and snapped like a flag of shame.

Rima's family was known to have the worst angel on the

block. Her dad was one of the first to get laid off, lose health insurance. Her older brother had developed schizophrenia and claimed that the angels gave him secret messages; the family didn't have the money for his medications. The bank had visited their house three times in the past month. When the hurricane hit, the oak tree in front of their yard not only punched a hole in the roof, but also fell onto the family car. The tarp they placed over it leaked mist and bugs and occasional angel guano. That they were the one Hindu family in a neighborhood of Latino Catholics was not lost on my mother, though the fact that they were even darker than the rest of us, my mother pretended not to notice. Rima was wild, a force of nature, and my mother was known to count this as one of Rima's mother's misfortunes. Nothing terrible had happened to Rima's sister, Shruti, yet—she was valedictorian, a national-prize cellist, who radiated beauty—but we were all waiting; there was a sense that she would not be spared. It was Shruti Rima got her strength from, though while Rima's came out in recklessness and force, all elbows and knees, her sister had merged it with a softness that came out in glory when she played music. I idolized Shruti for her ability to walk the line between strength and obedience, her ability to get away with doing what she wanted while still looking like a saint—unlike Rima, who fooled no one, and me, feeling caged and wanting desperately to do something unforgivable.

Rima winked at me and then resumed solemnity, leaning on her fists in their overgrown grass. Her long black braid flicked with the impatience of a cat's tail as she turned back, echoing how it often weaponized into a whip on the basketball court. Her sister, Shruti, inclined her head as if she were still at her cello, her own long black hair draping over one shoulder. I knew Shruti had woven Rima's braid, had raked her deft fingers through the silken mess, had crooned a Carnatic composition as she worked. For the moment, Rima's lanky brother, Rajiv, was quiet, his eyes sallow from sleeplessness, instead of having his usual energy. Their mother beat her chest with one hand and kept her other hand dug into Rajiv's elbow in case he started with one of his outbursts. Their father, still in his pajamas, gritted his teeth and barked, "Thoughts and prayers," like it was being dragged out of him. Back in Bengaluru, they'd had other words, other rituals, for the angels on their roofs.

The angels above us looked on into the distance, snapping their mouths to eat mosquitoes from the air.

How could I have known that this would be the last time I would see all of them together, that unlucky family? If I had known, what would I have done to protect them?

Sunrise bled hot over the roofs like a punctured yolk, another day given to us. Neighbors quieted and rose from kneeling on their lawns. Kids sprung up, suddenly released from piousness to get ready for school. I lunged for my backpack by the front door and dashed across the street.

Rima grinned in greeting, leaning against the crumbling stucco of their front stoop with a swagger. Behind a bush that had overgrown the half wall of their stoop, I showed Rima a tube of lipstick that I'd snatched from my mom, a cocoa pink. It wasn't Rima's style—she always went brazenly bare, glittering only with the sheen of sweat, though her parents forbade her nothing. But this small rebellion assuaged the hot throb in my chest.

"Yeah," she said. "Do it."

I painted my mouth jaggedly with the tube, my trembling excitement and the sharp line of my fear of my parents' no-makeup rule getting the best of me.

Shruti emerged from the house, backpack slung cleverly over one shoulder, her hair draped over the other. Shruti could wither anyone with a look, and her arm around your shoulder made you hum with joy. She clicked her tongue at me in pity, cupped my chin with cool fingers calloused by cello strings, dragged her fingernail along the edges of my lips to fix the colored mess.

Rajiv flung open the door, and he gave me a thumbs-up. His smile transformed his tiredness, and I noticed his bravery despite the voices that tormented him sometimes, despite what the angels told him. It was never good. The angels always said it wouldn't end well for him, but that for the rest of us there was still a chance. And yet he faced each new day with a bright smile. "Give 'em hell," he said now.

Surrounded by the bold three of them, I could pretend I was the fourth, fear of getting caught breaking the rules melting from me like candle wax.

"Stay good, kiddos," Shruti said, running a swipe of her hairbrush through her hair.

Rima rolled her eyes, any entreaties to behave sending her instead slingshotting off into trouble. "I'll race you, Paola."

Rima and I ran together to the bus stop, cutting through lawns, kicking up morning moths into a fraying cloud of white. She pulled ahead, her braid licking the air in front of me, and I followed after her, trying to close the gap. Shruti, Rajiv, and the other kids of the neighborhood streamed behind us, the daily pilgrimage. We had every reason to believe the day was bright ahead of us and we would survive it.

At school during recess, a boy on the basketball court got in front of us in a game of horse. "Wait your turn,"

I yelled, but that was as far as I let myself go. The boy turned around and said triumphantly as his wrist cocked and the ball swished into the net, "Go back to your country." Rage boiled in me. Rima grabbed his collar and flung him toward the back of the line. He tripped, spilled on the ground with his palms burned raw. Then Rima and the boy whirled in a fast-moving cluster as they fought on the court, him pulling her hair and her fingers around his ears, wrestling him to the floor. Police lights flailed once in the parking lot of the middle school. Two policewomen whispered to the teacher supervising recess, who turned pale and called for Rima. The boy, upset because he had always expected to have the right to call us whatever names he wanted, shook the hair out of his eyes, and stood up straight like he was innocent, and pointed at her. I thought the police were arresting Rima—for just being her fierce, untamable self. She'd been unlucky again, with her defective angel. I was afraid for her, and I knew horrible things could happen to people under police protection. I promised Rima that I would never leave her alone, that I would commit a crime just so they'd put me in jail with her, and I could be her witness if anything happened.

She laughed. "I'll be back before you know it." She squeezed my hand and let me go. She fixed her braid and walked toward the officers with a bounce. While I bucked the expectations that came with having a good angel, Rima owned that she had a bad one, wore her family's misfortunes with a grin that looked as dangerous as a lion's mouth. She made life bearable for me beyond my perfect handwriting, my straight As—life with her full of streaking across sidewalks and lawns like fireballs, secret desires whispered and let loose, the challenge in her eyes to reach for just a bit more than we were given. I knew that the only thing I ever did right was attaching myself to her, inviting her over even when my mother turned her nose up at their cursed family. When they led her away that afternoon, one of the officers putting a heavy hand on her shoulder, she didn't look back. I noticed, perplexed, that a few other kids were led away from their classrooms to the back of the patrol car.

After the end-of-school bell, my mother surprised me by being in the car line instead of having me get on the bus. I'd forgotten to wipe off the last of the lipstick from earlier, and my mother took a rough paper towel to my mouth. My lips stinging, rosaries swinging from the rearview mirror, my mother explained as she drove what had really happened:

Shruti had been in the high school music room. I imagined her curtain of hair swinging over her cello as she played. The arts magnate high school bused in musicians, painters, theater kids from across town, and Shruti was the only one from our neighborhood. It was study hall period for her, so there was no one else in the music room, and her continuous, transcendent playing must have covered the pops of gunfire, the gunman going classroom by classroom. After the boy—a white kid, someone Shruti had had no interest in going out with but who had never accepted "no" for an answer—left the music room, she was found slumped over her cello as if she'd given up on song. Fifteen other kids dead, twenty-eight injured. The boy, when he reached the end of the one long corridor, locked himself in the bathroom, looked in the mirror, and shot himself, sparing the hidden schoolmate who trembled over a toilet.

"So he's gone," my mother concluded. "And you're safe."

As we pulled into our driveway, my mother threw her eyes up to the roof where our angel was perched, as if not to anger its goodwill as she spoke. Across the street in Rima's house, their curtains were closed. Their minivan was gone. Their angel squatted between the chimney and the hurricane tarp, wings folded shut.

Rima's family didn't come home for hours, and I kept one eye on their empty driveway while I watched the news, looking for the Patils. I still couldn't believe it. Three shootings had happened across the country that day, but I only watched the coverage for Shruti's high school: cops swarming around the building, yellow police tape, reporters jamming microphones in the faces of kids who'd survived, shaken and sobbing. Someone's best friend, someone's boyfriend, someone's daughter. Someone saying the boy had given off all kinds of red flags. Someone else saying apologetically that he seemed like a really nice guy. I wanted to understand why that boy did it, incredulous that the balance Shruti had always walked between being good and being brave had betrayed her.

The news patched in an interview with a gun rights activist and then one with a member of the Mothers for the Sanctity of the World, who were still touring at the location of a two-days'-previous school shooting. The Mother focused on blessedness, on calling on the protection of the angels, and she punctuated her impassioned speech with a swing and rattle of small relics tied up her arm. She was full of prayers for the souls of the lost, but full, too, of threats for potential shooters. The Mothers, all of them white ladies, toured the country with their families, handing out guns, training, and T-shirts from their sponsors, staging armed marches protesting anyone who would stand against them, shooters and gun control pacifists alike. They were mothers of school shooting survivors, those lucky few children in the right classroom, who huddled behind the right desk, who asked for the bathroom pass at just the right time. In the background of the interview shot, their giant red tour bus grumbled its engine. They were heading to one of the new school shootings that had happened today, along with the Good Guys with Guns and the Innocents, what they called their husbands and children, their great pilgrimage through the year taking them from slaughter to slaughter.

"Turn the TV off," my mother said from the kitchen table where she had spread out her files and laptop. "Do your homework. You can't let this put you behind in school."

"What," I said, "I'm not even allowed to react?"

"You barely knew her. It's Rima that's your friend."

How could I justify the volcano inside me, the feeling that at any moment it could erupt out of me? I ran upstairs to my room and slammed the door, felt the walls shake, and hoped the trembling could be felt all the way to the roof.

Exactly what my mother had been afraid of. "Paola Margarita, we do not slam doors in this house!" she screamed. "Don't antagonize our angel!"

Later, my father came home, bags under his eyes packed full of others' misfortune. Usually he was at the bank until midnight, and I barely saw him but for tired weekends. There was so much failure in the world, he had tried to explain to me once, and it was his job to track it, predict it, place fund money where he could make a profit when tragedy struck. Today, like most days, he must have made a fortune. So many angels letting their families down. He plopped the takeout he'd brought home on the dinner table next to my mother's files. For a fleeting moment when my parents looked at each other, I saw that they felt helpless, powerless, worn down. But then I blinked, and they transformed into their usual disguises and defenses, the perfect successful family, the daughter who would go far, who would never be shot. Even their momentary weariness, their swift recovery, had been a lesson on being good.

After dinner, the Patils' minivan, still scraped up and dented from hurricane treefall, finally came down the street. When they all got out, the four of them, I kept waiting for one more, and then remembered that Shruti would never come out of that van again. A fever of shame and want, terror and grief, surged in me, and I ducked underneath the living room windowsill.

"Leave them alone," my mother called. "They don't need you in the middle at a time like this." And of course that's how my mother saw me: someone that needed to be restrained even in the midst of grief.

I snuck out the back door, the Florida sunset a blood red over the roofs, all the angels glowing a mourning pink. Rima saw me coming and let me in.

I'm not sure what I expected. Wailing, storms of human need, a funeral. Another part of me wanted them as they used to be: Rima's dad hollering to "forget about the angels, Paola" in the garage over the last woodworking project he was trying to sell on Craigslist after he'd lost his job, Rima's mother laughing at us from the kitchen where she prepared her catering as we ran amok around the couches, Rima and her brother joking with each other on one of his good days, Shruti's cello bellowing from her room.

Instead, there was mostly silence. Downstairs, Rima's mom was facedown on the couch in shock, the pale soles of her brown feet sticking out from a muslin sheet that covered her, too tender and raw and exposed. Her father sat blankly in the garage. Upstairs, Rajiv was quiet; the angels had stopped speaking to him.

Smothered with loss, I tiptoed up the stairs, trying not to step into the Patils' angel's ray of misfortune. Rima's shoulders rippled as we went up, her strength like she could hold up the roof if it fell. Except when we got back to her room, both of us on her bright orange comforter stained with ceiling popcorn and angel dung, the blue tarp waving and snapping above us with wind, Rima laid her head in my lap and began to sob, telling me what had happened.

I wanted to curl down with her, seeing even her, previously unvanquishable, laid low. Next door I heard Rajiv beg the angels to speak to him, but what he thought they could do, I couldn't hear through the walls. What could any of us do? Anyone with a gun could decide that the world was better off without us.

Ceiling popcorn rained down as her angel shifted above us and disturbed the roof. I soothed her heaving shoulders, ran my fingers over her braid. I felt the heavy emptiness next door to her room. Just a few days ago, we'd spent a Saturday with Shruti and her high school friends, a painter and a pianist, lounging on her stale carpet, radio blaring. They'd braided our hair into glorious updos while discussing their college futures and the painter's crush on Rajiv. When a song came on the radio that was Shruti's favorite and she sang along, we all hushed without her having to demand it. Later, when the three of them had headed to a party, Rima and I'd gone to the basketball court looking like queens slumming it, not wanting to shake the updos loose, not wanting to erase her sister's mark on us, the promise of her shining star ahead of us, that we could be deserving of everything we wanted. Shruti, the painter, the pianist—all three of them had been listed among the victims.

I thought about how lucky we were to be alive. But Rima, with her defective angel, might be the next one to go. It had happened before, whole families taken in multiple shootings, or someone who had survived one shooting being taken in the next. Why had I always thought it wouldn't happen here, to us? How could we ever think we were safe?

"There's something else," Rima said, sitting up. "We're moving away."

"What?" I said. I put my hands in my lap.

She told me that they were going as far away from this as possible. They would leave behind Shruti's empty room, go somewhere no one knew her brother's outbursts. The bank had been in the process of reclaiming their home, and now their fight was over. They would escape their disastrous angel.

"I'll go with you," I said. For a moment, I thought I could take Shruti's place, be the sister who balanced confidence and grace, rage in ways that only broke out in piercing notes. I squeezed my hands in my lap, trying to contain the wild thing in me that begged to be let out, to grow teeth and rampage.

Rima pushed me off the bed, mercurial and still wiping her eyes. "Paola, you'll be fine."

I was mourning, I was desperate. If she left, I didn't know what I'd become. I'd let the thing inside me out or I'd become what my mother wanted. Why couldn't she understand? "Stay," I demanded.

Her hands balled up into fists. "You think you can tell me what to do? Just like that boy that killed her? Get out," she said with disgust.

I knew that every command was a dare to her to do the opposite, and now I knew better than to explain or apologize. The rare times she was angry at me, there was no calming her down for days. It had always been Shruti or Rajiv who brokered the peace between us. The house descended again into silence as I closed the door softly behind me. I didn't know if I would ever get the chance to apologize again.

My mother hadn't noticed I was gone. In front of the TV— which blared another interview with a Mother for the Sanctity of the World—my mother pinched a landline between her shoulder and the crook of her neck. She was saying, "Qué tragedia," to a neighbor in a constant refrain. She always worried about what other people would say if our perfection slipped, but it was always her, the one drumming up gossip. Now, my mother held court as the neighborhood queen with the angel most blessed, the tragedy of Rima's family only a stage for her own sanctity. I wanted to scream at her.

But in that moment, my mother seemed the most powerful person I knew. She had always spent that power protecting the world from me, stamping down my desires, slapping my wrists at broken etiquette, disapproving from the first sleepover with Rima of the havoc we could wreak on the world. For once, I wanted her to protect *me*.

I kneeled at her feet, prostrated myself before her as if she were an angel. She tittered, uncomfortable, the phone dropping from her shoulder and clattering on the floor, as if I were the apparition we had always awaited. And wasn't I a miracle, alive in front of her, so much future, so much tragedy ahead of me? Wasn't I what she had prayed to the angels for?

"Mami," I said, a dam breaking open, my forehead touched to the tile floor underneath the fluorescent lights. I was thinking of the line of tragedies I was helpless to stop. "*Do something.* Why won't you do something?"

She picked me up off the floor, tucked my hair behind my ears. I knew I had reached her, and I suddenly believed in goodness again, in working to deserve it, in whatever my mother asked of me.

The morning after the shooting, families across the city kneeled to their angels in grief, the rest of us yelling our thoughts and prayers. This time we added, "Thoughts and prayers for the victims of Bayland High School Shooting!"

Rima's family stayed inside. And Rima, when I caught a glance at her through her window, seemed shrunken, a different person, like this was finally the misfortune that broke her. When they eventually emerged, Rima's mother didn't beat her breast, didn't say the words that allowed the rest of us to go on with our days. Instead she lay facedown in the morning dew of the lawn and wouldn't get up, her hair coming unpinned around her. Rajiv murmured to the angels, his eyes wide and red, his voice getting louder. Mr. Patil yanked Mrs. Patil up. Rima wouldn't look at me, pleaded with her mother like she'd turned into dutiful Shruti overnight. Rima and her father finally managed to drag her mother and brother back into the house, her mother's dress hem unraveling and splotched wet from the grass. The angels on our roofs bit the dew from their wings.

Just as Rima's family cloistered themselves inside their house, a red tour bus came roaring and sighing onto our cul-de-sac, MOTHERS FOR THE SANCTITY OF THE WORLD emblazoned on its side, air brakes exhaling as it came to a stop. The families still gathered on their lawns turned to look, some of them shaking their heads and going back inside, some of them slamming their doors, some of them waving in excitement, all of them adhering to the unspoken rule that one did not talk politics with the neighbors.

The Mothers filed out of the tour bus dressed all in black, scapulars and rosaries swinging around their necks, wearing giant makeshift belts that wove together their relics. Blessed objects made of the most ordinary things: old gym socks, stuffed animals, baseball hats—the touring Mothers had braved the scrape of roof shingles and the threat of long falls to touch the objects to the best angels watching over people who had never known misfortune, imbuing the new relics with blessedness.

Behind the ten Mothers came their husbands and guards, the Good Guys with Guns, machine guns crossed in front of them on straps, their arms slack at their sides as they fanned out across the sidewalk and into the street. And behind them, the Innocents, their children who had survived school shootings, lugged backpacks that sagged with homeschooling books, key chains of relics hanging off them like tails.

I knew from the news that once the tour group was here, they would stage marches, hand out relics and guns for protection, offer prayers and assurances that, this time, our angels would not fail us. If gun control protests competed with their marches, they sent the Innocents in front of them, instructed them to sing through the chants. Though my mother held more faith in being careful to deserve the angels, the Mothers felt that faith and guns were inextricable from each other. Being blessed somehow meant that you could hold weapons and be unscathed by their temptations, their mistakes. The Mothers and the Good Guys were known to say: the angels would make your vision perfect, your aim true. I didn't know how it was possible to know the difference between what you feared and what you were right to fear.

I could tell my own mother watched the crowd coming up the sidewalk with envy. They were social media influencers, leading the right-wing side of the debate on gun control. Sponsors like the NRA and various churches kept them flush in guns, ammo, T-shirts, homeschooling books, and rosaries. Their children corresponded with thousands of pen pal admirers. The Mothers posted Instagram pictures of their marches that got millions of Likes and comments: their children dressed all in white, their families still intact. My mother wanted to command that kind of presence, that kind of clear perfection—in the world, in me.

My mother rose up to her full height and went down the sidewalk to shake the first Mother's hand. I realized my mother had brought them. This must have been her version of what she thought I had asked her to do. She had brought the people who projected the most sanctity, the model children, the Good Guys to try to guide the angels' collective hand. Any house they visited was never known to befall the same misfortune. I had wanted more, had wanted Shruti back, my ignorance back.

Rima stared from her window, her palms up against the glass. Wouldn't she be safe now, now that the street would be adorned with relics, guards with machine guns trained on anyone who would bring us harm? As long as she stayed within the boundaries of their protection, stayed in the neighborhood. Now wouldn't they stay? Rima's mother yanked the blinds closed.

My mother led the tour group to our front door, invited them in. I began to follow, but my mother put her hand on my shoulder, stopping me before I entered the commotion unfolding in our living room. "Ni lo pienses. You're going to school."

I felt hot as a fever, the morning sun already burning down our street. "I don't want to go," I said. "Not after what happened. Not without Rima. And Shruti." What was waiting for me at school, for any of us? What was waiting on the bus, down the street, at the entrances of the mall, in the parking lot? "Mami, I'm afraid," I said.

"Do you think I don't do all of this for you?" my mother

asked. "I'm trying to save you so that you have the rest of your life to look forward to. This is how much I love you." She handed me my backpack and pointed me in the direction of the bus stop. I knew it was me she was afraid of, what was waiting inside to break free, whether in joy or destruction.

I paused in front of Rima's house. Angels pale on all the roofs. No one came out.

Before the school bus pulled me away, I saw Rima's house on one side of the street standing off against mine on the other. Rima opened her sister's curtains. In the back window of the school bus, I opened my arms.

At school, I tried not to look toward Rima's seat, empty as an omen. Our teachers mentioned the shootings, but then moved on to the day's lessons. If they had to stop for every shooting, they said, the whole world would stop. Shouldn't the whole world have stopped? But I didn't know how to stop it. The boy Rima had fought the day before smirked in his chair like he thought some kind of justice had been served by the angels. He mimed a trigger with his hands, the gun going off and pointing straight to me. I hid in the bathroom for all of recess not to have to face him. Was he the boy that in a few years would kill me? I was ashamed that, without Rima, I hid like the student at Bayland High who had survived by standing on a toilet. Then I paced in front of the stalls like a caged animal.

When I ran off the school bus back home, people in Good Guys with Guns T-shirts were patrolling the lawns and backyards of our neighborhood, keeping a lookout for any suspicious intruders. I recognized a few of my neighbors in uniform, guessed they'd been newly converted by the tour group. As I ran past them with the flood of returning children, some other parents snatched their kids inside, snapped their curtains shut, or hammered gun control posters into their lawns.

A bright yellow moving truck in Rima's driveway contrasted with the red touring van on the street. Had Rima forgiven me? Rima, who was straining underneath a small moving box, put it down to give me the X sign with her arms, her signal for now not being a good time to come over, usually to do with one of Rajiv's spells. Now it felt like a goodbye, like it would never be a good time again.

Two Good Guys stationed at the end of my driveway, who swiveled their machine gun scopes anytime they heard a sudden noise, pointed their guns at me. I held my breath, cringed, and made myself thread between them. I could tell they were particularly jumpy, uncomfortable in our suburb full of well-dressed Latinos.

When I opened the front door, Mothers and Good Guys packed the living room, extra guns stuffed in portable lockers lining the entrance hallway. My father was still at work, as usual. I could hear children playing upstairs. They had been blessed, I reminded myself. They had survived. They could teach me to survive.

The Mothers conferred with my own mother and her neighborhood prayer group. They were planning a March of the Innocents. I'd seen the marches on TV before. The children who had survived previous shootings formed a line, walked all the way to the school to bless the halls with their presence. The Innocents paraded through town, singing, swinging relics, handing out pamphlets, cutting through gun law protests. It was part blessing, part dare to anyone who was thinking about killing a mass of children to try to finish the job—not that any of the Good Guys would let that happen, surrounding the children with avenging semiautomatics. The pamphlets they handed out boasted, *Try doing that when we're all armed. Let them pick on someone their own size.* And behind the line of children and their guards, the Mothers prayed, calling on the angels of the roofs they passed.

My mother looked pleased to see me. "You'll be leading the first march," she announced, putting her arm proudly over my shoulders, smoothing down my hair.

Inside myself, I leapt. Finally, I could do something. I could sing at the forefront of something, a Joan of Arc figure leading the charge. I could be both good and brave and empty myself out with yelling.

Through the window, I heard the door of the moving truck rolling down with a crash. Rajiv shouted, then Rima told him that food was ready back inside.

"They're one of the good ones, aren't they?" I heard one Mother whisper nervously to the other.

"That Rajiv," my mother said to the Mothers. "I wouldn't be surprised if one day he was on the news as a shooter."

Alarmed, the Mothers began tittering. "Are they Muslim? Do you think they're terrorists?"

"Oh, no," my mother corrected. "He's never been violent before."

"That's fine," one of the husbands said. "We keep an eye on everyone."

I yanked my arm from my mother and stomped up the stairs, never being able to stand when my mother criticized Rima's family. Before, I had stilled myself with tense restraint, breathed slowly. But now with Shruti gone, her grace disappeared from this earth, for the moment I didn't care if my behavior embarrassed my mother.

Upstairs, dozens of kids plugged up the hallway and my

room, homeschooling books discarded around them. A group of kids my age sat on my bed with a lit pillar candle on a used paper plate, and they were holding hands and singing.

"What are you doing here?" I wanted to bury my face in my pillow.

"Practicing," said a chubby boy wearing a GOOD GUY IN TRAINING shirt with a sponsor list on the back, stopping the song.

"We're right underneath the angel," another said.

I nodded. Rima and I had often jumped on my bed with a broom, pounding the ceiling every time we reached zenith, daring the angel to respond.

Then the door opened with a bang, and Rima stormed into my bedroom. Her red eyes were a rage.

"I'm sorry," I said in a rush. She had wanted me to let her go, and I could, I swore I could.

She scoffed—at me, at the Innocents overrunning my house and sitting on the bedspread my mother had picked out for me where just days ago we had prank-called grocery stores, Rima dialing the number and holding the earpiece. The other line had picked up with "Hello?" and for a moment we had been held in trembling anticipation at what we might do or say.

"So you're the one we're here for," the chubby boy said to Rima.

All the children stopped talking to appraise her. Between them, they had seen so many school shootings, so many survivals, arrived at so many houses of tragedy and slept in the beds of the absent. What was there to say? "We're sorry about your sister," a girl said, finally.

Rima nodded, closing her eyes, setting her jaw against crying, and when she opened her eyes, she was again the Rima whose strength I always trailed after.

A girl took a quick selfie with Rima in the background, uploading it to Instagram with the tags: *New march location! Stay tuned! #theInnocents #survivors #ontothenext #blessings #thoughtsandprayers.*

"We're here to bless you," the chubby white boy said.

"Like hell you are," Rima said.

The boy shrugged, undisturbed. "Want to play good guys and bad guys with us? You can be the good guy this time."

Rima glared at me, stood across the room. But they didn't give her a chance to refuse. They moved like a rehearsed theater group, so used to this, so quick and polished.

They passed out toy guns that felt real, even the metal heft of them, even the tiny speaker that made a discharge when you pulled the trigger. Rima started as a good guy on one end of the upstairs hallway and the boy started as a bad guy on the other. The rest of us were innocents, hiding, kids caught in the cross fire.

When we heard the first gunshot from the bad guy's toy gun, the rest of us scattered. I ran toward my closet and huddled over my shoes, helpless as I was supposed to be. This was how they had survived. I could hear footsteps running across the carpet in all directions, gunshots, kids yelling "Good!" and "Bad!" so that others could tell the difference. The game wouldn't end until everyone had been unearthed from their hiding places, declared for one side or the other. I hoped that Rima would come after me.

Then someone threw the door open to the closet, and there was Rima, the daylight behind her too much to look at, pulling me out. She shot me in the heart with the gun, the hard barrel pressed against my chest, her eyes wide. I flinched, frightened. It sounded so real.

"Good!" she shouted, and then she softened, slipped her fingers into my hand. She had forgiven me.

I wanted the game over. What did it matter which other kids fell around me, which didn't? We were surrounded by shrieks, gunshots, and laughter. "I don't want to play," I said.

"Then we won't play," she said.

The dormer window to my bedroom was open. Rima pulled me to it, climbed onto the roof. I followed, hesitant.

We shuffled toward the angel that perched beside the chimney, trying to keep our balance on top of the fresh angel guano. The angel watched us, calmly chewing whatever was in its mouth despite the shrieks underneath us from those who'd been caught. There it was, the most blessed angel in the neighborhood, and I, the child my mother was constantly trying to whip into shape to deserve it.

A bird smell, sour and musty as a pigeon roost, made me dizzy. Below us was twenty feet down. Over the edge of the roof, the yellow moving truck waited in Rima's driveway to take her away. In the yard, a group of Good Guys led my mother and some of our neighbors through target practice against bulletproof Kevlar they had stretched against my back fence. My heart thrashed against me, my tongue plunked heavy as lead as I swallowed. Our sneakers slid on the roof.

"Stop," I called, just as I slipped forward on all fours and my palms landed in fresh white ooze.

"Since when are you scared?" she said, her hands on her hips at the top of the roof.

I would have given anything to discard my fear then, to chuck it down where it would burst on the sidewalk like a rotten fruit. Instead, I found my mother's voice bubbling out of me. "Maybe don't antagonize them," I said, nodding at the angel.

"You think it's the angels that did this? You think we deserve this?" She was echoing her parents, too.

"How could you say that?" I said.

"Nobody's *doing* anything."

I pointed to the people target practicing underneath us. "They're doing something."

"I've never heard you defend your mother." Rima pulled out the toy gun that had dangled out of her pocket. She was right in front of the angel, which ignored her to peck at its wingtips. She pointed the gun at me. "Are you good?" she asked.

"Don't," I said, trying to keep my balance with my hands up.

She closed one eye and put the other against the barrel, aiming. Her right foot was sliding down the roof.

"Yes, I'm good," I shouted, and it felt like a defeat.

Then Rima slipped, the gun falling out of her hands and clattering down the roof. She collapsed backward against my angel.

It folded its wings over her. I blinked, and it was suddenly like she wasn't even there, disappeared behind white down, only her basketball sneakers poking out from the bottom of the wings enfolding her. I couldn't breathe, the thought of touching the angel after such disrespect sending my heart plummeting like a cut elevator. I wanted to go after her, but there was my mother's voice again, telling me to follow the rules, to wait for the impossible moment when the angels would speak. Rima momentarily disappeared, this was what the rest of my life would be: no one to tempt me, push me, no one to release what was caged inside. Did I feel relief? Instead, I felt like I had lost my own sister. I resolved to be better, to be good, once Rima was gone—but only then. I dove after her.

I forced the angel's wings apart and wrapped my own arms around her, the wings closing back over us. Tiny feathers whirled around us in the sour air. The giant bird at our backs breathed softly, and its muscles twitched. Rima's dark braid draped over my arm, studded with down, the gravel of shingles and crusted angel shit underneath us. The shots below from target practice and the game were distantly muffled. I thought about what it might be like to have wings, where we would go. Certainly not to perch on the roofs of unhappy families. No protection but the rushing air, we would let loose an endless screech over the swamps, release our lament and our triumph. Our fragile, hollow bird bones a strength that pushed us higher.

Rima was gasping shuddering breaths. She leaned into me. I remembered a night we had streaked naked across the street while our parents were sleeping. Rajiv laughed with us when he saw what we were doing, chucking socks out his window into the grass, and Shruti leaned out her own window, still humming, straining against the windowsill like she wanted to join us but she'd left such childish freedoms behind. The grass was cold under our feet, the humid wind startling on our exposed skin. Yet us sitting on top of this roof, the commotion of the Innocents underneath us, the angel exhaling hot breath at our backs, felt more like nakedness. Had the neighborhood looked up, they would have seen two flightless girls on the roof, wings over them, coming to grips with what was being taken from them.

Then the wings parted, and there were the rest of the children, already climbing up the roof from my window. There was the sky, all those roofs gabled with white birds. If only we could keep this vision: every roof identical, every roof as blessed as the next, every human sheltered beneath them promised to survive the daylight.

In awe of us as we rested against the angel, the other kids whispered among themselves about relics. They started taking off various things they were wearing—friendship brace-lets, headbands, watches, socks—and touching them to the angel's ruffling feathers, soaking up whatever blessedness resided in angels. They were making new holy relics for their moms to wear or for selling on Etsy to those who wanted protection.

When Rima's father had first lost his job, I'd had the idea to switch our angels to give her family a bit of good luck. I hadn't been brave enough or strong enough then to capture the angel twice my size, to try to drag it off the roof. But that had been years ago. Now, I started pushing the angel in the direction of the roof sloped toward the street and Rima's house. "Help me," I said to the other kids.

Thirty of us pushed the angel's body, dug our hands in its feathers, its heat, its quivering muscles. All of us good guys and bad guys trying to change what was about to happen to us. But this was a lark, a game. We were only pretending, like every morning on our knees. No matter how we rocked and pushed and pulled, the angel stayed.

That night, Rima didn't go back home, and my mom was too busy handling the adults downstairs to notice Rima sleeping in my bed. The Innocents slept in the hall-ways and across my room in sleeping bags they'd brought, packed as tightly as Legos, their toy guns hugged like stuffed animals. The Good Guys drank beer in the living room with the neighbors who had been eager to hold guns and aim at targets in my backyard. Shruti's parents were not with them, and I knew they were forever separated from those lucky few whose families had survived and wanted to arm the world to protect what they had. My father stumbled in from work, and through my closed door, I could hear him talking to the rest of the fathers about what he did. "Lots of failure today. It was a windfall."

"What we do isn't really all that different," a Good Guy replied. "Just planning for the worst. Another school shooting today in Texas, and we're going there next. Gotta get face time for our sponsors. There's going to be a gun control protest there, too. Lots of press."

"Yup," my father said, his phone clacking as he typed on it, like he was taking notes.

"No one to protect us but ourselves," a neighbor said, slapping something with a metallic rattle.

"It's our right," someone else said, slurring. "It's what we deserve."

The moonlight pierced in from the window. I clutched Rima, breathing in her hot metal smell, the hairs that escaped her braid tickling my face every time I inhaled. What had I done to deserve her, and what had I done that she was being taken away? What was there to protect me if it wasn't this? I pushed my fingers into the weave of her braid, trying to fuse us together. Rima's breath caught, and I could tell she was awake now. I stilled. Instead of her rolling over, instead of me kissing her, instead of anything we could have done, we lay there with shadows on the wall like beasts clawing themselves open. Neither of us made a sound.

I awoke to an inky form hanging over me. Bodies were strewn across my bedroom floor in the aftermath of darkness. I whimpered, clinging to Rima. I knew in that moment that my luck had run out. Whatever rushed in when blessedness left, it had come for me, for all of us. The bodies on the floor the wreckage of our childhoods.

But then I realized they were only sleeping. It was my

mother standing over me, hissing quietly, wanting not to wake the other kids she had stepped over to get to my bed. I saw her take in the length of me, my arms around Rima.

"Don't disappoint me," my mother said, as if I already had.

She pulled me out of the bed, Rima groaning with sleep, the other children silent at our feet. I abandoned Rima. My mother watched me brush my teeth and comb my hair as if I were anointing myself, and she handed me a white dress, immaculate and frilly at the shoulders like nothing I'd ever wanted.

The parents streamed up the stairs to wake their own children, and clattering in the kitchen announced breakfast. We were buoyed up by food in the orange predawn lights of the house. I saw Rima descend from the stairs and slip out the door.

I ran after her. From every roof, angels watched the sidewalk pockmarked with streetlamps. "Wait," I said. "March with us?" I wanted to hold on to her again, but I didn't dare.

She whipped around, her braid nearly lashing me in the face. "You still think you're doing something?"

I did. I wanted to lead that march like a burning saint, show all the news cameras and shooters that we were bright as gold, too blessed and wild to capture. I wanted that boy at school to see Rima and me arrive hand in hand, glowing with righteousness. I could feel the ache in my hands, which held only air. And if she wasn't next to me, I could turn that ache and emptiness into a raucous clapping, make the angels witness, the shooters listen.

Rima and I were silent for a moment, each intractable. Finally I said, "At least promise me you won't leave until I get back from school."

She shrugged. Her parents would leave when the truck was packed, and no later.

"What do you want from me?" I said, knowing how much life there was to want.

She took the baseball hat she had mashed over her braid, put it on my head. "Stay good, kiddo," she said, as if she were Shruti provoking us into trouble, as if she'd already grown up and left me behind. She would bear her grief like a tornado in the next place she landed.

The parents lined us up just as the first gray wisps of dawn stretched from behind the houses, our march to coincide with the usual morning rituals. Good Guys and our neighbors who had volunteered went out the door first, taking a gun from the many lined up against the wall cluttered with our backpacks and shoes. My father picked up a gun, nodded to me. He was excited, I could tell by the buoyant way he lifted the gun. So much failure. Look at how this world has failed us.

"Trust me. I love you," my mother said, just before she walked through the door and fanned out with the rest of the Good Guys. And what could be trusted, if not love?

One of the Mothers prompted me forward into the street, all the rest of the Innocents following my lead. They were adorned with relics: sweaty socks and the bracelets they'd touched to every angel worth touching, gathering sanctitude to protect them from bad guys and guide the Good Guys' aims true. We paused for the Mothers to arrange themselves behind us.

Rima and her family were already out on her driveway, bags with their last possessions at their feet, their truck glistening with morning dew, a For Sale sign the bank had put up in the night swinging beside them.

Now dawn was coming. The white on the roofs brightened; lights turned on inside houses. The lawns glittered like dark fields of stars. News vans were stationed in some of the driveways. Scopes glinted from the roofs where gunmen had positioned themselves. But were they protecting us or pointing at us? How many of them, their fingers on the trigger, would never in their lives have a momentary thought that the world would be better off without someone? Without the girl playing her cello in the music room, without the neighborhood of Latino Catholics praying their way to blessedness, without the Hindu family in the ramshackle house on the corner? I positioned myself by my mailbox.

"Please," Rajiv begged the angels, in the midst of one of his bad days. I waved at him, my only good-bye, hoping he'd remember it on his next good day.

Rima's father looked at me with pity and sorrow, like I was the daughter he'd already lost.

There was nothing I wanted more than to hug them all, than to be taken away by that unlucky family.

Other families opened their doors for dawn's oblations. Even if they disagreed with the politics of the march, they were enthralled with the spectacle. I could see my mom hiding behind a mailbox, keeping her scope aimed down but her eyes roving across the neighborhood, looking for the bad guys that wanted to take down the march, gun down children. For a moment she looked majestic, powerful as St. Sebastian, the cordons of her forearms tensing as she held the gun aloft. A few news cameras and selfie sticks aimed her way. All the angels glinted in the dawn, their tow hair shining like halos.

The first Mother shouted, "Thoughts and prayers!" beginning the morning's ritual, and that was my signal to start walking. The rest of the Mothers took up the call, and the neighborhood joined in, kneeling in front of their angels. So many thoughts rose up around us, I could almost see them in the tendrils of our breath, so many prayers. The Innocents began singing. I prayed for Rima to be safe in the next world she ended up in, that one day we would meet again as old women who'd been allowed—who had demanded—to live our lives to completion.

I promised to be good this time. I would be strong. I would keep the angels on our side. I wanted a way to survive. I kept marching down toward the end of the block where the yellow bus waited to take us to school, but I would keep marching past it, walking all the way, blisters on my feet. I would be brazen in innocence. I would make the world safe for wildness like ours. Except the cadence of my legs kept feeling less like a march and more like a prowl, a hunt.

Behind us I heard yelling that didn't match our chants. Over "Thoughts and prayers!" I could hear something else. I saw the Good Guys point their guns behind me.

It was pounding feet running toward the front of the line, Rajiv's voice, shouting a message from the angels or maybe a good-bye to me, something his sister could never say herself. I turned around. Rajiv, arms waving, brandishing Shruti's hairbrush, the only relic he had to protect him, to remind him of what he had lost. But I would never find out what the angels had told him.

I heard first one pop, then a series of pops, a sound that barely registered above all the shouting behind us. Rajiv crumpled to the ground, hit several times, his shirt blooming with red. Rima and her mother sprinted toward him. Her father stood blank and unable to move. I looked back at who had done it, ready to rage, to become an avenging angel, to bring justice down upon everyone like a cleansing fire.

My mother, my father, the neighbors, all of them looking incredulously at their hands, the AR-15s in them. Good Guys closed in, a practiced cordon around all of us Innocents. I locked eyes with my mother then, looked at her protection, at her love. I opened my mouth, a burning wail sliding up my throat and erupting from me, a sound that clawed and pierced and stabbed.

The Stones of Sorrow Lake

pressed my face to the car window to see Jackson's hometown, the place we'd just spent all our money moving to after graduation, the place we would be stuck in. It was June, the month of green. On the outskirts of town, wind from the lake fanned waving cornfields and decaying barns overgrown with ivy and rich black with rot. As we pushed closer into town, houses of old siding and paint flayed up with age sat haphazardly along potholed roads. Willows wept over the roads and one little girl riding her bicycle. At the center of town, brick buildings crumbled around businesses that had been passed down for a century.

Beyond downtown, as the road came close to the waterfront, I could see the lake shining bright over the town, the last border before the Great Lakes it fed into and then Canada. Instead of sand, the shore was made of smooth stones, large and small. Townspeople gathered at the rocky shore, some with arms outstretched, balanced on boulders, staring into the waves, others sunk into a pile of pebbles, kneeling with palms open, as if to catch something falling from the sky.

"That," Jackson said, "is our lake of sorrow."

Jackson often flashed the pockmark scar on his
forehead when he swept aside his hair, but I didn't know
what sorrow had caused it. He said he'd been too young to
remember. The scars, and the stones that dropped from
them—they happened to nearly everyone in that town.

When the townspeople encountered their first great
grief—not something small like a broken leg or a bickering
between friends, but real grief that brought you to your
knees—the first time they felt that, their stone of sorrow
would form. Sometimes it happened when they were still
children: a father who left, a twin who died. Sometimes it
happened when they were teens. A few were lucky enough to
escape that kind of grief until they were older, or had somehow steeled themselves against it.

But whenever they felt that sorrow, that's when the rock
started forming—in their fists, in their praying palms, in
their throats. At first it was as small as a grain of sand they
couldn't wash away, irritating. Then it would roll into a
pebble over a matter of minutes or years. Sometimes it only
grew as big as a skipping stone, sometimes as big as a con-
joined twin they had to carry wherever they went. Everyone's sorrow took its own course and speed, and no amount
of forced catharsis or closure could make the rock go away
when you wanted. In its own time the stone would dislodge,
but only when it could fall on the shore of the lake. You
could see the pilgrimage of townspeople at the shore every
dawn and sunset, orange light scattered on their faces, hoping their rocks would dislodge, would lie down with their
comrades of sorrow, all those generations of them along the
waterline.

You knew which rock was yours. It called to you if you
went too far away. You could see as you walked on the shore

where people had carved their names on their rocks in acknowledgment, as if to say, here is the one that came out of me, that won't let me go. The townspeople were tied to that lake—so few of them were ever able to leave town for any long period of time, if at all. Even Jackson had wanted to move back when we graduated—though only temporarily, he said, just until we saved up, had better luck, could find jobs in the city and move downstate.

He'd wanted to move here alone. He said he was embarrassed to be moving back with his parents, and we could be long-distance for a while. But something about that story didn't sit right with me. I thought it must have been his sorrow calling to him—the lake, his stone he said he was too young to remember. What if it called again so strong he could never leave? And I wanted to be there for him through that. So, I told him I was coming with him and kept at it until he gave in.

The way he talked about home was so different from my own family stories from the Dominican Republic. Mine were full of heat, jungles, politics, and the sea a thousand miles away. But in the stories Jackson told, I imagined the snow and ice of upstate winters as if peering into a snow globe. I could shake it, and down fell that white glitter with the promise it would keep swirling and swirling around those tragic, trapped figures, and if I stared too long I might find myself inside it. And here I was, moving there, not knowing if I should expect to hate it. I wanted to give Jackson new stories to tell, ones about us, ones where the joys between us, the sorrows we would hold each other through, about our first summer in town, the kids we would have, were as important as the ones from his hometown.

After the twenty-hour drive and final pass through
the town, along the lake and down a winding road to Jackson's parents' house, we were ready to uncurl, shower, sleep. But when we turned the corner around a barn half-scavenged for scrap wood, Jackson said, "Oh, no."

Streamers were strung across trees by the driveway, and a giant sign clamped down by two crooked-hung windows on either side of the house I knew his great-grandfather had built said WELCOME HOME. It seemed like the whole town had turned out, milling over Jackson's parents' land. There were kids playing with toys, dogs running about, people heaping food on paper plates. A woman I recognized from pictures as Jackson's mother waved from the porch and called everyone to attention while we parked.

I took a deep breath and got out of the car.

"Surprise!" they yelled. "Welcome home!"

Jackson's father shook my hand. "We didn't think you would come."

"Bill . . ." Jackson's mother said. "He means we thought you'd never get here."

"Surprise," I said.

The town whirled around me, clutching my hand and saying "Finally," and "Welcome," and "Nice to meet you." They all clapped me on the back, introducing themselves in a mad rush. A few of them had stones on their shoulders like parakeets. One girl shook my hand and the stone in her palm felt smooth and cool. Many of the rest had visible scars. The children, for the most part, ran around unburdened, unmarred.

It was the kind of small town where everyone's sorrow was memorized in a litany. Jackson had told me their stories. Their families had lived there a hundred years or more, off the land and the lake, planting in the summer, ice fishing and hiding from the lake-effect snow in the winter. Most of Jackson's friends were drug addicts or ex–drug addicts—your options for escape when you can't leave a place and you can feel the stones on the shore calling. Three guys hugged me with trembling arms, pinprick-pupil eyes.

These were the kind of people I had been taught to look down on, theirs the sorrows I was meant to pity. You could tell they thought the same about me, poor me, without a stone. But I'd felt pain before. It came to everyone, eventually. And any new sorrow of mine would happen with Jackson by my side. There was nothing about this one town that made them holier than the rest, just because they wore their scars on their skin. Still, I laughed and smiled, because what else could I do in the face of all those visible sorrows?

There was Jackson's high school best friend, called Panda because he was giant and cuddly. But I knew that Panda had killed someone in a fight one town over while he was still in school. That had been his sorrow, even though the other boy had started it. And even though the fight was years ago, Panda still hadn't lost his stone, which grew between his shoulder blades—a boulder that hunched him over and made sitting in chairs impossible. He worked construction despite the disability of the boulder; he needed the money. And then he had been laying bricks on the top story of a house while on painkillers and lost his balance. The boulder tipped him right over. He fell two stories straight down on his back and survived. He was telling the story now and saying he was suing the construction company for an unsafe workspace. He was winning the suit, too. I heard him say to someone in the crowd, "Oh, my back, my back." To someone else he said, "We're about to be millionaires."

As he went to give me a hug, Panda said, winking, "So

you're the new girl," and kissed me on the cheek the way he must have heard my people do it.

"Have you heard about June?" he said to Jackson.

Jackson put his arm around my shoulder and squeezed. His lips were pressed thin. "Best month to see upstate for the first time, isn't it?"

Panda had married a woman named Barbie with one jagged scar down her cheek where a stone had grown and fallen off within a single day, so big when it appeared that they had to carry her to the lake, where she lay kneeling, cheek to the shore. With her, it was that she got married to her first husband at seventeen, and then he had died in a car crash, just slipped off the ice on a road cutting alongside a cliff. She was supposed to go out with him that night but had been feeling sick. Panda was her third husband. The second one she'd married at nineteen, and he died by drowning. It didn't matter how many sorrows you had—only the first one grew a stone, made physical the memory that would tether you to those shores your whole life.

Barbie tried to keep everyone away from Panda because she was convinced he would divorce her before the millions came through. When he handed me a beer, she shuttled him away toward the picnic tables, her scar caving into a grimace.

I touched my cheek.

"Don't worry," Jackson said. "We're not staying long enough for you to get one of those. We'll just save up some money, be out of here before you know it. In the city before you can blink."

He pointed out others from the town: the mayor, his high school basketball coach, his two sisters, his brother's new baby who had Down syndrome. The shy sister, now a fifth-grade teacher, barely spoke to me as she sat her two beautiful

boys at the picnic table with cut-up chicken and melting Pop-
sicles.

One of the sister's knees was swollen, and she had her leg
stretched out from the bench, so I had to step over. She had a
tumor in there that had spread, and they couldn't operate.
At first when everyone had seen it growing, they thought it
was a stone, a second one under the scar of the stone she'd
dropped. But they should have known that wasn't how it
worked, and eventually they figured out it was cancer—
which explained the new stones clinging to the foreheads of
her two little boys. The boys played Wiffle Ball beside us. I
said hi to them, told them how great I thought their batting
form was, but they wore their distaste for me on their
Popsicle-smeared faces.

Jackson whispered, "They do that to everyone but their
mother. I promise, you'll get along fine here."

But why wasn't I sure? The night before, we had slept on a
pallet of blankets on the empty apartment floor. We held
hands over our heads, ran fingertips over the lines of our
palms. I loved him—his scar, how his smile always ringed his
eyes with lines, how he was the stronger of the two of us,
how he was the one who could pull himself away from the
sorrow on these shores calling to him. Even though he had
had to come back, eventually. I didn't think I could be that
strong. On the long drive we had only fought once, because
of me making goofy animal noises to a song and giggling, a
laughter that somehow had grated on him. "I'm just being
silly," I said, but then he asked me to drive for a few hours.

In line for food, Jackson introduced me to his friend
Samantha. I knew there was a stone inside her mouth, big
enough that she couldn't speak around it. It glinted gray between her teeth when she smiled. With her, it was the fact
that her brother—the valedictorian, the one they thought was

going to get out but couldn't pry himself away from his first sorrow—had killed himself in the back room of the pizza shop where he worked. It was the only pizza shop in town, and it closed soon after, bankrupting that family, which in turn became someone else's sorrow. Samantha handed me a paper plate, pointed at my Maná T-shirt, and moved her hips around a little as if she wished she could dance merengue. I was relieved that she couldn't ask me questions and I didn't have to make conversation. I could feel myself relaxing a little for the first time since we arrived.

Every time someone looked at us, Jackson took my hand underneath the picnic table. I kept hearing people whispering the word *June* all around me, and I'd never seen a month so beautiful and new. The air still smelled slightly of chicken shit, but then the wind would pour through the trees surrounding the clearing and I'd catch wafts of jasmine and lavender. The sky was blue and clear like an ocean I could walk into and float on. Spiders ran across the table, and big fuzzy bees landed in the children's hair. If this was what Jackson was called back to, the June in his memory, I could dream it with him. I saw him as a little boy with his same tight-lipped smile, skipping other people's sorrows across the lake.

"Let's talk to Grumps," Jackson said when we were done eating, and we threw our plates away and stepped over the extension cord juicing the refrigerator on the porch. I knew Jackson's father had added the porch the summer after he'd been accepted to the FBI. Of course, he'd never left the day he was supposed to go to Quantico; Jackson had told me he was too afraid of straying from the shore of the lake. For Jackson's father it was that some boys from out of town held him down and made him watch them rape his girl-friend, Jackson's mother. Jackson's mother already had a stone growing over one of her eyes from a previous sorrow, so she just shut them tightly until it was over. They never found the boys, never knew who they were. So he couldn't leave for Quantico, of course he couldn't.

Jackson's grandpa, nicknamed Grumps, and the other old men stood by the beer fridge trading stories, the creaky porch shifting with their weight. It seemed like they'd heard them all before. Most of the men had large scars on their forearms or biceps, and they spent much of their time drinking at the VA. Grumps still hadn't lost his stone—since Jackson's grandma died, he refused to go to the lake to let it drop. The stone bulged under his shirt like a beer belly. Jackson hugged Grumps around that belly, challenged him to a game of Ping-Pong he knew he would lose.

"I'll do you one better," Grumps said. "Why don't we take this little lady off your hands?"

"Can I trust you not to get her drunk?" Jackson asked.

"Sure," said one of them, winking.

Cups appeared from the vets' pockets, the telescoping metal kind that come with flasks, and a small table was unfolded in the center of the porch. One of them pointed at a camping chair for me to sit down. Jackson stepped back a few feet. We made a circle with the cups in front of us, all of them filled with moonshine from someone's barn.

"What are the rules to the game?" I asked.

The vets harrumphed, and Jackson stepped back close to me. "It's not a game," he whispered. "Just listen."

"Just leave her with us," Grumps told him. "We'll take care of her."

Panda beckoned Jackson from another corner of the yard.

"I'll be fine," I said.

"I'll be right back," Jackson said, walking down the porch stairs.

His grandpa began talking: "I fell in love when I was sixteen with a girl who could speak to animals. Fifty years of happiness with goats, squirrels, deer living in the house. Then she died. That was worse than war. I was lucky that my sorrow didn't come until I was old. I didn't even stay in this danged town because of sorrow. It was for love. I stayed for her and because she had a sorrow—her best friend, her dog, dying in her arms. Then I get stuck here as soon as she quits this place." He patted his stomach, the stone there.

Another vet said, almost in a chant, "What is love but an eventual sorrow? What is love but a stone waiting to happen?"

Everyone took a drink and I followed cue. Dust caked everything I touched. Our first shot, I swallowed whiskey-floating balls of it.

The vet to Grumps's left, with so many pocked scars across his arms and face, said, "When I went to 'Nam, I had a baby with a girl from Da Nang. Then a friend stepped on a land mine and I got peppered by shrapnel. They sent me home. The fall of Saigon happened while I was out of it. Been looking for her ever since." He touched one particular scar on his forearm that he'd tattooed over with the insignia of his company.

Everyone drank. The kids laughed and yelled just beyond the porch banisters. Samantha came onto the porch and sat down on the floor next to me. The vets pulled out another metal cup for her, and when she drank I could hear it clink against the stone in her mouth.

The third vet, his bottom teeth missing and his lips curled around the gums, started. He said his older sister, the one who let him sleep in her bed when he was frightened, had died from pneumonia when he was ten. Another said his best friend died next to him from a gunshot. He'd had to be given an honorable discharge because his stone had grown into his brain; after this vet's homecoming, townspeople had to carry him to the lake. His skull was still soft in that spot.

Another had tried to start a feed store before he went to 'Nam. It had taken all his savings, bankrupted him when it failed. He didn't even get drafted; he'd enlisted out of shame.

Panda lumbered up the porch, his arm around Barbie, who shouldered some of the burden of his weight. "Can I join?" he asked. He sat on the floor, where the stone on his back wouldn't get in the way.

Samantha was next, and then soon would be me. Samantha couldn't say anything. She just tilted her head back, opened her mouth wide. She hummed with her mouth open like that, a gray song. We drank.

"What about you?" Grumps asked me.

I was already pretty tipsy. I was so sure that I, too, had my own pain. But after hearing all they'd suffered, how could I, without wearing a rock or a scar to prove it? No great loves before Jackson. My parents and friends were all still alive. The relatives who had died had been on an island across the ocean, and I had barely known them. In that moment, drunk as I was, the only thing I could remember that hit me the hardest was how my face fell when Jackson turned away from me if I horsed around, like somehow my lightness was an insult. But that was such a small thing.

"Don't think I have one," I said. "Not yet."

They exchanged looks, and I was sure they were thinking, *One of those.*

Barbie sniffed, crossing her arms.

The circle kept going, and now and then Jackson beamed his smile across the yard. Once, I saw what I thought was a young girl throwing a ball at his face, but then I realized the ball in her palm was actually a stone and would not dislodge. Eventually Jackson walked toward the porch to check on me.

Barbie saw him coming. "Hey, Jackson!" she said. "Come join in. Give us yours."

He shrugged. "That's okay," he said, glancing at me.

"He doesn't remember it," I said, pretty drunk and glad there was something I could talk about as if I knew the answer.

Everyone looked at me, brows furrowed. Samantha started humming again. Jackson put his hands in his pockets and backed down the stairs.

"Come on," Panda called to him, "June's getting married."

"Forget it," Jackson yelled back.

June, the month of bees and welcome. June, a girl. I imagined her clad in weeping willow branches, her eyes like honey, always taking everything seriously. I was too drunk to stand up and pick my way around Jackson's grandfather, who was blocking my way off the stairs. "Grumps," I said, "I need to go."

"Go ahead," he said, "hit me in the stomach. I promise it won't hurt."

Panda punched him, and Jackson's grandfather fell down from his chair. I think I gasped, and then he stood back up, laughing at his prank. "Told ya it wouldn't hurt," he said.

Everyone was grinning, but I could see they were sad for me, suddenly. They were the kind of people who could laugh as they cried.

I stumbled across the lawn to where Jackson was tossing a Frisbee for one of the dogs. "Who's June?" I said. "Why do people keep mentioning her?"

Jackson looked down at the dog while he yanked the Frisbee out of its mouth.

"Who is she?" I asked again.

Finally he said, "It was so long ago . . ."

"Okay. I'm listening."

"June," he said, squinting into the sun, "was my first sorrow."

I let out my breath, fell backward into the grass, and lay there while the sky spun over me. "I thought you didn't remember it."

"It doesn't mean anything, just because it's my first sorrow," he said. "It doesn't have to be my biggest or my last. I'd rather not think about it."

"More," I said.

He ran his fingers through his dark hair, avoiding his scar. "She was my high school girlfriend. We were young. She left me the fall I started college, except she waited until I came back for Thanksgiving to tell me that she'd met someone else. This guy from just over the town line. He was training to be a mechanic. He wanted to see her every day. She said I had my eye on leaving, that I didn't have a stone yet forcing me to stay, so why would I. Nothing I said would make her change her mind . . ." He trailed off. "But I hadn't met you yet." He stood over me, blocking the sun, so serious, waiting for my verdict.

My palm itched where ants had gotten on me. Even at that moment, I wanted to joke with him. In my drunkenness, I wanted to blow a raspberry on his arm to make him laugh.

"I have something to show you," he said as he pulled me up, the sky rushing down to meet me.

At the front of the property, the gray barn door

creaked open with an ancient weight. Inside was an old sailboat, the mast folded down to fit. The whole room whirled, and I heard people outside saying good-bye, heading home. Jackson pulled the cord to light one bare bulb, while I drunkenly flopped onto the seat of an old tractor.

He said, "It's my brother's old boat. He hasn't looked at it in years, and he said if I could fix it, we could keep it."

"It's beautiful," I said. Already I could hear the ropes creaking in the lake wind, feel us sailing far past the shore, ignoring the siren song calling Jackson back. We could sail on the Great Lakes, large enough for shipwrecks and millennia of sorrow. In this dream, he's not swimming for shore.

I put my hand on his shirt and pushed it up to lay my itching palm on the warm, bare skin of his back. I pulled him to the tractor. I said, "Sit down."

"Oh, *really*," he said.

"Please sit down," I begged.

I pulled his shirt over his head as he slid onto the tractor's seat. I straddled his lap, kissed him, and buried my face in his neck. The room spinning threatened to throw me off him. He kept his body taut, holding me so I wouldn't fall back, and his eyes were distant. I wanted to snap him out of it. I wanted to be the stone his fingers traveled over like a prayer bead.

"Pretend I'm June," I said.

He pulled my arms down from around his neck. "Stop," he said. He put his hand to the scar near his hairline, his fingertips brushing over it.

"It's just a game. Call me June."

"Why is everything a game with you? This is not a game. This is real." He gripped my back with a desperation I'd never felt from him before. His hard-on grew underneath me. "I don't even think of her anymore."

"June," I said. "June. I already know."

He clung to me harder. "Please stop," he said.

I knew I wouldn't stop pushing until he said it out loud, until he drove himself to that stranger's feet, calling out her name under her window, insisting he would stay this time. And me—I wouldn't stop following him down the sidewalk while he went looking for her, while he pleaded with her. Why couldn't it have been me?

My hand felt painfully gritty, like I'd fallen on the pavement and sand had grated my palm, and then I knew what was happening. The grit was growing into a pebble right before my eyes—the kind of sorrow that comes on quick.

Jackson lifted me off him. Outside, voices wild with painful joy let out great whoops, hollered for the party to continue. He tried to hold my hand, to cover the stone so that neither of us could see it. But it pushed against him and our fingers were pulled apart. We heard our names being called. Crickets started their pulsing countdown.

Then Panda and the rest of Jackson's friends swept into the barn. I was still staring at my hand. They could all see it, what had grown there.

Samantha cupped my hand, rested her cheek to the cool stone. I could tell she had taken pills, her world made numb and wondrous. They all trembled around me.

Lake, lake, lake, they started chanting.

I could hardly stand to resist, and they set me aloft on the sailboat. Jackson helped, taking hold under my armpits. He gripped me hard, not wanting to let go, but whatever I was, I was not a stone, not an anchor. I was not enough. He did not climb up with me.

"I have to take a walk," he said.

Panda grabbed the chain hooked to the sailboat's hitch and started pulling. "Oh," he said, "my back!" But he kept pulling. The rest of them joined with cheering, a procession towing the sailboat down the tree-lined, winding road to the lake. I lay down on the deck, the sun already set, the green light of dusk jostling between the tree canopies above me.

At the lakeshore, they helped me down to place my feet on others' sorrows, the stones worn slick as mirrors. The lake lapped at us in the gaps between the stones, the world veined with water. I could see Jackson's sister farther down the shore, heading toward the downtown pier, holding her two little boys' hands, performing the daily ritual of lake-waiting.

Barbie and others kneeled at my feet, hands cupped underneath me to catch the stone if it fell. I knew the lore: if you could catch a sorrow in midair, just as it was breaking loose and before it touched the shore, you might be able to escape the lake's pull. Jackson did not join them. He started walking down the shore, and my heart reached for him. He bent to pick up a stone.

"He's found his," I said.

Panda said, "That's June's stone."

My rock was forming out of pieces of me, and the pieces were being dragged out. I held out my palm, my offering to everything we'd lost. All those sorrows shoring up that great lake. The waves kept beating—not the biggest wave, not the last—all that water polishing those stones to glass.

I could already see my sorrow clearly, how it would tie me to this place even while Jackson was strong enough to escape, for a while, before being yo-yoed back. His parents would let me sleep on their couch after he had gone. I would waitress at the lake's marina, learn the litany of sorrows, weave my own into their net. I'd wait on serious June and her new husband, lay dinner in front of them, take orders from the both of them. "You're like a daughter to us," his parents would say. Somewhere, someone's stone would claw out of them. Samantha would silently teach me how people lived with the holes and scars the stones left behind, would hold my hand every evening as we waited on the lakeshore just past downtown, her lips open as if in song. And when Jackson came back into town, he wouldn't come to see me. I'd have to show up at the one bar in town after my shift when Samantha dragged me there to catch a glimpse of him, to see if he'd stay, to see if, while not his first, I could still be his biggest or his last. Jackson would turn away from me with that tight-lipped smile I had learned to love.

Of course I would laugh. I would close my eyes and laugh.

The Whitest Girl

From day one, Terry Pruitt was too good and too white, the whitest girl we'd ever seen. Most of us at Yama Catholic Girls High School were some version of Latina. But Terry was whiter even than those whose families were high-class or blessed with Spaniard instead of Indo or plantation genes and shot out of our mothers' bellies as pale as little Europeans. There were other Anglo girls, of course, but they lay in tanning beds, wore too-dark makeup that made them glow orange, studied Spanish, and flashed gold hoops. Terry Pruitt didn't even make an effort. Her skin was so pale we could see the web of veins underneath, including one throbbing blue line that split her forehead in half. Her teeth were jagged and yellow, pocked with metal fillings. She had pale gray eyes the color of dirty dishwater, and her hair dulled mouse brown, not like our shining dark locks we gelled up into ponytails or our pelo malo we ironed straight as sheets. Her first day of school, all we could do was stare at the audacity of her whiteness.

A group of us followed her home after that first week of school and discovered that she lived in a trailer park with a herd of brothers and sisters, all as translucent and bad-toothed as she. Their parents had died, and their grand-mother was raising them. She was too old to drive, so they had to walk everywhere. We were horrified. How did she get admitted to our school? When people that white yelled at us in the grocery store, or assumed we couldn't speak English, or that we were somehow unintelligent, their anger mystified us. When others wanted to dismiss us, we were lumped together with Terry's kind of trailer white, these people we didn't understand. We watched her run after a chicken that wandered underneath the trailer, watched her pluck its eggs from their hiding places to feed her siblings. When the kids screamed and ran around her and she looked about to break, we saw her put a pillowcase over her head. Suddenly she looked peaceful, faceless, that sack of white sagging over her shoulders. We were fascinated.

After that, we only wanted more from the whitest girl we'd ever seen. We were like circus-goers who gasped at the bearded lady and then wanted desperately to know if, underneath all that hair, she was beautiful. We wanted to know Terry's secrets, we wanted to know who she loved, who she hated, what she dreamed of in the bed she shared with her sisters. We didn't admit this to each other, of course. We said that we wanted to ruin her life, or at least get her kicked out of school, and hazme el favor, how dare she? So we became her dark shadows, assigning shifts for every moment she might have been alone. Some of us protested at our cruelty, but the rest of us framed it as a game. Then it all seemed harmless.

One of us reported back that she had joined the choir, but she sang like a cat in heat. Another said she tried to play the clarinet but couldn't muster enough breath for anyone to hear the notes. She spoke with a lazy Southern drawl that made us wonder if she was, in general, slow, except we heard she had a scholarship. We discovered she was religious in a sanctimoniously abstinent way, and not in the ostentatious kissing-crosses-and-crying-Jesus way, which was the one we understood.

She seemed not to be bothered by us turning up out of nowhere: in the next aisle at the grocery store, behind her when she walked home from school, crowding by her locker. She seemed not to notice. We *could* have just befriended her. We could have invited her to everything we did, asked questions, pried her open with all the bluntness of an oyster knife. But we didn't want to. We imagined it would look like she was running the show: a white girl, nearly glowing, surrounded by a sea of brown and tan and orange. So instead, we trailed behind her in line as she cashed her grandmother's social security check, circled her lunch table where she lingered over a single slice of bread. She did none of the normal things, like hang out at the movies, socialize with the guys from the all-boys across the street, or anything that wasn't school or taking care of her siblings.

Once, she hesitated for just a moment, turning toward the parking lot where the boyfriends from other schools waited to pick their girlfriends up. Then she continued down the street. We thought this meant that she wanted to be a part of our lives, that she regretted never inviting us over to her trailer filled with trash and her grandmother's doll collection, that she wanted to be invited to our quinceañeras. We thought this meant she wanted to be us.

One day after the closing bell rang, we caught her in the broom closet, hand around a fluorescent bulb, her eyes cast down, the young janitor explaining to her how to connect the wiring to a light switch. We'd barely noticed him before, except to know his name was Joseph. We'd heard he was a dropout from the all-boys, but he couldn't have been much more than college age. His hair hung past his ears. He was tall and muscled, arms as hairy as forests—a man. This is what had made us discount him, that he was older and dropped-out and scrubbing our toilets. But at the moment he extended his hands to show Terry Pruitt something in his palm, his long sandy hair framing his face, we thought he looked as soulful as Jesus. We wanted his honey eyes full of mercy to glance toward us instead. Then he and Terry bent their heads over his hands as he twisted two ends of stripped wire together, and their pale backs in their uniform shirts looked like the outline of a white elephant.

After that, we caught her in places she'd never been before. She went furtively into the makeup section of the grocery store, but then counted her change and put back the glistening tubes. The youngest of the Pruitt children played on a swing set at a playground near their school, and Terry drifted two streets down, head in the clouds. She walked into a bar during a local band's ska set. Having assumed she was at home and asleep for the night, we stared from our seats with surprise. She was dressed in a turtleneck with sleeves down to her wrists, despite the heat. Always that throbbing blue vein in the middle of her forehead. We thought she was alone, and then we saw Joseph bring her a Coke, unsheathe the straw from its paper for her pale, thin lips. Then we saw her terrible smile.

We were horrified. His eyes slid past us. Didn't he see what we saw? What magic did she have that we didn't? We were the color of smooth pecans, our eyes dark and full of mysteries, our plump lips deep purple and moistened. Some of us were even blond or blue-eyed. Some with tamed afros that waved into halos. Some willing to do things with him that Terry could only have dreamed of. Some just as virginal as she was, though no one would have guessed, people always commenting on our cuerpazos. Some in the running for valedictorian. Some of us would end up scattered to colleges across the states, dragging our boyfriends with us to more exciting lives. We could entertain anyone with stories about how our families had crossed this ocean or that desert or were pursued by so-and-so evil dictator. Some of our dads were even janitors, too, though we were embarrassed by them. Our futures were still bright. None of us were white trash, we told ourselves. We wouldn't phosphoresce in the moonlight as Joseph walked us back to our cars.

The next week at school, we analyzed her in desperation. The way her mouth opened to screech out a note, her fingers soft around rosary beads at weekly mass, the frail hunch of her shoulders, the throb of her forehead. Joseph, who was watching her through the classroom windows as intently as we were, was on to us. Although Terry was not able to imagine that her running into us held anything but good wishes, Joseph had been cleaning up after our messes for years, had found our crumpled notes. The first time his car passed by one of ours as we trailed Terry from school, his eyes catching the hunger in our own, he knew what we were up to. After that, she waited after school for him to drive her home, and he drove fast, shaking us every time. Our constant eye on her dwindled into only what we could observe from school hours. She had slipped from our grasp.

Quinceañera after quinceañera rolled by, each of us despairing that despite our elaborate ball gowns, the relatives and people we'd invited, the boys who were our dates, none of it was enough. The clinking of our bangles sounded like chains, the gel in our hair felt too much like grease and dirt, our clothing tight and suffocating. We started wearing less jewelry, leaving our nameplates at home, as if we had forgotten who we were. We wanted to be loved so badly—even though we knew that *good* and *love* didn't always mix. What did it mean to be as angelic as Terry? But we saw glimpses of her at school that disturbed us. Terry hiding from the nuns, Terry refraining from Eucharist during the weekly mass, Terry forgetting to mouth the words to the rosary after school, the beads hanging limp in her hands.

Finally, we spoke to her. "Did you have sex?" we asked her, as if we were her friends. She turned bright red, the only color we'd ever seen her be besides white. But she said no. We didn't think she was capable of lying.

In the month of Yasmín's quince, we had an idea. "Invite Terry," we told Yasmín. That one night, she and Joseph would be in our grasp again. So Yasmín sent her one of the invitations tied in a mint-green ribbon, which began, *Dear Terry, Special Guest.*

The days leading up to her quince, we planned. We would be dressed as elaborately as princesses, but we suspected Terry would sew her own dress. The one of us who wanted to be a movie star said, "We have to set the stage." The one of us most chonga, gesticulating wildly, said, "Let me get my fingernails on her if she even touches my boyfriend." The one whose uncle was an ousted president of a South American country said, "Please, no need to get ugly." One white girl, honorary member of the group, who had refused to discard her nameplate and gold hoops, said we could throw self-tanner on her to ruin her paleness. Someone proposed talking only in Spanish, but only half of us knew Spanish. All of it seemed too much. All of it seemed not enough. What had she done to us? She was just one shimmering, pearlescent drop in an endless sea of what we hated, what hated us. And hadn't we learned, after the insults thrown at us when we walked down the street, after the landlords who wouldn't rent houses to our parents, after the relatives rounded up like cattle and thrown back across the border, that hate was as useful as love?

Terry arrived at the quince on Joseph's arm, her sloped shoulders bare in a silver dress. She wore no makeup, and the lights that had been arranged all over the ballroom floor drowned out her features, so she looked like a ghostly blob. We'd planned the lights, of course. There were other white girls there, people from other schools, and dates that Yasmín's cousins had brought. Yasmín's parents were old-school Mexican, which meant her quince was the biggest and fanciest we would ever go to. Everyone she knew was there, dresses puffed with lace like icing on cupcakes, everyone as graceful and immaculate as high school girls could be. Her quince happened during many colleges' spring breaks, so everyone who had fled for the year, cousins and older friends and boyfriends, strolled about looking fresh from a war. Some of us took to the lights like we'd been born in them, flashing our smiles and teeth. Some of us were overwhelmed and kept going to the bathroom to escape. The room, where Yasmín and her court spun the opening dances in their poofy gowns and tuxedos and we waited to join in, was hot and made for thirst. Some offered Terry and Joseph cups of spiked punch. We watched the ruby liquid pour down their throats.

Of course Joseph knew that the punch had alcohol. This made him no less eager for refills, for himself or Terry. We tried to talk to them in passing. She was quiet and kept ducking her head behind her hair, which sprouted from her forehead frazzled and stiff. She was sweetly shy. We were drinking, too, and though we would never have admitted it, the fuzziness of the evening, the unreality, was bringing us out of our hatred. Her eyes were wide. She was drowning in the grandness of everything she didn't have, and we were sorry for her. Joseph kept his grip tight on her arm. With his other hand, he tossed back his long hair. Everything in his manner said that he was above it all.

"Who is that guy?" asked some of the out-of-state cousins.

We started to explain that he was our janitor and he was dating Terry, keeping our motivations behind tight smiles, but the dates and cousins back from college interrupted us. "He's your janitor?" they said, incredulous. They shook their heads. "At an all-girls?"

"What's the matter?" we said. "Can only women serve women?"

"Haven't you heard why he got kicked out?" they said. "Why he never finished school?"

The story they told us was that, some years ago, he had been at a party thrown by his friends from the all-boys. Another girl showed up, a white girl from one of the public schools no one had been friends with, who only came because her cousin's parents made him bring her. She'd gotten drunk to deal with the awkwardness. Later that night, the cousin found Joseph in one of the bedrooms with his pants around his ankles, hunched over the girl, who was so drunk she couldn't make coherent words. He had just finished. Most of the guys there were his friends, so they quieted the cousin, although the party ended soon after. But the cousin, he wanted to ruin Joseph. The girl refused to press charges because she didn't want her name on the public record. But her cousin's parents had donated a lot of money to the school, and they got him kicked out almost at the end of the year when no other school would take him. He never went back. A few years after that is when he must have shown up at our school—rag, mop, and bucket soon in hand.

We shook our heads, for the first time feeling so dumb despite all our months watching them. "It could have been one of us," we told each other. Except that it had been a white girl.

Then the court's performance was over, and people flooded the dance floor. We looked over at Terry. Her ghostly figure swayed with drink. The hem of her dress swished up, and we saw she wore tattered, dirty sneakers. She looked up at Joseph with those drowning eyes that meant she was in love. We saw through his facade then. He no longer looked like Jesus, more like a rat with pinched features and uncut hair. The music rocked us against our dates. Some of us joined the dancing, sliding our bodies in the air like snakes. In some of us, pity sank like a stone.

We all wanted to tell her. Some of us felt that telling her would be a kindness. Some of us who had suffered at the hands of men before wanted to save her. Some felt that telling her would be the last revenge, the last betrayal of this girl who in our heads was no longer a girl. She was a Frankenstein's monster cobbled together of every horrible thing that had been said to us about our families, of our powerlessness when we left the bounds of our high school, of the nuns' eyes watchful against the apparent sin of people who looked like us, of the disregard that bunched us together with her kind of people, with their potato casseroles and bad music, bad manners, their self-satisfied boredom, their blinders that meant they could only see their own bare patch of ground. Others felt that we could take with one hand what the other gave. No matter what our motives, each girl would be fulfilled. Our whispers hid underneath the reggaetón and merengue and bachata. At some point a real mariachi band walked in, sombreros and jackets flashing wildly with golden brocade and rhinestones, trumpets and violins held aloft. Some of us kept dancing with straight faces.

We tried to pry her away from him. We said, "Terry, come

dance," but he followed. She shifted her feet from side to side, beaming at the fact that we'd asked her to do anything. We said, "Terry, come sit," and he pulled a chair out for her. We had our dates glare at him to make him feel unwelcome, but it seemed like he enjoyed this. Finally, Terry had to use the restroom, the one place he could not follow.

We recognized her old sneakers poking out under the stall, white strips of pleather flayed off and dangling. "Terry," we called.

"Yes," she said.

"Terry, we just heard something we have to tell you."

"I'm so grateful Yasmín invited me," she said.

"Oh," we said. The music stopped for a moment.

"Quick," she said. "Tell me before the music starts again." So we told her.

We heard the toilet flush. "That's impossible," she said. "He's been more kind than anyone." Then the toilet flushed again and there was silence.

We waited. "You shouldn't be alone with him anymore," we said. "We're so sorry."

The music began again, muffled by the bathroom walls, the bass notes trembling the mirrors. When she finally came out, her eyes were puffy but dry and her fingers twitched like they were fingering rosary beads for novenas. The vein in the middle of her forehead throbbed and tapped. She seemed full of a strength we hadn't seen in her before. As she washed her hands, she said, "Have you never heard of forgiveness?"

"For that?" we called after her as she walked out. "For *that*?" And what right did *we* have to be the ones to forgive him for his sins? What did forgiveness mean, when he could do it again, when it could happen again to any of us?

Then we were divided. We started to see the differences between even ourselves. Some of us wanted to leave her alone. Those of us who felt the hate that had been poured into us chilling and condensing wanted to prove it to her, what he had done. Some felt we should try to convince her because who knew what kind of danger her naïveté would drag her into. Couldn't we protect her? But how could she not stand with us against what he had done? A few, who had never believed anything and were becoming the outcast atheists, said, "How do we know it's true? How do we ever know it's true, what we believe?" Most felt he was the one we should break. We dispersed on the ballroom floor.

Joseph put his arm around Terry. We could see her stiffen, then smile that horrible smile. She seemed determined to stay until the end.

Some of us felt sick and asked our dates to take us home. Those of us thrilled by the dark caught Joseph's eyes, full of all the danger we wanted to tempt, and gyrated for him, our hips carving up the smoky air. Some lied through perfect teeth and said, "Terry, you look so beautiful, you could have any guy here."

Then Joseph had to use the bathroom. We noticed, when he walked out of the room, that he stumbled. Then one of us, when he came out, told him Terry was outside.

The smokers saw him squint out the door into the dark, then trip outside. "Terry," he called. Crickets and our voices met his call. Some of us blocked his entrance back inside.

"Is it true?" we asked. "About why you got kicked out? Does our principal know?"

"Little girls," he said. It was the first time he'd spoken directly to us, done something other than pick up our trash. "Would you believe that none of you know what you're talking about? None of this is your business."

"What do you want from Terry?" we asked. "Why did you do it?" we wanted to know. We didn't ask, *Why not us?* When he could have picked the noblest of us to ruin, the most beautiful of us, the darkest of us, the palest of us, the one from Argentina who spoke five languages, the one who looked like she'd crawled out of the Garden of Eden, dark hair down to her waist. We didn't ask, *Why that one girl? What did she do to you?* We knew full well that hate did not require an initial offense. Only the original sin of being born.

He clenched his hands, but we knew there was strength in numbers, an entire group, easy to misunderstand but impossible to ignore.

Meanwhile, Terry had ventured out onto the dance floor with the rest of us. She did her strange swaying, and then a few of us ditched our dates and grabbed her hands and pushed her hips around like ours. She even mouthed the words to one of the punk songs. She seemed both rattled and happy but holding no grudges about what we had told her. For a moment, we thought she could have been one of us. For a moment, we were just a mass of dancing bodies in the strobing smoke. The mariachi band with their gentle guitars and brazen trumpets captured us in an amber wash of music so we were all waves in a single sea. Some of us wondered if that was what forgiveness felt like. We were girls celebrating our fifteen years on earth.

Then Terry asked, "Where's Joseph?" and one of us said, "I saw him go out."

We had pushed him toward the parking lot. We held hands like in a game of red rover, and we tried to pin him out by the dumpster where he belonged. Why did we terrify him? The fear in his eyes was what we wanted. It was the eternal paradox, that you both longed for and wanted to destroy what you feared.

He must have thought he could take us all. He ran toward the smallest girl with the highest stilettos. The girl went toppling, and Joseph tripped and fell on top of her.

This was when Terry walked outside. She saw Joseph on top of a girl on the ground, struggling to get up, all of us yelling and crowding behind him, and, finally, she was not an idiot. Her face, all of its whiteness, seemed to fold into itself like dough. She turned softly on her ratty sneakers. She started walking home. None of us in our high heels or our bare feet could keep up with her, the ones who wanted to explain. Joseph called after her on the sidewalk.

For just a moment, she turned toward us on the sidewalk. She glittered translucent and unsmiling, beautiful as the moonlight, rays of pale light piercing through the trees to surround her. Our exclusion of her trembled in our guts, on our skin. We felt the very edges of us shred apart, our safety in numbers dissolve. We were only each girl, one and one and one, alone in a terrifying world that wanted us to love what would hurt us. Then she stepped into the woods in the direction of her trailer and was gone.

She would never come back to school, but we'd see glimpses of her in town, her hair cut short and ragged like she'd allowed each sibling to cut a lock, that blue vein coursing like a river. Years later when we would hear she'd joined the nuns, our guilt would drive us to visit her, but she was cloistered away, the nuns told us as they clucked about Terry's innocence, eyed the shapes of our bodies as if they wanted to cover them with drab wool. She would never marry, never bear children, never pass on those terrible genes. Then our pride settled on our heads like thorns. After that, the only time we'd remember her was driving by her old trailer, where a few of her sisters still lived, the moon-blue glow of an old television flickering, us uninvited.

Later that night of the quince, after running to her trailer and back, coming up empty-handed, Joseph did sleep with one of us. Loss engraved on his face, he sat in his car. We sent out the one of us best at martyrdom, the best at being a mirror for what boys wanted to hear. She said, "Joseph, I've left you notes among the trash." Later, we saw him hunched over her, then over the steering wheel as the rest of us leaving the party passed by the car, satisfied and terrified.

Yaiza

The day my mother hired a new housekeeper to replace the last one she caught stealing was the same day Yaiza arrived on the tennis courts. It was almost summer. Our first official tournament was coming up, one hosted at the same tennis academy where we took lessons. We came from all over the neighborhood to congregate at those courts after school. Our parents didn't let us walk there, across a busy highway, but we all lived less than a mile away. It was a mostly Latino neighborhood— some big houses, some small. Everyone who could afford the tennis lessons and the gear came from the big houses. But not Yaiza. She had only one racquet shoved in a ratty backpack, not the racquet bags with backup racquets, key chains, and USTA zipper pulls that we had. She was eleven like the rest of us, but darker. She had a Miami accent when she said hello, those Spanish *l*'s that flicked from the back of the mouth instead of the front. No mother dropped her off; she had walked.

When Yaiza first arrived, she threw open the clubhouse door so hard she nearly took it off its hinges. My friends and I had been rewrapping our racquet handles with matching purple cushioned grips, the boys tossing tennis balls back and forth. We flinched, took her in, and turned away.

I was used to being the favorite, and one of the women who coached us let me drive the golf cart before lessons. I was the hustler of the group. My form was less than beautiful, and I didn't hit winners left and right, but I was the fastest. I could run down every shot and keep a rally going until the opponent tired out. I had a strange grip, a one-handed backhand with my left, which meant I had greater berth and could reach shots that should have been winners. In school I behaved the same as on the tennis court. I did all my homework, chugged through the books at the library. This doggedness was why the coaches always called me over to drive the golf cart, dragging behind it a wide brush that erased the footprints and ball marks of the previous age group's lessons. Afterward I would excavate the white tape of the court lines from beneath the clay I had smoothed over them— more hard work I was glad for. The thuds of the tennis balls, the soft, dusty smell, the way we were powdered green after hours of sliding and kicking up clay—I wanted to earn it all, to feel like those moments were my own, the dust mine.

I watched Yaiza out of the corner of my eye while I whipped the cart around. She warmed up jumping rope by the entrance of the clubhouse, her dark braid swinging back and forth. The coach's whistle blew. We lined up, keeping the new girl at the back. But from the first thwack of her racquet, Yaiza's shots flew farther than ours, faster than ours. Her volleys were examples of perfect form: no windup, just short, deft caresses that made the balls drop dead at your feet. It was the kind of playing we'd only seen older kids do, ones who were state ranked. When we touched the net and ran back for our overheads, most of us would throw our weight forward, spinning with our weak arms. Yaiza's overheads were effortless, her arms crossing her body with grace instead of desperation. She grunted with each shot, and when she missed one she yelled. Clearly she had already been taking lessons, but so had we.

A girl who lived three streets down from me, a mean girl who didn't like to lose, pegged Yaiza in the back of the head with an overhead while Yaiza returned to the end of the line after one of her gorgeous shots. Yaiza turned, not knowing who had done it, her eyes wide and enraged. "What, so you want to play me?" she yelled.

But none of us said yes, and—like that—we had a respect for her. I did, anyway. She didn't work hard, but she worked *hard*, if you know what I mean. I did things over and over, for longer than anyone else. I made people weary. Even my mother tired of me. But Yaiza didn't do something twice at fifty percent if she could do it a hundred percent the first time. She didn't waste her energy outlasting anyone. She didn't need to. I could already see that a match between us, the natural against the hustler, was inevitable.

When the sun got low and our mothers came to pick us up, we heard them, leaning on their parked cars, whispering *scholarship girl*. My mother said she'd just hired Yaiza's grandmother as her new housekeeper. As we pulled away, I saw Yaiza running across the eight lanes of rushing traffic, her racquet stuffed in a lopsided school backpack that sagged and jumped as she ran.

At home, my bed was made. I never saw our housekeepers; they were always gone by the time I returned from school. My fresh laundry was organized in a basket at the foot of my bed by unknown hands. I was perpetually embarrassed, my underwear folded into little squares, strangers handling my most precious things. I imagined a grandmother who looked just like Yaiza, but old and hunched, scrubbing our toilets and mopping our floors. I felt ashamed, like they could see some dark part of me even I didn't know about, just by the trash I left scattered on the floor, the books discarded under the covers, the drawings I penciled at night.

When I got to the courts the next day, it was Yaiza who was riding the golf cart, already swinging those brushes around, powdering the clay up behind her like a whirlwind that matched her. Yaiza who called something out to the coach's sun-ruined face with its million brown, benevolent wrinkles. Yaiza who turned the cart away as we pulled up, who wiped her sweat in our direction.

"That girl is certainly earning her lessons," my mother said.

The coaches were tightening nets and pulling out the shopping carts full of felted yellow balls. When Yaiza jumped down from the golf cart and pulled out the wheel that would clean the tape lines, I walked beside her. My plan was the same as all my plans: I would wear that girl down.

"So, where'd you play tennis before this?" I asked, the first words I had spoken to her.

Yaiza shrugged. "I was in Miami."

"That's great," I said. "I'm sure if I'd had lessons in Miami, I'd be hitting like you."

"Never took no lessons," she said. "I found a racquet in a park, and I played against the wall."

"Oh," I said. "No net?"

She laughed. "Drew a line on the wall. Nets just give you an excuse to stop when you miss."

I hated her. I'd told myself people earned what they got, and I wanted to believe that if I just kept running down the world, I'd emerge on top. "Well, why doesn't your mom drop you off?"

"It's my grandma," she said. "Why, you afraid of crossing the street?"

"Not afraid," I said, "I just don't need to." By then there was a ruckus of other kids arriving, and I left her to the tape lines.

After that, I watched her closely. I copied her form. I even started putting two hands on my backhand like the other kids and felt how hard you could hit that way. The tournament was coming up, the last weekend before summer. We were all hitting our hardest and ignoring Yaiza because we were naive enough to think we might still win. And even if we didn't, there was always second place. We ran suicides, sprinting from doubles line to doubles line, a competition I shone at, sliding into each tape-touch with the quickness and drama of baseball players sliding into home base. After lessons, Yaiza crossed the street, her form bisected by the court fences as she dodged cars, her backpack threatening to jump over her head with every running bounce.

Two weeks before the tournament, while we were racking up balls between drills, one of the boys said, "You're bleeding." I looked down at my knees and my shins, which were often scraped without my realizing, but another of the boys said, "Gross!" and pointed to my white tennis skirt, where bright red had sprouted.

I ran into the clubhouse with my racquet behind me, even though the strings would cover nothing. I slammed into the bathroom stall and pulled down my bloomers and my underwear, which were soaked with blood. I knew what a period was; my mother had told me about it, but she hadn't told me to prepare for it so soon. I had nothing with me, and the clubhouse bathroom was not the kind of place with pad dispensers. I locked the door and tried scrubbing the cotton in the sink, but that made it worse, and instead I had wet, red bloomers and a stained skirt. I texted my mother, but she must not have been looking at her phone.

On the next break between drills, the boys pounded on the door, calling me *bloody vag*, but none of my friends came to rescue me. I knew nobody else had gotten their period yet.

Then a softer knock on the door, and my name in that Miami accent.

"Go away," I said.

"I have some pads at my house across the street and some shorts if you want to come with me," she said. "Everyone else is drilling."

"I'm not walking out in front of everyone," I said.

"*I'm* not your maid," she said. "If I'm going, you're going."

I took a deep breath and weighed my options. I had never crossed the highway on foot, but I wasn't going to give her the satisfaction of seeing me afraid. I stuffed a wad of toilet paper in my underwear and unlocked the door.

So I found myself walking behind Yaiza, my drenched bloomers seeping into my skirt, hoping everyone was too busy hitting to watch me down in the parking lot. I tried walking with my legs slightly crossed, but then I couldn't keep up with her. The soft thuds of balls, the noises that seemed to me clean and pure, receded, and the ruckus of the highway loomed in front of us.

At the curb, the cars rushing by, hitting us with engine noise, exhaust, and air, she crouched a little, like a runner at a starting block. "Go," she said when she saw an opening. But I hesitated, and then my window closed, cars zooming across like they were practicing warp speed. Yaiza was at the median, waiting for her next break, balancing her sneakers on the log of concrete. "Come on," she yelled.

A wall of cars barreled down. There seemed no way I could make it, but I tensed my body, leaned into the pavement. She said, "Now! Run!" and this time I didn't hesitate, feet pounding across the blacktop, pumping my arms like a suicide race, air smacking me in the back as I reached the median and the cars rushed past again. The next half of the street we ran together, me outdistancing her as we ran into a ditch, using it to slow ourselves down.

When I looked over, she was laughing. She said, "Yeah, yeah," like she was answering a question I had already asked.

We walked past the wall that separated our subdivision from the highway, past the small houses and the big houses, past the playground I had conquered, the trees I had climbed all my life. A few cars slowed in the residential streets and I kept my head down, embarrassed in case they noticed the stain on my skirt and recognized me.

Yaiza's house was the smallest on the block, a flimsy pre-fab square, no bushes or palm trees, only a dried-out brown lawn that crunched under our feet. We were ten streets away from my own, but I had never felt farther. The people who lived on this street, had they not climbed high enough, had they not run fast enough?

Inside, Telemundo yelled from the TV in the kitchen and a gnarled woman I assumed was Yaiza's grandmother sat at the table, a fist under her chin. This woman had folded my bras, had seen the porcelain figurines of children I still kept on my dresser, had probably even sat on my bed and passed her hands over my pillow. She possibly knew me better than my mother did, who seemed to not even see me for who I was and kept wanting me to quit tennis for dance. I clasped my hands in front of my ruined skirt. I stood there, not wanting to interrupt Telemundo, not wanting to be caught trying to disappear before announcing myself. I wanted her to see me—not the random leavings of my life but *me*—and I wanted her to tell me I could do anything. Yaiza's grandmother didn't turn around.

"What are you doing?" Yaiza asked. She pulled me into her room, where two sets of bunk beds were pushed against opposite walls. Dirty clothes and a soccer ball littered the floor, and the room smelled like onions and metal, like unshowered boys.

She pulled a box of pads from a black trash bag deep in the closet. "Got to hide it from my brothers," she said. I realized she slept there with them, and that she had carved a space out for herself by playing tennis while they were playing soccer.

She pulled out a pair of jean shorts and handed me them plus the box of pads. I didn't have extra underwear and mine were soaked, so I pasted the sticker of a pad to the crotch fold of the shorts.

"Yeah, you're fine," she said when I walked out of the closet where I had changed.

We didn't say good-bye, and I never saw her grandmother's face, that woman who would always be invisible to me although her presence was everywhere in my room, her sweat on my sheets.

On the walk back, I still kept my head down and clutched my bloomers and skirt, rolled up in a trash bag. We crossed the highway again, cars honking, me pulling ahead as we lunged toward the other side. I looked back at this girl, her dark braid bouncing, her biceps and shoulders lean and sinewed. The sun blazed, pinpricks of sweat on our skin glimmering, like the sun washing us in gold could make us the same, two girls made from hot metal.

Later, her kindness would be my consolation prize, and my gratitude burned. I would never thank her. I felt a hot fire in me to win, to beat her for her kindness. Who can explain why we feel it necessary to be cruel when we do? I ran faster.

A car horn broke the moment. My mother in her gold Honda Odyssey, pounding the horn in the fury that took her over when things didn't go the way she'd envisioned them. She had gotten my text and come to rescue me, too late but not late enough to miss us running across the street, my mother slamming on her brakes before U-turning at the median so that she wouldn't hit Yaiza.

Of course, my mother started with the Spanish *what were you doing what were you thinking you could have died santa marias.* Yaiza kept her head down as she walked past. My mother rolled down her window and told me to get in.

"No," I told her. I kept pace with Yaiza, and we walked down the driveway to the clubhouse like that, my mother doubling down on her authority, yelling out the window, rolling slowly beside us, Yaiza saying nothing, even when my mother turned her famous rage on her.

That night, my mother informed me I would quit tennis and she would start me in dance classes the following year. I raged, yelling, inconsolable, and I knew I would win if I just kept at it, the way I always did. "Why?" I yelled, and my mother exploded back, "That girl is trouble." Finally, my father came into the living room to mediate. Tennis camp somewhere far away for the summer was the negotiated settlement, which seemed to me more like a reward than a punishment, but I made sure to still look angry and slam the door to my room.

Those final two weeks before the tournament, my mother began staying in the lot until the lesson was done: car on, air conditioner blowing, a magazine flipped open on the steering wheel, or talking on the phone, her mouth flapping with gossip. I didn't dare talk to Yaiza with my mother watching, and she didn't talk to me. She shrugged when we caught each other's eye. But when a boy mentioned blood to me, she pegged him in the foot with an overhead he could never return. I still had her shorts, which I'd hidden in the corner of my closet, too embarrassed to give them back yet or have her grandmother find them. And then I forgot them.

Meanwhile, Yaiza kept trouncing us, graceful topspin arching the balls over the net to lunge away from us before we had even taken a backswing. I was the only one who could run them down, by staying near the back fence and sprinting for my life if she delivered a drop shot by the net. Those last two weeks were scored by the grace of her swing and the sliding and thudding of my feet. I went home powdered green and smelling of must. A few nights I refused to shower. I wanted that dust to be mine because I'd fought for it, wanted it to color me permanently, to claim me back like I was made of it and nothing else. Long after college, when I had quit tennis, I would ask myself what it was all for, and my eleven-year-old dirty self would point at her own skin and say, "This."

The day of the tournament came. I was convinced

I would finish second to Yaiza. None of us had played in a tournament before, which meant none of us was seeded. We'd be paired with opponents at random. I envisioned myself outlasting several players and even some seeds before facing Yaiza in a final match.

The bracket sheet was taped to the clubhouse windows. When I saw my bracket my stomach dropped. I'd been paired with Yaiza in the first round. I spotted her in the parking lot with her scuffed racquet, the grip rubbed raw, jumping from foot to foot to warm up. I splashed water on my face, pulled down my new tennis dress my mother had bought me as an apology, and walked onto our court. I shook her hand as if I'd never met her before. My mother parked right behind the fence and pantomimed clapping. No one came to watch Yaiza.

The match went almost like I had dreamed. She slammed killer shots with perfect form and force, a terrifying angel, and I ran them down. Every once in a while, she'd miss when I wore her out in a rally. I got some points like that, and I wasn't that far behind, though she was winning. But I always came back in the second set, when my opponent tired out. Tongue coated with dust, I felt I had almost ground her down.

Then we were nearly even in the second set, 4–3 her, and she threw the ball up to serve. Arm cocked, racquet behind her head, hand pointing up to the ball, hips leaning into the court, body coiled. Then the beginning of the swing, her explosion, and it was like I could see it in slow motion, the ratty grip slipping out of her hand, the racquet slamming down with all the force of the ball on the ground, a sound like a stick breaking.

She picked the racquet up, examined a seam through the fiberglass frame. I knew she didn't have another. I waited for her to approach the net. Instead, she shrugged it off and got ready to serve again. Confused, I walked back to receive. Same swing, same explosion, but this time the racquet made such a dull thwack when it made contact, I knew the ball wouldn't make it over the net.

For a moment I felt relief, a wash of happiness. She would have to forfeit; she couldn't keep playing. But then I remembered going to her house, her toughness in the face of our mocking, that racquet the only thing she seemed to have. I had three racquets. I looked back at my mother, who was deep into a phone conversation and not paying attention. I pulled one of my backups from my bag and held it over the net to her. If I won, I wanted to say I had beaten her fair.

She didn't thank me. She didn't even hesitate. She took the racquet like it was her due and walked back to serve, calling out the score like nothing had happened and I better get ready.

Maybe my quickness finally left me. But more likely my racquet suited her better than her old one did. Suddenly my feet weren't enough. She was hitting winners past me, drop shots so delicate and close to the net it was like she was placing an egg without breaking it, like she was a witch enchanting the ball in the cradle of her strings. All she had to do was stare a ball down and it would go where she wanted it and bounce away from me. I had to play the rest of the match trudging from lost point to lost point. I had to shake her hand at the end, tell her, *Good match*, and know she deserved it. She didn't pump her fist or yell out *Yes!* like some of the other kids did. She shook my hand in seriousness, as though it held no joy for her, the fact that she'd trounced me.

Out of spite for my mother, I told her to keep the racquet. She shrugged and twirled it in her hand.

"You know your problem?" she said as we were walking out. "You don't keep your eye on the ball. You look away at the last second. You flinch."

I made my mother take me home, instead of staying to watch anyone else. Yaiza did win, a neighbor boy told me, outsmacked a girl who was state ranked, first seed. A golden trophy the size of her arm.

That week, my mother packed me off to a tennis
summer camp in Sarasota. The coaches there made me watch

the ball until it hit my strings, until I hit it harder than I remembered Yaiza ever hitting. By the end of the summer, I was ready to go back and beg for a rematch, show Yaiza the new person I'd grown into, flaunt my new boobs, which had come in just in time for the boys to notice, boys I kissed, sweaty in the darkness of the tennis courts, perfumed with that same musty smell of home, the clay I was convinced would always be mine.

But at the end of the summer when I returned, I rollerbladed past a For Rent sign in front of her house. When I mentioned Yaiza, my mother said, "Just goes to show what you get instead of gratitude. I caught her grandmother stealing."

Dread filled me. "What did she steal?"

My mother could hear the tremor in my voice, my temper coming on. "*Your* things. I saw Yaiza with one of your racquets, with that ugly purple grip you always use. And I was willing to admit I could be wrong, maybe it just looked like yours and she had gotten the same grip. But then I caught that woman leaving the house with your clothes. And you know, I would have given her all of your discards for her granddaughter, but since she stole it . . . No. They all went back to Hialeah."

I tried to explain about the shorts and the racquet. I thought if I just tried hard enough, just wore her down like I had every other time, I could bring them all back.

"What's done is done," my mother said. "She didn't even leave a number."

I raged. But for the first time in my life, there was no way out, and I was trapped by my guilt. When I walked back onto the courts, it was clear I could outplay the rest of the kids my age, and they moved me up to the older group, but this just left a bitterness in my mouth. I would never know if I could have beaten Yaiza, or why I needed to. I would never know what part of me could be seen now, the secret self she could convince me I deserved.

I should have forgotten her. Instead, I kept looking for her name in the rankings. I never saw it.

My senior year of high school, I went to a football game against a rival school. The nighttime haze of fall and the stadium lights seemed to hide all of us in plain sight, those of us who were there holding hands and trying to make out, those of us who were coming into our own and didn't want to look at what we were becoming. We seniors had our sights set on the future. We had already been sorted. I was number two in the state and getting a scholarship to UF.

My friends chattered around me. Near the opposite bleachers, I saw Yaiza, or a girl that looked like her, dressed chola, wearing giant gold hoops and her lips outlined dark in pencil. A boy from the rival school had his arm around her. I ran up to her, calling her name.

"Yeah?" she said.

"Tennis," I said, "remember? How's your tennis going?"

Her shoulders tensed, like she was curling up to swing, but then her lips stiffened into a straight line.

"Naw," she said. "I don't play no tennis. It's a rich-people sport."

Her legs were as strong and thick as ever, her shoulders wide through her jacket. I never got the chance to ask if she was playing something else, soccer maybe, before the boy put his arm around her and led her away. She laughed at something he said and then punched him in the arm.

I wanted to lob a ball at her back, or a taunt, trick her into swinging at a ball out of instinct. I wanted her to turn around and face me. But what was it I wanted her to see? What could I beg her to see? What was it that I still flinched away from at the last second, that I couldn't follow?

She walked toward the opposing bleachers, holding her head high, projecting that nothing could wear her down, not me, not life, not anything I couldn't see. Just like when she used to carve her way to the net among the soft thuds and pats of sneakers, a sun forging the myth that we were equals and our joy was our own, a rain that cratered the green clay and made us close our eyes when it came pouring down.

YAIZA

The Drownings

ater glimmers in the corners of our eyes. The pools are always within sight: in patios behind our houses, through the glass doors opening to the kitchens, in bright reflections of blue threads sliding on our ceilings, the water waving in the windows of our bedrooms. It's Florida, the end of a sweltering summer before eighth grade. We all know someone who drowned, hundreds this summer alone. We've all had our own close calls, bear scars from slipping and falling in the deep end. Barely any pools are left unsanctified by drowning. Still, we return to the pools daily. The water calls us back, all that blue jagged with light. We want to be swallowed: the splash, the cool weight slipping over our heads, the rush of sinking.

The new girl, Rosa, arrives from somewhere north and cold on the first day of school. Rosa cannot swim. When the homeroom teacher introduces her, Rosa's dark hair slants over half of her face, and we remember *new* means depths we do not yet know. In Mr. A's science class, Zach throws paper airplanes at her, meant to antagonize her into giving up her secrets. The airplanes are badly made; they dive-bomb quickly in the air, swimmers out of their element, and do not reach her.

The teachers at school often explain things to us using liquid. When we were little, we saw how the porcelain tiles sank underneath a rising water level when we all jumped into the pool. "What did it mean?" we asked. "Displacement," said the teacher. In sixth grade, our science teacher explained chlorine and how pH imbalance can kill cells and other life. The music teacher explained rhythm as waves or swimmer's strokes.

Our parents explain nothing. They are the ones who survived the childhood of drownings, who escaped the close calls. When we ask why they were the ones to survive, why the water that takes so many of us children spared them to grow up, they have no answers. They seem afraid. They can't help us with our homework. We feel, this year, like growing up means losing something and also that we want to be lost. We have the hubris of the young, think that if we pay attention, we can catch the moment of transformation, we can hold on to whatever it is the parents have lost even while we rise. Which of us the water will choose to take, which to survive, doesn't matter to us as much as the moment just before. After all, the water has already claimed so many, almost a third of every generation: curious babies who crawled into a gap of the pool fence before anyone noticed, clumsy toddlers who couldn't yet swim, kids who just got tired and couldn't keep their arms going, kids who hurt themselves jumping in and couldn't get back out.

After school, Rosa sits on the ledge in her brand-new bathing suit, watching us screech and splash. We can see she wants to be one of us. In the water, none of us are awkward. When we plunge our heads under the skin of the surface, we watch others' legs kicking and standing, the way they glimmer, surrounded by pinprick bubbles of air. The muted screams of laughter above. The girls and boys we all want to be are those who slip sharp as knives into the pools, those who dive the deepest, those who hold their breath so long that when they emerge, they are gasping. Zach can hold his breath long past all our fears. At parties, Jocelyn waits until everyone is watching her, eyelashes clumped wet and black, smooth ponytail like an eel behind her. Then she jackknifes, plunging straight down beneath the wavering surface, waiting until the last possible moment, until we're sure she's hit bottom, before pulling up. She tells us she kissed the glimmering quartzed floor. We gasp on her behalf. We want the pressure of crushed stone on our lips. All of us are drawn to the depths, where we're beautiful and hungry as mermaids, tempting the drownings that come every year.

Mr. A tells us that where there is water, there is life. All those dry planets, dry as deserts, dry as husks, they are meaningless except to describe the motions of the stars. In the lab, we separate H_2O molecules into gases that dissipate in the classroom atmosphere. Zach, who dives the farthest and holds his breath for longest, who never does what he is told, tries to inhale the vapors. His eyes open wide, and he dances around the classroom shaking each of our hands. He even pulls at Rosa—Rosa with her strange memories of snow, of water frozen still and safe, of layers of jackets between her and everyone else. She gasps at his touch and turns away. Zach says the oxygen is making him do it. He says it is too much air.

After school, Rosa remains on the edge, splashing us with awkward kicks that throw her chest back, pull her slim line into a V like a system of counterweights. Her hair, frizzed in the humidity, is tossed back with the rest of her and slips off her face like opened doors. The mysteries that tempt us are many. We think knowing things means growing up. Even Zach calls her to at least come step into the shallow end. We wonder if she doesn't come in because she has her period, which only a few of us have so far. We cup our hands and toss water at her in messy, jagged rainbows. We close our eyes against the chlorine. Momentarily blinded, Rosa accidentally falls into the shallows, the brick edge sharp as glass all the way down her leg. We gather around her: the scraped, white flesh trickling one red river. It looks like life.

Jocelyn splashes loudly, annoyed at the attention the new girl has received. We pull our eyes away. Recovered, Rosa dangles her legs off the edge again. We let our eyes slip under. Beneath the water, we watch Rosa's legs flutter in the shallow end, the one that looks like life and the one that looks like death switching places in front of our eyes.

When we fall asleep at school, we dream of swimming in the air, holding our breaths to tread water above treetops. We start awake, interrupting Mrs. Z's health lesson on taking our vitamins and the effects of scurvy on sailors lost at sea. Mrs. Z is obsessed with the lost. Her best friend and her two sisters drowned in childhood like so many. We've heard this same nostalgia in our parents' voices, the way they watch us, with our desires and our fears and the way we must chase both. Our parents no longer take the risks we do. Drownings among the adults are rare. The temptations have gone stale for them; they dip their ankles from the steps, recline in lounge chairs beside us, but rarely do they let themselves get pulled in. Even car crashes, a kind of land-drowning—glorious wrecks that the teenagers tempt by rushing down the highway at a hundred miles per hour, sitting on the driver's lap, making out and covering the driver's eyes—even these are rare for the adults. They have so much to lose now, they say. "You've already lost it," we say. Perhaps our parents are still drowning in a way that we can't see, changed by age. Perhaps we are the ones drowning them. They tell us to go play in the pools. They try to remember—through us—the way they felt when everyone they loved was consumed by water, one by one by one.

After school at Matteo Aristes's house, the school

year's first drowning. Jocelyn stands on top of a diving board, arms waving. We are so rapt with her performance, her lithe body, her smile (the same smile she gives us every year at the talent show when she dances ballet to music soft as mermaid dreams). Jocelyn releases the board, cuts into the air, plunges below with barely a sound. We hold our breath, savoring the anticipation she works on us. But then she doesn't come up. We gasp. We look around at one another. It's a joke, surely. But Mr. Aristes leaps in to pull her out by her hair, slopping her on the ground like a caught fish, breathing into lips no one has kissed. We've seen this drama before, during the previous years' drownings. Rosa watches, pale and horrified. We are sun-browned, our wet bodies trying to hold on to the feeling of being in between life and death, the electrifying high of losing what we love, the moment when our whole world reveals itself to us in the glimmering light of something that must end: the puddles growing around our feet, the breeze brushing us with chill, our pruned fingertips, the rare silence of the water but for small slaps against the tile, Mr. Aristes's gulping breath that we can almost taste.

Finally, Jocelyn vomits, coughs, and breathes. She holds her chest and her head, where it hurts, she says. "You didn't drown!" we exclaim. We seize the moment to brush her shoulders softly, to feel the cold still hovering there. "It still counts," she says.

At the morning assembly a few days later, Jocelyn speaks into the microphone about living life to its fullest, how we never know when it could all be gone. She gives us that brilliant smile. It's a speech we've heard before, the words so predictable we could sing them. And we're already living to the fullest—this means courting the very dangers that cut life short. Jocelyn's dazzle begins to look gaudy; her smile, tired. The adults nod, lulled by the familiar. To us, they look like they're just treading water.

In the school hallways, we ask Jocelyn what drowning was like. Not the boring stuff she thought afterward, about appreciating what she had, but the very moment her lungs filled with fluid. When she was one with the water, when she closed her eyes—the moment that separated her from us. She closes her locker, gives us her smile from right before she launches off diving boards, says, "I couldn't possibly put it into words." We wonder about it; would we feel fear? We are very curious about fear.

Mrs. Z drones on about cardiovascular flow in the body, how first the oxygen gets sucked into the lungs, the bronchial sacs. We look over at Jocelyn, eyes bright and open in the classroom fluorescents. We hold our breath. We let it go.

We dream of what it's like to die. For a few of us,
there is a black nothing that we crave. For others, death is heaven: just like living except hardly anyone is lost. For most of us, death remains a mystery that cloaks our desires. Every time we bring our dream selves to the brink of drowning, we wake up. Sometimes it's an alarm that stops us; sometimes

it's a classmate's touch, fingertips like licking waves. The boys have started waking up in wet sheets. Do your homework, Mr. A tells us. Mrs. Z tells us to make sure we're getting all our vitamins and minerals. We want to ask them how that will help.

When bathing suits cling to us, we watch each other's outlines. Some of us are growing breasts; others' shorts tent at the crotch in bewildering responses. We pull each other under, bodies shifting with the current. We brush against skin with our stroking arms. We are captivated by the startling paler edge revealed when a bathing suit shifts away from tan lines. We chase each other in circles outside of the pool, the water at the center ready to catch us if we fall. Our parents don't drain the pools. They know what it is like to crave something and have the thing held back from you, and they don't dare forbid us. There are unacceptable risks and there are the ones we embrace. We keep diving. We put our dry clothes back on carefully, our cool skin burning with touch.

Rosa avoids puddles after rain, those sudden thunderstorms that send us all shrieking for cover, the lightning that strikes the pools with a booming crash. She stays dry, a refusal of our hunger. An anger unlike any we've ever known boils up in us. We liken her to our parents, who've lost the magnetism toward the water, and we can't decide if this makes her more adult or more childish. We test her by excluding her from the pool invitations. We see her rollerblading down the sidewalks and the driveways, let our delighted shrieks ring out as she passes. Jocelyn kisses Zach under the patio eaves. Rosa swings on the abandoned playground with her toddler sister. She sits on the whirl-around with a picture book in her lap, her rollerbladed feet hanging heavily off the edge, trying to teach her sister how to read. The scab on her leg is completely gone. She sits on the outskirts of the lunch tables with girls who pretend she isn't there. Jocelyn holds court over lunch trays, people guessing what she saw when her eyes closed, and she says, *No, that's not quite it.*

Zach tries to get close. He tells his older brother to

hold him under for two minutes, just past the point when he feels his lungs exploding, when he usually lunges for the surface. His brother, a football player who pushes his body to lift more than anyone else in the weight room, who has taken his convertible flying down an abandoned road, his girlfriend whooping with each turn threatening to flip them over, understands. His parents see them from the kitchen window, the brother pushing down in the deep end, elbows locked, face already straining with grief. The parents drag them both out. "Did you feel it?" we ask. Zach shakes his head. Not long enough under.

Zach tells us he'll settle for drowning in our eyes. He sets up a station at the picnic tables with a pencil cup beside him and a sign that says LOOKING BOOTH. A quarter from our lunch money and Zach will take turns looking into each of our eyes for three minutes. The girls do it, even the boys; each person presents a different contest. When it's over, we blink; we feel like that's the longest anyone has looked at us in all our years. We think maybe this is like drowning: feeling naked like there's some core of us, some light, suddenly raw and expanding and taking us over until the rest of us is gone. We want it again. We trip over ourselves for him to look at us in the hallways, even Jocelyn, who whispers into his ear when the timer sounds. She says she'll see him later, at her house. All he says is: *Next.*

Rosa sits down last of all. She turns off his timer and never plunks a quarter into his cup. "Look until you don't want to anymore," she says. When the bell sounds for fifth period, Mrs. Z pulls Rosa away. Even then Zach doesn't move.

Zach invites Rosa to his house along with the rest

of us, and to our surprise, she comes. Fully clothed, this time she kicks listlessly from the edge, barely splashing those who pass. Zach swims closer and closer to Rosa as we play. He is lithe as a shark. "Come in," Zach says. Rosa says, "I didn't bring my bathing suit." We tell her one of us brought an extra one. Rosa says, "I'm not going to change." The rest of us can feel ourselves transforming, forgetting what came before. Our bodies feel full of light, buoyed up, rising, raw. Every sensation electrifies us: currents dragging across our skin, sun evaporating droplets, towels rubbed across us, even a stare we can feel on our skins.

We are told Jocelyn isn't coming back to school. She's touring the country as a motivational speaker. Our parents call us in to watch Jocelyn on late-night TV, bright stages illuminating her. She's somewhere that looks like a desert, everyone dry, bone straight, moving stiffly. We guess Arizona. She talks about out-of-body experiences, how right before you die, you can know everything about your life. As she says this, she walks down into the audience, puts a hand on a woman's back, and leads her up to the stage. The woman is taken behind a curtain. The show always ends before we see what happens to her. "Yes," our parents say, nodding, aging toward death, toward knowledge, reaching for what they've lost.

Mrs. Z tells us about our reproductive systems, information that's been withheld from us until now. She describes the baby floating in placenta. She shows us horrifying videos of births, mothers screaming. We lean forward in our school desks. We imagine ourselves before we were ripped from the fluid darkness, spilled out into this world of land and air. The violence of our first breath. How our warm, unknowing silence chained itself instead to hollow sounds we can't fill up with our desire: words, questions, and their infinite answers. We are distraught.

In consolation, Mrs. Z describes the mechanics of sex, something she says we are never to have, though we sense she's lying to us to avoid accelerating our curiosity. "What does it feel like?" the boys ask her. She turns red. The girls ask among themselves, dragging fingertips on each other's arms, giving each other burns by twisting skin. Those of us with parents that still love each other listen at their doors at night for their movements, their gasps and cries. But how can they still love each other, hold on to each other, without the threat of drownings?

Zach slips Rosa a secret note in Mrs. Z's class. *I can show you how to swim*, it says, *at night when no one is watching*. Rosa throws the note in the trash. "If only you could feel what I felt," says TV Jocelyn with her secret smile.

A month later, Tyler hits his head on the steps

after a front flip and drowns in the deep end. It happens at night while his parents are out and he is alone. The principal announces our loss at the morning assembly. "Tyler," we say, "gone." We roll the words around our tongues like jawbreakers, the sweet terror. "Live life to the fullest and with no regrets," we sing with the principal, who gives this speech often. For a week we dive from higher, run faster, punch ourselves in the chest in his honor. A month after that, we barely remember him, his death only a condition of our life.

Rosa, though, she repeats his name. Down the halls, she mumbles a litany against forgetting: Tyler, Tyler, Tyler. He joins the pantheon of the drowned. We've forgotten our first drowning, even our second, but seeing Rosa this way kindles a new fascination in us. Why can't she let go? It's so easy for us to toss aside memories, release fear and love, grasp them again for a fleeting moment, like when we first jump into the pools: flying, then the slam of resistance, then the weightlessness.

At school, we are drawn to Rosa and her persistence. At night, Jocelyn's mystery show flickers blue in our living rooms.

Zach waves at Rosa with pruned fingers when she bikes past his house. He watches her at the lunch table, slides her a carton of milk. She ignores the milk. She says she wants to go home. "You live here now," Zach says. She glares at him.

"Okay, you're stuck here," Zach says, "I get that. But at least let me show you how to swim. Maybe then it will feel like home. You'll forget how hard things were at first."

We play games of rooster, boys hanging on to the legs of the girls, who try to push each other off the boys' shoulders. The boys feel legs smooth as dolphins. They catch glimpses when bathing suit tops are mistakenly yanked down. In the water, everyone pays more attention. When we call out *Marco*, our hands reaching out in our imposed blindness, Zach never calls *Polo*, waiting silently while our fingertips grasp his body, brush his skin. "Come in," Zach says, splashing Rosa.

The other boys take Rosa by the arms and legs, throwing

her in the deep end. She screams, and the boys remember she can't swim. Zach yells and dives in after her. He pulls her into the shallow end, hands under her armpits. Rosa splutters and coughs. She bikes home sopping wet. After she leaves, Zach's chest feels tight and his breathing rasps. All we wanted was for her to feel our thrill; we wanted to push her to get over her sadness. "That was her choice," Zach says. Mr. A practices his lesson on equal and opposite force, on the reason why the water punches us back when we cannonball.

Two nights later, a pebble cracks against Zach's bedroom window. Zach lets Rosa in the front door. Upstairs, his parents snore heavily. They are dreaming about becoming old, surviving, treading water, and someday resting on the shore. They are always so tired. Zach's brother turns the TV up to cover the snores as he curls over his weight bench. On TV, Jocelyn tells sleepless people to imagine their own out-of-body experience, watching themselves like in a dream. We know she will never come back to school. She will never give us what we want. She wants to remain a perpetual question, a throbbing desire, a choice we can never have. She asks the camera, "What does it matter what I actually saw? Your whole life is a near-death experience. We are all living dreams."

"The pool looks different at night," Rosa says. "Electric. Or like glass, like if you went under, it would suddenly harden and you couldn't get back out." She's remembering the cloudy frost of frozen lakes. She knows Zach's tried to drown before. She's reluctant to get in the water with him. "I'm afraid, too," says Zach. "Of me?" Rosa asks. Across town, Mrs. Z mumbles the next day's lesson in her sleep,

"Vitamin A the lungs vitamin E your hearts." In our beds, we dream of sharks and long slippery trees we can climb just by breathing, our lungs like ballooned floats.

Zach holds Rosa's hand as they descend the pool steps. Lights flood the water from below. Rosa lies on her back. "Breathe in," Zach says, "and hold it." She floats. "Now kick," Zach says. His hands, warm in the chill of the pool, hover under the small of her back. Zach's wrinkled fingers drag over Rosa's stomach. She feels like she's deep underneath an ocean of everything she doesn't understand. "Are you going to try to drown again?" she asks. "Not while you're here," Zach says. Rosa's eyes burn. Her head slips under.

Zach holds her up higher. "Extend your arm and stroke," he says. She extends her arm, pulling loose the string of her bathing suit top. It floats away from them. Her skin is tender with newness. Zach's lips are warm on her mouth. Nets of light tremble over their bodies as they move together. They try to look at each other, to take each other in, as they start the new forbidden thing, but their eyes keep closing as they gasp.

"Remember this," Rosa says. "We're already gone," Zach says.

Afterward, when they pull up out of the pool, elbows locked to push up against the ledge, the chlorine rushing off them, their sudden weight feels like returning to the realm of the living. Out of the water, they are both awkward. "I still haven't learned to swim," Rosa says. In our dreams, we are heavy. We roll over in our beds.

Rosa throws pebbles at his windows the next

night, but he doesn't come to the door. She calls him through the weekend, but he does not answer. At the Monday morning assembly, we learn Zach has drowned himself hugging his brother's free weights. We look to Rosa, who confesses she was the last to see him. We remember his goofy antics, when he took all the science frogs home and let them loose in his pool, when he looked into our eyes for quarters, how he chose his desires and drowned in them, how he lived the edges we chased.

Rosa wonders if he believed that the moment he lost consciousness, he would release the weights and float to the surface. Why did he have to try again? We seek the answers for her. We retrace his steps that last night. A few of us pass our fingers over Rosa's stomach just like he did, but we don't get very far. We touch each other in forbidden places. We pretend to teach each other how to swim. Finally, Rosa learns the breaststroke, her head craning out of the water as she tries to keep it out of her mouth. Rosa remembers Zach passing her milk across the picnic table, the moment he looked into her eyes, saw her, and then let her change.

When we say his name the way Rosa does, we can taste the sadness. But then we kiss each other and the newness of one taste replaces the other. Metallic braces, mint Chap-Stick, cinnamon gum. The words lose their meaning. Soon, we will graduate to high school. Soon, we will leave the water behind for land-drownings, for hot metal and fiberglass, tires burned, brakes squealing. Already, we are using the wrong words for the unanswerable, like Sex, and We're Burning Up, and Love. Already, we are feeling more adult, like we have just a bit more to lose. Rosa pulls her hair back into a ponytail, takes a deep breath, and dives down to reach bottom. If only we could live in every moment forever. If only the answers to our lives could be captured in a bottle we could drink from again instead of looking back across unreachable chasms, our own out-of-body experiences. At the end, we will know what all the lost knew. The liminal moment when a fluid darkness answers all the questions there are to ask. Rosa touches the rough, quartzed pool floor to her lips.

The Great Escape

As her Alzheimer's got worse, my tía Chani retreated behind her apartment's locked doors and white curtains, sold her car, disconnected her phone. "To keep out the thieves," she said, by which she likely meant us, her family. Most of us only visited because we were vultures waiting to inherit her things. When we whispered among ourselves, it was about what she owned. Paintings worth un cojón, sculptures by dead artists, furniture carved out of caoba, jewelry that Dictator Trujillo's nephew—who married her by force—had bought to chain her. The paintings were of herself: young and naked, sometimes dressed in slinky kimonos and caftans, posing before a landscape, always from the back or the side. Before the Trujillo, she'd wanted to be an artist. Her father had sent her to art school, where she befriended painters who would become famous, men who would return to her form again and again to immobilize her on canvas. All of that had ended, of course, after she married the Trujillo.

For some reason, tía Chani always listened to me, and the relatives pushed me forward like an offering. Her daughter, the person who was supposed to inherit, had a big falling-out with her and moved across the country, close to the border of Haiti. Heydí had been adopted from Haitian cane cutters and wanted to be forgotten, to go back to the people from whom she'd been plucked instead of living a life she felt was forced. Tía Chani, once her daughter left, degenerated rapidly. She lost things so diligently it was like a religion. She sent away nieces, brothers, nephews, claiming to not remember them, insisting that the lobby security escort them out even though the guard remembered when they'd visited just the week before. He had to stand behind them awkwardly while they got into the elevator cursing and calling her a selfish crone. I never had to suffer that humiliation. For whatever reason, my name she remembered. Perhaps because I was the same age as her daughter.

She kept forgetting where she put her keys, changing the locks, then finding the original keys. Sometimes she changed the locks so the daughter could not get in, even though the daughter was *not* trying to get back in. She was paranoid that someone had in fact stolen her keys, and she added more locks. Her door looked like a game of Connect Four from all those round keyholes. She added metal gates outside her front door, chains around the joints, bars on the windows, even a grate on the trash chute. She'd gotten stuck inside a few times for days until I managed to convince her to call the locksmith.

Discarded keys and old locks piled up in mountains outside her apartment door. She planted bamboo in buckets of keys. She made sculptures of women with magnetized keys clinging to each other in triumphant forms. During Navidad she made thorny wreaths of keys to hang on her door.

Despite what anybody else said, I liked the old chueca. She had traveled off the island to places I was dying to go. I told all my friends about her, how she was unpredictable and independent. I brought my boyfriend to meet her. I had warned him that if she let us inside he'd be surrounded by naked pictures of the young her: large globes of her breasts, a face that challenged with the eyes, black hair that flowed like lava over her shoulders. They said she'd once looked like Elizabeth Taylor.

Of course, she lost her keys the day of the visit. Bars and grates and rejas stood between us, although she never closed the actual wooden door anymore. She liked to feel the breeze from the sea, she said. We visited with her through the bars. We couldn't see inside her apartment, only her front hallway, so he did not get the eyeful. She squeezed pillows through the bars for us to sit on and passed us a bowl of hazelnuts, which my boyfriend had no idea what to do with.

"Act mannered," I whispered to him. "Do not act like you're from the campo."

When she excused herself for a moment, I told him to crack one to be polite, but then he kept trying to put the shells in the sculptures of keys and I had to hiss at him to behave. He hid the shells in his pocket.

When my tía returned she had changed, dressed all in white with a string of turquoise chunks around her neck and her hair poofed up. She looked thirty years younger.

"Wow," my boyfriend said, and elbowed me.

"A white suit is a blank canvas," she said, and winked at him. "What was your name again?"

He asked her about her travels, as I'd instructed him to if things got awkward.

She smiled and sat down again on the floor. She passed us pictures from a silver engraved box: her on a camel in Egypt, her in a headscarf in Pakistan before that was what it was called, her skipping down the streets of Paris in a fur coat.

Most of these pictures had been torn and all that remained of the other half was a hairy arm around her waist, sometimes fat fingers resting on her arm, sometimes just a shadow.

"Tell us about the Louvre," I said.

She smiled, animated. It occurred to me for the first time that she remembered me because I was more like her daughter than her daughter. It made me momentarily sad that neither of us could really be what she wanted us to be.

I'd heard her daughter had gotten a boyfriend in the campo. "Tía," I said, "why don't you make up with Heydí? Call her."

"She wants to be invisible," she said. "I approve."

Then she told us something that I'd never heard before. She had another daughter, one she'd adopted with the Trujillo. The night the Trujillos had to leave the country in exile, he snatched the little girl up on a plane. Tía Chani never saw her again, except for once, forty years later, in Miami. The girl, now a woman, believed she had been raised her whole life by the next woman he married. "She didn't seem to like me or the lies I implied," my tía said. "I could see she didn't know who she was."

"I'm so sorry," my boyfriend said.

"Was I talking about my first daughter?" she asked. Then she repeated the story.

"I'm sorry?" he said.

"What was your name again? Anyway, these things disappear." She shrugged. Then she got up with the silver photo box to put it away and vanished down her hallway.

My boyfriend started grabbing keys out of the discard pile and the bamboo planters. "We've got to get her out of there," he said. He tried key after key in all of the locks.

"Don't bother," I said. "Those are all the wrong ones. She's probably forgotten we're here anyway."

He held out his hands, helpless, full of keys and hazelnut shells.

Then tía Chani came back to the door, and he closed his fists.

She announced, "I hope you juice everything you can out of love while it lasts, like the pulp of a rare fruit you will only have once. What was your name again?"

His eyes opened wide. On the way home, I clapped him on the back. "You survived," I said. "Haha!" And when tía Chani called my mother to say how much she loved him, I wondered what in the slightest she'd gleaned, besides his manners, about who he really was.

Finally, she lost the keys for good. This was the week she was robbed going to the grocery store, and when she yanked her purse back, the man gave her a black eye. She called me in hysterics. "What do I look like," she said, "a vieja? Someone who won't put up a fight? Is that all I am to anybody?" She liked to say things like that: not, *Who am I?* but, *Is that what I am to you?* Made you feel sumamente guilty, like you'd wronged her terribly.

Even my mother was jealous that she'd asked only for me. Maybe she suspected I looked forward to my visits to tía Chani more than returning home to her. Once, my mother asked tía Chani what it was she saw in me. "So responsible," my tía had said, "so intelligent. She will be more than what you expect." When my mother told me that, I almost choked with laughter. I wasn't any of those things, but I was glad that was how she saw me.

A few days after the robbery, my tía accidentally sent the keys down the trash chute, and by the time she told us, trash day had come and gone. The relatives congregated in the hallway of her apartment on cushions, like a harem. We wasted a few days convincing her that the keys would not turn up and she needed a locksmith.

"Why do I even leave the house anymore?" she asked with her hands on her hips, chains and locks swinging around her like heavy wind chimes. She sported a white suit and sunglasses inside her house to cover her black eye and she did look like Elizabeth Taylor, back from the dead.

The locksmith we hired had heard stories about her from other locksmiths and charged us a fortune to get her out.

"Thief!" she yelled. "Ladrón! I'm calling the police!"

She banged his fingers with a marble statue as he tried to cut the metal. She stabbed at his eyes with a silver letter opener. No amount of reasoning could get her to stop.

We waited on the bottom floor so we wouldn't be implicated in disobeying her. The elevator door opened. The locksmith's fingers were swollen, and he had a cut on his cheek.

"Is she out?" we asked, hopeful despite it being too quick for all those locks.

He shook his head.

"You have to go back up," my mother insisted. "We'll pay you double."

"Doña," he said, "there isn't enough money in the world for any locksmith in all of Santo Domingo to go back up there."

The other relatives decided it was time. She was too old and could not live alone. They tried to get her classified as mentally unfit so they could do what they wanted with her and her things. I was against it. I had nothing to gain. I was the youngest of all the relatives and knew they'd never let me be the one to make decisions for her. I was already sure everything was coming to me, and I preferred the old chueca to all of them. Luckily, when the judge interviewed her through the bars, all the relatives gathered around the door as witnesses, she dazzled him with her wits. Plus, she knew the judge from back in the Trujillo days, and he knew what she'd been through. He promised her he'd never let them sign her away.

I begged her to come out. She said, "This apartment is like a seashell. Inside, I can see the malecón over the other houses, I can hear the sea, I saw the revolution flooding down the street fifty years ago. I saw the ships getting smaller when the Trujillos ran away, my daughter getting tinier like an ant. Outside, there's just the Bolívar Avenue, cars that won't stop for me to cross, the orange shell of the apartment complex.

"And everyone who cares about me is right here." She stomped her age-gnarled feet on the floor. But there was no one inside with her.

Then I was to be married. He proposed to me by promising we would travel everywhere my tía had gone.

"The boyfriend you met," I reminded her. "Please come out, for me."

"I don't want to burden anyone," she said.

I told her I had a dress waiting for her on the other side. I said, "Wouldn't you like to see all those people watch you walk in, looking better than ever?"

She said, "That's all I've ever seen, all those people watching me walk in. You're the one walking down the aisle."

"I'll never ask you for anything else," I told her.

She smiled at me and cocked her head like a parrot. "I'm so glad," she said, "that the young are happy, and that we have this friendship. But my wedding day was the saddest day of my life."

She didn't come out.

The day of the wedding, the dress was too tight; I

felt suffocated in folds of lace. It had a little loop sewn into the end of the train, so I could walk with it in my hand without dragging it. We were getting married at a beach and not a church, and I could see footsteps in the sand all the way to the gazebo where a priest and my soon-to-be-husband waited. His eyes gleamed. I wondered what it was about a woman being a bride that made her more beautiful? Was it the dress? Was it happiness? The glare of camera flashes washed out my vision. Faces blurred. My mother-in-law, who saw a vessel for grandchildren; my mother, who saw the upright, diligent daughter my tía Chani had professed me to be; other relatives, who saw me as the anointed one who would inherit the cojones when tía Chani passed. To my husband, I was the one with more class, the princess, even though all my childhood I had been the wild one. But then, it seemed he saw my wildness in that moment, too: that at any moment I could bolt. His eyes half lidded like he was seeing through my dress to the core of me. As I approached, he waited for me to reach out my hand before taking it. Then the words of our vows passed over me like the sweetest spell. I felt myself uncurling like a flower, dropping old petals at my feet.

I didn't visit my tía for a long time. First it was the honeymoon, then moving to the new house, then pregnancy and kids. The relatives were always calling, "checking on tía Chani," they said, but really checking to see if I'd fallen out of favor. I had set her up with a daily meal service, so there was someone paid to look in on her every day. I still talked with her over the phone. She told me grand stories about all these people who had already died, asking me when they were coming by to visit. "They're on a long vacation," I told her. More and more she was calling me by my mother's name. I worried, but then the baby started crying or the toddler hit her head on the coffee table, and I had to be a mother. Or the housekeeper started asking me what she was to do for the day, and I became the ama of the house. Or my husband came home, my trusting husband, who thought he had fully tamed me, who liked to be the savior. When he came home from work, he would swoop the girls up on his lap, give them sweets, refuse to say no, me following behind, cleaning up their mess. The promise my husband and I made to each other—that we would travel—was still unkept. For a while, I forgot who I was, besides a nagging wife, a resentful mother. She glared back at me from every mirror. I wondered if I would end up as alone as my tía. I decided to visit her.

I told her we were coming to show her my children. My husband had the youngest in one arm. I had the four-year-old by the hand and a food basket in the other hand. Each girl was puffed up in frills and lace. I squeezed my husband's hand in triumph in the elevator. We were a family. We were going to have a picnic, albeit through bars.

When the elevator opened, a locksmith appeared, tinkering around her door, tía Chani on the other side, hovering. I felt incredible relief. Then I realized he was not getting my tía out, but adding more bolts.

She was wearing a pitiful little batica, sweet pajama roses all the way to her swollen ankles. "They're after me," she said. "At night. Trujillo's after me, and those painters want me again."

"Nobody's after you," I lied. "We've brought you cake."

Then she saw my children. "My daughters!" she said. "You've brought my daughters!"

My heart stopped. The oldest rushed forward with my tía's cry and fingered the locks like they were beautiful toys. She shoved her tiny pinky into the keyholes. She'd turned out like my husband, so trusting. Tía Chani was reaching for her. For a moment, I thought it wouldn't hurt to pretend, but then I had this crazy urgent feeling that I'd made a bargain I couldn't keep, that she'd suck them to the other side of the gate like the Enano Saltarín and I would never see them again.

"They're mine," I said. I had my husband rush them back down to the car.

She almost fell to the floor, leaning heavily on the metal gates to support herself, the locksmith stepping back in terror. "And who are you?" she yelled.

After that, we all speculated she was close to death. I visited her each day, sure it would be the last. She grew skinny, hair paling to bone white, her skin sagging off her skull in delicate folds, heavy with all those years of being a mirror for others' desires. She couldn't keep down solids so I brought her shakes with long straws she could sip through the bars. Sometimes she wouldn't even come to the gates; she didn't want anyone to see her. She wanted only to be a voice. She kept getting younger and younger in her memory.

She was twenty and she trembled and asked me when the Trujillo was coming back. Then she was seventeen and an art student, and Trujillo had killed her best friend, Lario. Then she was fifteen, and she was happier than she'd ever be in her life because no one yet noticed she was more beautiful than all her sisters, and she had painted a prize-winning abstract. The teacher told her she'd created a whole new ocean of light without forcing form around it. Her mother was so proud. Then she was finger painting on the floor. She was so weak. She thought I was her older sister. "You're so diligent," she kept saying, like an incantation to keep me just the way she needed me to be.

One morning I found her passed out by the iron gates in her batica. I thought she was dead. I choked on my own spit, and I felt guilt hang on me for letting her pass alone. But when I reached through the gate, coughing and tearing up, her eyes opened. She said my name for the first time in months. "I'm so glad you've come," she said. "I'm so embarrassed. I must have drunk too much with all my friends." But then she was back in 1960 again.

That night, I packed a bag, and I slept on cushions at the outermost iron gate, like a dog. My husband brought me food. He tried keys on the locks when she wasn't looking.

"You're not helping," I said. "She's only ever going to come out of her own volition."

He said, "I know you feel like you have to do this, but I am ready for you to return to being you whenever you are. Come home. You don't need this."

I pushed him away. I had married, I had borne the children, I had been diligent, I had not yet inherited. What would I be at the end of my life? My tía had no one. Heydí had stopped responding to phone calls. The two things my tía wanted most were a daughter and to be an artist. Didn't I owe her the one she could possibly have, or at least the semblance?

"It's only for a little while," I told my husband.

I felt myself becoming older, tired, stiff from sleeping on the floor, while my aunt remembered herself younger and younger. The neighbors stepped over me with pity. The relatives, when they saw the bags under my eyes growing like suitcases packed full for more trips I would never take, said, "That crone sure is taking ages to die." They meant it to hurt me. But I was ready for her death, too.

Then she refused to put on clothes. She said clothes were a burden. They were all about making it easy for other people to see you, easy to be who you looked like in them. She didn't want to wear costumes anymore. She wanted to feel. She rolled her sagging skin on her marble floors. She was so fragile, I worried her skin would tear as the slick stone tugged on her. When she stood up, I was moved almost to tears with how differently she now stood from the paintings I remembered. I passed her towels to wrap herself in, but these she flung at the neighbors when they walked to the elevator. The towels flapped against the bars and fell at her feet. She was in the finger-painting stage, so in the end I convinced her to roll herself in a floor painting of navy blue, and it wasn't so obvious to the neighbors that she was naked and wrinkled as a chinola.

Finally, I called to her from the gate and there was no answer. I thought maybe she'd passed out on the toilet. It had happened before. Or fallen over one of her many marble coffee tables, and I had no choice but to wait for her to wake up. Or maybe she was ashamed at her nakedness suddenly. I kept calling.

When I was sure she couldn't hear me, I called a lock-smith. He said it would take days. Everyone heard they were opening her place up, that she was likely dead. The rest of the relatives gathered outside like witnesses to the passing of royalty. While they were cutting it open, I couldn't figure out if I should feel sad for my tía or happy. Outside in the hall-way, the sculptures and wreaths of keys still glittered, the bamboo shoots that had grown tall as the roof swayed with the ocean breeze from the malecón.

The locksmith and a team had to open her apartment with the jaws of life, the iron gates and locks prying away like the tops of cans. New air gasped through the hallway as the locks fell to the ground with clinks, lost keys that had been wedged between layers of iron doors clattered free, the bars groaned as they bent toward us, the doors creaked and popped and finally gave way.

When the bars were pushed open, I was ready to see tía Chani laid out like a queen in all that splendor she'd hoarded for decades. The mob of relatives crammed into the apart-ment, pushing and shoving in excitement. They were all de-termined to get in first and pocket what they could in the moments before I pushed past them. Then, turning down the hallway in front of me, I heard a collective gasp.

There was nothing inside the living room. Nothing in the bedrooms. Nothing in the kitchen. Not even furniture, not even anything on the walls, not even a single plate in the cupboard. Nothing in that apartment left of all the riches I'd convinced myself I didn't even want, until that moment. The only thing left was the actual stone of the floors that climbed up to the tops of the walls, shining and marbled like a com-plicated shell.

The theory was she'd spent all those years breaking the fragiles, tearing the paintings, pulling apart the chains of gold into pieces small enough she could fit them through the grate over the trash chute. But then they couldn't explain that even tía Chani was gone. Not even a smell of rot anywhere to suggest a body. She would not leave us even her bones as relics. The more spiteful relatives theorized that she had keys the whole time, and while I had been sleeping, she had escaped the apartment. This I did not believe, that she wouldn't have even told me.

There was nothing to see. The relatives left. The lawyer informed us she'd left the apartment to the daughter, who would end up selling it from Barahona through a real estate agent, without ever going back to the place she'd been raised. My husband stayed with the girls back home, leaving me time to collect my things from where I'd camped out for so long, to become what he trusted I would now become.

I sat in the middle of the living room, saying my tía's name over and over. Nothing but my own voice curled back to me, a sweet timbre I'd never bothered to hear. The sound of ocean waves slapped against the walls. The marble veined with delicate pink glowed with afternoon light. I took off my shoes, let down my hair. I lay down, my skin tingling with the cool polish of stone. My very scalp felt alive. I felt wild. For the first time, there was no one but me.

The Kite Maker

You haven't truly seen a kite fly until you've seen an alien fly one. Dragonfly wings on their backs trembling with anticipation, deep sighs from their purple mouths as they're unrolling the spool. They run with their slow, spindly legs to let the kite pick up speed. When they release the diamond of cloth from their skeletal hands, you can see their armored shoulders strain to rise up with it. As the diamond dips then swells on the string, you can hear great yips, then these wavering trills and the desperateness of their song, how badly they want to be up there. There were thousands of them at the park the other day, and I swear I almost cried hearing those songs ripping from those alien throats.

Some of them try to hide this surge of emotion when I put the kite in their hands. Tove was like this. First time he came into my shop, he tried to keep his eyes closed, his black eyelids flickering with the effort. He walked in pretty stiff for his kind, pushing his skinny feeler legs barely out in front of him, like he was sneaking in on tiptoe. But the little hairs on his legs bristled, and finally he flicked open his black lids.

"Can I help you?" I asked. I never knew what to say around them. It seemed like everything I said was wrong, loaded with some hidden meaning I didn't intend. I still remembered the moment they first arrived, their spaceships burning through the atmosphere like comets, like falling angels, and how we'd surrounded the ships in horror, aiming for their thin legs with anything we could find, because the rest of their bodies were armored but the legs snapped like pencils. I had done these things myself out of fear, when the boys were small, but there was no taking it back now. The ease of killing bugs that looked like them was so natural to us from when insects had encroached on the territories of our houses. Now the aliens kept my shop afloat, seeing as they were the only ones who wanted antique toys. These days, humans wanted tech gadgets, anything with a hint of alien aesthetic, a taste of the exotic. Kids weren't even flying remote helicopters anymore, not even drones. Now you could roll into a suburb and the kids in the front yards would be flying around mini Dragonfly arks, playing at intergalactic war, the losers crashing down into the home base dirt patch they called Earth. Kites, spinning tops—these were ancient toys, more unfamiliar to kids than the Dragonfly tech we'd dragged out of the broken arks. Teenagers tattooed themselves in alien symbols.

Tove inhaled, his Dragonfly body puffing up for a moment. He looked around my dusty shelves of wooden and metal toys. Miniature trains, yo-yos, weather vanes, carved boxes, maracas, tin soldiers. The pegged wall of kites, bright and colorful like those old collectors' rooms of dead butterflies stretched open to display their wings—this was the only wall he didn't look at, as if he was too aware of where it was.

"I am Tove Who Battles Photons," he said in the strange way they announced themselves, his voice flickering in and out of human range.

"Anything you need?" I said.

THE ROCK EATERS

112

He said, "A wooden top. Maybe a kite? Or a game of the dominos?"

I used to be able to scalp them for all the technology they could spare just for the kites. Since, they'd learned to feign nonchalance, but a good antique dealer knows the market. I led him straight to the kite wall, the sailcloth breathing with the breeze he'd let in.

Tove scanned the price tags and shook his head. "Maybe not," he said in that gravelly voice.

I knew what they did for money. Because their wings and legs were built for gravity and an atmosphere thinner than ours, they didn't move fast, couldn't fly, were unsuitable for heavy lifting. Jobs like construction and fieldwork were reserved for humans. But Dragonfly fingers were nimble, so thin and skeletal they swished through our atmosphere like singing blades. Needlework, precision jobs, diamond cutting. They would do all of this for less money than our most menial jobs. They slept in giant warehouses that companies had built for this purpose. But everything they made felt strange, built for another world. Their cloth rasped, jewelry they'd cut reminded us of scales. Alien-made. All the brawny, tough-man jobs were sources of human pride, if you could have them. In this way, I was more like the Dragonflies than the humans, my craft a sign of weakness.

I heard people passing on the sidewalk outside. I held my breath. Sometimes I got a hard time from angry groups who still weren't pleased that the aliens had landed, no matter how much they'd assimilated, no matter that there was no decent way to get rid of them. A group of anti-miscegenation skinheads had been roving the strip, and it wouldn't be the first time they'd come into my store looking for trouble; I'd had bricks thrown through my window a few months before.

But the footsteps passed.

"Next time," I said to Tove, exhaling.

It wasn't about the money. It was about pride in something I'd done, about art. I'd made each kite with my own hands, thread and needle, stick and lathe. I dyed the cloth myself into tapestries that could be seen from the ground. Sometimes the Dragonflies tried to make their own kites from paper bags and twigs. Sometimes they even made them out of scraps of nylon they'd quilted together, stolen from the factories where they worked. But the alien craft makers reflected their own predicament in everything they made. These clunky, make-shift things flew poorly. Mine were art, the aliens told me; they were more than the sum of their parts. Mine had the lift, the weightlessness that pulled your heart up with their string. They told me it made them feel like they were back home, like they had never been stuck here. Dragonflies dropped into my store often, like moths to light. Profits went up. Now I could make the kites as big as I wanted. I had one as big as a hang glider in the back room. Eight hands would have to hold it at once to keep it on the ground.

He lifted one of the kites from the pegboard wall, his antennae straining toward it. I went to return it from his hands to its wooden peg. I brushed his feeler hands as I did, the millions of hairs on his black fingers tickling me, rushing me with a sensation I hadn't felt in years. I felt my face go hot.

Tove withdrew his thin arm as if he'd been burned and said nothing. He left the store in the same tiptoeing way he came. It would be months before he would return.

I went home to my human-made house in the suburbs. In the dusk, I always half expected another ark to fall, the parabolas of broken ships littering the sky. But it had been twelve years since they arrived, more since they first headed for Earth, their home world destroyed by a large meteor, only enough fuel and years to reach the closest habitable planet, break their ships open like eggs in the atmosphere, and never return. Now, when I rolled into my driveway, the kids roamed the neighborhood playing humans and aliens, hitting each other with electronic wands that dissipated on contact so that no damage could be done. We didn't have any actual aliens on our side of town; the children considered weak played the aliens: eyes big, offering no resistance. If they fought back, they were scolded, *That's not how it happened.*

I closed my car door. As I struggled with a heavy bag of groceries, mini-ark toys floated above my head, bobbing as they fought or crash-landed in the sandpit in the neighbor's yard. My boys sat around the kitchen table watching holograms instead of doing homework.

"Help me with my bags," I said, and it took them several seconds before they jumped up to indicate they'd heard me.

My oldest, Aleo, brought in my bag of nearly finished kites I would work on later that night and tossed them in the corner of the kitchen without looking. He had a disdain for the things. Nobody at his high school wanted to look like poor alien kids, who were always flying kites and never wore clothes, only threadbare baby shoes that protected the ends of their delicate legs from the pavement. Of course, no human would ever be confused for a Dragonfly, but looking poor or brown was almost as bad. We passed as white and we weren't poor exactly, but no matter how much money I made off of the kites, it never seemed like enough.

Benon hugged the paper sack of groceries. He was wide-eyed, and I knew he was bullied when Aleo wasn't around.

"How's the schoolwork coming?" I asked as I threw broccoli into a pot.

"What's cooking?" Aleo asked without looking up from the hologram he was watching again.

Benon held his nose. I didn't make any excuses for my cooking.

When we sat down to eat, Benon said, "About home-work . . ."

"Shoot," I said.

"I have a history report. It can be about anything."

I froze. I knew what he would say before it was out of his mouth. Of course he would, always playing the alien in the neighborhood games.

"I want to write about the Fallings," he said.

I pressed my lips together hard. Aleo shoved more food in his mouth than I thought possible to swallow. Something black flashed from under Aleo's sleeve as he reached for more food. I grabbed his hand and pulled up his sleeve. "What is that?"

"Nothing," he said, yanking his sleeve back down again. But I'd seen it. Alien script: the swoops and careful circles, the spheres with the arrows shooting out.

"Is it permanent?" I said. "Do you even know what that means?"

Aleo mumbled.

Benon said, "Mom, you were there at the Fallings. You *saw* it."

"So did your brother. Aleo, what does it mean?"

"I don't remember," Aleo said, glaring at me. "I was only a few years old."

Yes, I remembered him on my hip, three years old, and Benon only a few months old. We left Benon with a neighbor, but Aleo was too much, was walking and running and always breaking everything he touched. I remembered him crying when he saw the Dragonflies emerging from their ships, his cry the call to arms that I needed to rush forward, his body on my hip the ballast when I swung. "What does the tattoo mean?" I insisted.

Aleo slammed his fork down. "It means Aleo Laughter in the Air."

"Laughter in the Air? Really?" I snorted. When was the last time I'd laughed, felt levity? "Can you even read it?"

He didn't answer.

"Mom," Benon whined, "I want to know what it was like."

I didn't say, *How could you own up to all the things you've ever done that shamed you? How could you look backward while stepping over the dead bodies in the way?*

"It changed everything," I said.

"It's permanent," Aleo said. "It's a part of me now."

"Good. Great." I got up from the table. I was no longer hungry. I shut myself in the garage for the rest of the night, turning a group of sticks smooth in the lathe. One thick, long branch was earmarked for the large kite. When I picked it up, it felt just like the weight of a baseball bat, the only weapon I'd had when I'd headed to the first arkfall. I swung it in the air, the heft just right for making contact.

In late summer, the skinheads started setting fire to some of the shops that catered to Dragonflies. It was illegal, and also ridiculous. The world would change without them whether they wanted it to or not. But a bakery down the street that hired a Dragonfly to decorate the cakes had been burned to the ground.

The skinheads were already on the wrong side of history, but it only made them cling harder to their hatred. Some groups were angry because the Dragonflies were taking up resources; others because they'd taken jobs. Some were staunch on no human-Dragonfly love. Our species were so different we couldn't procreate together, and the religious zealots claimed that without the sanctification of children, the union was unnatural, disgusting. Bestiality, which was a sin. Religious pundits tried to justify our cruelty by saying the Dragonflies had no souls. Some of them believed that the aliens were playing a long con, coining the adage: *There's more than one way to colonize the Earth.*

Some months after I first saw Tove, I came home to a Dragonfly in the backyard, the neighborhood kids encircling him with their electronic sticks. Even the older kids were out, excited by the new development. "What's going on?" I said.

Aleo shrugged. "Ask Benon."

"He's for my project," Benon said. "I asked him to come home with us."

"Are you fine with this?" I asked the Dragonfly kid.

"I'm cool," the Dragonfly said. He looked at me and popped gum from his tiny, pursed mouth. I waited for him to announce himself the way his kind did. It was hard to tell their ages, but this one must have been born here, was already starting to lose the customs of his parents.

Finally, I asked him, "Who *are* you?" more combatively than I would have liked.

"I am Yeshela Whisperer of Mist," the child said begrudgingly.

"Wonderful," I said, and went back inside.

I was not against the kids mixing, unlike the other parents who were prying their blinds open to watch from across the block. It's just that I didn't think the kids were ready. Not after I'd seen what we'd done as adults. But I was willing to bet against myself. I left them to it and pulled aside the curtain.

They were reenacting the Fallings again. Benon sat atop our old swing set and directed. He was using the Dragonflies' name for it, the Arkfall Massacres. It seemed like this time they were trying to get everything exactly right. They even had a giant hologram of one of the arks cracked like an egg projected in the sandbox. Benon was reading the history out loud.

Millions died. We hadn't known what they wanted. When they crawled out of their broken ships and picked themselves up out of the crashes, we were sure they were invading, they wanted our children, they wanted more than we could give. We defended our Earth. We aimed for their thin legs, their eyes, their delicate fingers. In our city, a ship crashed into the main fiber-optic tower. It wiped out most communications, and city officials were too panicked to fix it. Other cities made other mistakes. We couldn't call each other directly, and so everything we knew about the crash that boomed into the city at dusk, the other arkfalls across the world, was through a rumor mill. Was the National Guard coming? Were they too busy with other arkfalls? Were there too many of the ships to defend against? How many of us could they kill before we reacted? By sunup the next day, we were at the crash site with any weapons we could find.

The neighborhood kids were making the Dragonfly kid crawl out of the hologram. Then a line of them stood ready with their e-sticks. Benon knew I was watching. He couldn't help but flick his eyes in my direction. That kid always had the uncanny ability to know when I was looking, unlike Aleo, and then perform the son he thought would make me proud.

Benon directed the neighborhood kids to approach and

demand what the Dragonflies wanted. *Tell us what you want. Hand over your weapons. Speak in our language. Give us everything.* Benon kept pausing the action to ask the boy what he felt, what he would have done if he'd been there.

The moment came that I was dreading. The boy, as directed, stood up slowly, testing the thick, heavy atmosphere. He put up his thin arms to shield his eyes from the alien sun. Benon said, *Look, he's going to shoot us.* The humans approached, sticks raised. The boy's wings fluttered, an unconscious reaction, trying to fly away even in a game, finding this atmosphere a noose to the ground—just like his parents did then. Had he been like us, he would have yelled for the humans to stop. The e-sticks flew at him, whaled on him, and went for his legs. The e-sticks worked as they were supposed to, dissipating into gas upon contact. The blows weren't hurting him. Aleo had once flung one at me in a childish rage, and the dissipation had only felt like the strangest whisper. The boy closed his eyes as the sticks hissed over him, his sensitive body hairs feeling the ghost movements of a long-past massacre. Benon looked to the window, it seemed, for approval, his eyes asking, *Is this right? Is this how you did it?*

I closed the curtains. A spray of police lights flashed past the window. Someone must have called the cops when they heard a Dragonfly boy was in the neighborhood.

I opened the curtains again. Yeshela was cowering on the ground, trying not to move, lest he hit the handles and fists holding the e-sticks, which would not dissipate. The humans were still going, their joy at having their game more lifelike than it had ever been before, like a drug. How could they know what they were pretending to be? For them, it was just a story. They never got to the point of horror, the point when we were sorry, when the tide turned, after we wanted them to surrender in the human way, arms up, after we wanted them to fight back to absolve us, after we realized they could not be pushed to fight back, when we began to carry them into the hospitals and the morgue, the doctors trying as best as they could to understand our differences, how to get under their armor, how to splint antennae together, where the vital organs were.

I burst through the screen door. "Stop," I yelled.

"Mom, it's a game," Aleo said.

"A game," I scoffed.

The cop car parked across the street.

"I'm taking you home," I said to the Dragonfly boy.

I loaded Aleo and Benon and the Dragonfly into the car. The boy directed me to a side of town I'd avoided since the city had changed. Otherwise the three of them were silent the whole way. The streets changed from our suburbs and waving neighbors to downtown and sky-rise apartments and expensive alien-batteried cars to cheap construction to, finally, giant warehouses in a maze of parking lots. In our city, they had been installed in old complexes of customer fulfillment warehouses. In other cities, they had been pushed into condemned and rotten buildings at the center. In others they were given cloth FEMA tents. In some they were given nothing and wandered from public park to public park.

The warehouse the boy pointed me to was almost as big as one of their ships. Rows of them lined the industrial complex. At the gates of the boy's warehouse, I parked, pushed my own boys out. "You're going to apologize to his mother," I said. Benon hung his head.

"History makes no apologies," Aleo said, repeating something he'd heard in a bad hologram, winking at Benon.

The Dragonfly boy did not say, *Please don't come, please do not meet my mother, please do not tell them what you did.* Instead he said, "The warehouse is not a place you'll like. My mother will not like this. We are far in the back."

Which did not deter me in the least.

A smaller door had been cut into the giant loading dock door. Inside, the old product shelving stacks had been repurposed into bunks, layer upon layer of bed spaces where as many as four or five of them slept at a time. Whole families of Dragonflies curled into each other's bodies. We stepped over standing water on the concrete floors, the smell of mold, flies swarming in clouds. There were dragonfly feeders hung up on the long scaffolding—I mean actual dragonflies, the tiny Earth kind, which the aliens hatched from eggs and studied. There was no electricity, no running water I could see. Just rows and rows of bunks, each bed like a tiny home, some decorated with my own kites, wind chimes, feathers, and mechanical fans.

When we reached the bunk the boy said was his, his mother climbed down, buzzing. She didn't announce her name because it was her turf, not mine, but I didn't give her my name either. It was easier this way. I pushed my boys in front of me.

"I'm sorry," they chimed in unison.

"For what?" asked the mother.

"They—we—" I said.

"He wasn't hurt," I finally offered.

"I don't understand," she said. She chattered to her son in their own language, the hums and silences, and he sullenly responded, his legs curling and making him sink in stature.

I wanted to run back the way we came, past rows and rows of these broken families, but I made the three of us stand there in penance.

The mother turned her head back to us. She said, "I think

forgiveness means different things in our language. We do not ask for it."

We were silent, rebuked, looked down toward our shoes.

"I'm sorry we make you sleep here," Benon said. "It's so horrible."

For a moment I was proud. I would have pointed out every failure in the warehouses so my boys would learn how much we had.

Then the mother said, "It's our home." She turned away from me, bundled her child's legs up, and lifted him, laboring slowly in the heavy atmosphere up the ladder.

That night, I put my sons to bed for the first time in years, checking on them in the bedroom they shared before turning out the lights. Their childhood progressed across the walls from Benon's side, with its cartoon spaceships and innocent pale stars, to Aleo's side, with museum diagrams of arks and telescope photos of suns that roiled and flared and irradiated.

Benon was still chattering about his history report, how he could use what he'd learned.

"Please," I said, "don't do that again."

Aleo rolled his eyes, turned over.

"But I'm trying to understand them," Benon protested.

"*Them*?" I said.

Benon gave a large sigh. I was afraid for them, my kids, for what they would discover about themselves, for who they wanted to be but would soon discover they couldn't.

I tried to hold them both, one arm in each bed. Aleo shrugged me away; Benon stayed rigid.

"Mom, we don't need you," Aleo said.

I thought of their father then. A year after the Fallings, he had left us for another woman across the country. The Fall-ings made you realize you didn't even know yourself, he'd said, that we didn't even know who we'd become. He wanted to start over with someone else, with this new understand-ing. He said, as he closed the door softly for the last time on me and the kids, "How can you love like that, not knowing what's inside of you?"

I hadn't argued.

It was months before Tove walked into my shop

again. I wouldn't even have recognized him—I had a hard time differentiating them—except he had that strange walk, like he was feeling his way around a cage. The bell tinkled, and he tiptoed in again. From Benon's history report (he walked around the house spewing facts), I knew that their religions focused on the legs as the expressions of the body. The rest of their bodies were so rigid, but the legs could curl like delicate antennae. If they could express their souls, it would be through the way they moved their legs.

"We're closing soon," I said.

Tove's top antennae drooped.

"But if there's something I can do?" I said.

He tiptoed through the aisles, ending up at the kite wall like I knew he would. I hopped off my stool. He let his fingers glide across the sailcloth of the cheapest kite, a red one that pictured the deserts of Mars. I could tell it wasn't his favor-ite. His purple eyes, remarkably human, roved all over the wall.

There was one on the bottom shelf that was my own fa-vorite, dyed mostly blue so it would melt into the sky. A big no-no in the kite trade; amateurs stuck to reds and oranges, colors that would be easily seen in the clouds. But I was an artist and hated rules. I wanted the kite to blend in. I wanted the kite to look like a ripple across a mirror, like a great tide welling up under the surface. It wasn't the cheapest, but I was determined to see it in the sky. I always made my customers take their kites across the street to the park. I told them it was to verify that they were satisfied, that the kite worked. But mostly I was watching them, trying to understand the alien emotion that racked their bodies as they let them loose.

"How about this one?" I said, picking it up.

He purred from his throat, smashed his eyes shut against the blue.

"It is not for me," he said. "I would have to ask."

"Who is it for?" I asked.

"My sons," he said.

Benon had informed me that the Dragonfly women gave all of the material gifts to the offspring, so I knew something must have happened to Tove's mate. If it had happened twelve years ago, I did not want to know. I could tell myself he and I were the same, trying to figure out the world alone, no one by our side who had seen the best and the worst.

"I'm sure they would love it," I told Tove. "These sell quickly, so I can't promise to hold it."

"It is about choice," he said, his accent terse.

Benon had told me that back on Sadiyada (our approximation of their home planet's name), none of them gave orders. If a shuttle full of Dragonflies were about to drive over a cliff, the passengers would say, *A cliff!* rather than *Stop!* or *Turn around!* They believed in pointing out what was there rather than compelling action. When they had realized an asteroid was about to decimate their planet, they merely built the ships, let anyone who wanted the one-way trip board the ships that would fall apart on atmospheric impact.

The others just stayed behind, burned up with the asteroid's impact and fireballs of debris raining from the sky. Mothers, sons, lovers, all of them separated, and no matter the love between them, not a one would beg, *Come with me*. They just waved good-bye.

And then they got here, and they were assaulted with demands. *Come out, come out unarmed, give us everything you have, defend yourself, fight back so we can excuse what we've done, proceed this way to the camps, work, work, buy, buy.* I pressured them all. I couldn't imagine the shame, on top of everything else I had caused.

I nodded to Tove, who put down my favorite kite to look at another. "Choose whichever you'd like," I said, a demand disguised as a choice.

Two teenage voices began yelling outside the store.

Tove dropped the kite in the middle of the aisle. I pushed Tove quickly into the back workroom. He screeched softly, his hairs smashed down underneath my palms. "Stay here," I said, "and don't come out until I tell you." Tove said nothing.

"Trust me," I pleaded. I had to leave him there, stuck among my half-finished projects and the cardboard boxes.

I got to the front counter before the bell tinkled, before bald heads rushed into the room, the baldness a physical refusal to be like the Dragonflies with their million bristling, feeling hairs. They blew in with chants of *Bugs are bugs!*

"Any bugs in here?" the leader asked.

"No," I said quickly. I stared them down.

I recognized one of them, an older girl that Aleo had brought over once after school. Then, I thought she'd been nice, shy, had always called me ma'am. Did it matter that before the Dragonflies arrived, she and I would have been hated instead—for our dark hair, her Chicana roots and my Dominican ones, that we knew how to speak Spanish? It did not. All of us had a choking fear clawing at our chests. Her baldness was new, her scalp paler where hair used to be. I could tell she recognized me, too, the way she wouldn't meet my eyes, and she hunched her shoulders and tried to melt behind one of the others, a burly man with a sweatband around his forehead.

"Lady, I could have sworn . . ." the ringleader said.

"See for yourself," I said. I knew it was best to let their anger wash over the store with the least provocation. I had called the cops before, and I knew from experience that they waited until any damage was already done before intervening or blamed the victims instead.

They looked around the store. Their eyes settled on the kites. They knew who my customers were. They started to poke through the dusty racks, the afternoon light arriving in golden, violent streaks to illuminate what we were all capable of.

The girl I recognized pushed a display case weakly, so that it tottered but didn't fall. One of them brushed a row of yo-yos onto the floor. Another was heading in the direction of the workroom door. The burly man with the sweatband picked up the kite Tove had dropped on the floor in our rush toward the back room. I kept staring at the girl I recognized, who finally looked up and caught my eye.

"Nothing here," she said.

The burly one with the kite handed it to the girl like it was evidence to the contrary. The girl looked at me, snapped the wood of the kite. She ripped the cloth in a struggle of arms.

She tossed the flail of broken kite, the spine akimbo. She led them out of the store. I could hear them whooping on their way down the street to the next establishment.

I picked up the broken kite and put it behind the counter.

I wasted minutes picking up the scatters of wooden yo-yos, just in case they changed their minds and returned. I shook, my arms trembling as I replaced the yo-yos to their stack.

When I finally went in the back, Tove was under the giant hang-glider-sized kite that took up most of the ten-foot room. His shape flinched when he heard the door open.

"I'm sorry," I said. "You can come out now."

He moved the giant kite off and nodded.

I held my still-trembling hand out to help him, but he stood up slowly by himself, his legs curling under his weight, the air pushed from the flutter of his wings tickling my skin. A breeze when there was none. I remembered brushing his hand the first day I met him.

"This one," he said, pointing at the giant kite. "This is the one I want."

I had painted it with a mosaic that looked like stained glass, so when it flew, it was like we were inside some great cathedral. Like we were supposed to pray underneath its great glass.

"How much?" he asked.

I understood Tove, wanting the biggest, best thing you couldn't have. I was trembling still. I wanted his unexhausted hope. I wanted forgiveness without having to name my sins. I wanted tenderness to feel real to me again. Some part of me wanted to fly in the face of everything those skinheads represented, but another part of me wanted the world before the Dragonflies fell in. Could we be tender again? Benon had informed me that the Dragonflies were so fragile—all those hairs on their legs and arms and feelers, all those thin appendages—that they were so careful with each other when they loved, they barely even touched. Lovemaking was mostly an act of anticipation, their wings manipulating the air around the beloved like a cyclone of foreplay, sending all their hairs and feelers singing with touch. It was like being loved by the air itself. Even this was left wanting from Earth's atmosphere, their movements clumsier now, the work so much harder on them. But human lungs! We had always been clumsy, but we had more lung force than their wings had now. Instead of answering Tove, giving him the simple price of a kite, I pursed my lips and whistled air in his direction.

"Oh," he said, eyes closing. "Oh, he—me—na." His throat buzzed. His voice sounded like a bad radio, their own language spoken on a frequency that sounded to us like only silence and hums, like what he was trying to say couldn't ever reach me.

I whistled again, pushing air across his face in the circular pattern Benon had described. For a moment, I thought what I was doing was a boon. A moment of tenderness between us. Proof that we could connect despite what had happened.

"Oh, I feel unarmored," he said. "Oh, hemenalala, I am defenseless."

It was like I was pummeling the words out of him, he said them that painfully. Suddenly, I realized he wanted to say *Stop*. He wanted to say *Desist*. Were those nicknames he had given his fallen mate? Was he trying to call her ghost back across the years? But it was my name I wanted on his purple lips. I was angry. I didn't want him to be defenseless.

I blew all the way around him to the back, where his four wings trembled, my breath blowing their wing-dust off until they shone translucent. Had he still been able to fly, stripping his wings of their powder would have been even more cruel. Benon had said that their wings were electric colors in the home atmosphere, but in this one they had turned a dusty brown. Now they were like drab ghosts. Benon had never told me what came after, what consummation was for them. Had I known, I might have done it. I know I would have done it.

"Oh, hemenalala," he said as I made my way back to his front, where his thorax armor glistened and tensed.

I stopped, held my breath. What had I done?

When Tove was finally able to compose himself, I couldn't look at him. I said, "The kite isn't finished. Come back in a month."

He didn't answer me, and he didn't turn around. His eyes stayed closed the whole way out of the store.

Weeks passed. Tove did not come back. I wasn't expecting him to. Where would he get the money? And after what I'd done. Benon got an A on his history report, the note from the teacher saying, *May there be no judgment in truth.* The skinheads came again into my store after another one of my customers, who was able to slip slowly out the back door. Benon was still spouting Dragonfly facts routinely, like, *Their language doesn't even have a grammar for commands,* and *Didja know they had prophecies about ending up here eventually? But this is only the third epoch in their religious texts—there's still a fourth and a fifth about going to other places and saving us along with them.* Apparently, they, too, had stories about arks, wandering through deserts, how many of them would fall when they got to their new home. Aleo got another tattoo, this one a poor translation of a command they had no word for, *Remember.* But remember how?

One afternoon, just before closing, I heard people yelling outside my store, saw the lighters flick on the other side of the frosted glass. I ran outside.

"What do you think you're doing?" I yelled to the group

that had gathered, the same group of skinheads that had plagued me with Tove. I meant to distract them with words. I meant to drain the fervor out of what they were doing. I meant to inject them with the moment I had years before, when I dropped my bat.

The leader said, "Stay out of the way and you won't get hurt."

The lighters were licking strips of cardboard. I thought of how much money was inside that store in wood and cloth, what I would lose. I let my temper loose. I started yelling, calling them the curs of the world, disgusting creatures, more animal than the bugs, not fit to inherit the Earth. I spat because I'd seen it done in holograms and at some point my words failed me.

The girl who had been Aleo's friend, now confident and grown into her role, said, "Lady, I wasn't even born when they got here, and I didn't even have the chance to do anything. What did you do when they came? You're just like us."

"That was before I knew," I said.

"And now we know what we are," the girl said. "You're just pretending."

The rest of them chanted. *More than one way. Bugs are bugs.* The cardboard strips touched the storefront. They all stepped back.

"There *is* more than one way," I said. I rushed forward, trying to put out the flames with my jacket, but the flames seemed to glow and leap up brighter with every swing and fan. I yanked open the shop door, burning my hand on the doorknob, and ran inside.

Inside the shop, you could barely hear the crackle of the fire. I stopped. I was panting. I looked around at the shelves, the kite wall illuminated orange from the flames outside the window. Did I want to let it burn? To let everything I had done in conciliation disappear, burn up, leave no trace? For any guilt I had to disappear, to be forgiven by flames?

And then I smelled smoke. I snapped out of it, ran in a craze pulling kites down off the walls, rushing back and forth to my car parked out back, dumping everything I could and going back inside. One of the kites caught on the door-jamb, the cloth tearing like muscle, the frame snapping like bones, like legs, like antennae, a feeling I remembered. In my memory I stood over a Dragonfly, arms lifted to protect a small one. I left the baby, but I killed the mother. We were methodical in our frenzy. Dragonfly after Dragonfly, if they moved, if they didn't move, if they made sound, if they were silent, we killed them. We were afraid. I was afraid.

I pulled all the kites down off the wall before the flames reached inside. I pulled the giant kite out of the back room, the frame still heavy as a baseball bat, the cloth still fragile as skin.

I started driving. What did I have left in the world? My sons, my kites. The certainty of moving forward and beginning again. My fear. I wanted to scream. For a moment I let go of the steering wheel and let the car drift over into the other lane. Another car was coming down the roadway, driving along like everything in our world was normal, metal body swinging toward me. Then I thought of Aleo and Benon and jerked my wheel back.

I drove my car in circles. I was like a sleepwalker. I don't even know how I got there, but eventually, I ended up at the Dragonfly warehouses.

Inside, I asked, "Please, does anyone know Tove Battler of Photons?"

They bristled, and too late I realized I'd said his name wrong. Long black antennae-like fingers pointed me to another warehouse, down corridors, up racks of bunks. Then I found him lying on a third-floor bunk, eyes closed, his sons chattering in their mother tongue beside him.

"Tove," I said.

He sat up.

I did not say, *Come outside,* or even *please.* I said, "My store is burning. There is something outside. It is for you."

He stared at me for a good while. Did he hate me? I deserved it. He could have lain back in his bunk. Instead, he labored down slowly. He waved his antennae at his sons, and they followed at a distance.

There were tears sliding down my face. "Why didn't you defend yourself?" I asked. "Why?"

He led the way outside, tiptoeing as if walking toward a dangerous secret. Finally, he said, "Wouldn't you have killed us all, if we had fought back and lost? You have books that say only the weak will inherit the Earth. In our prophecies, the only way to stay was to not fight back."

I didn't mean twelve years ago, I meant in my back room. I wanted to tear my hair out, hearing that—for him, his mate, the self I had lost that would have let them be. I said, "But why did *you* not fight back?"

"I wanted to live so badly," he said. For the first time I noticed seams on his legs where they must have been broken before, the source of his strange tiptoe walking.

"And if you inherit the Earth, what would you do with it?" I asked.

Silent, he waited for me behind the trunk of my car. A crowd of Dragonflies gathered behind us to see what this human woman wanted.

I opened the trunk, began passing out the kites I'd saved. Of what use could they possibly be to me? I handed the end of a rope to Tove, two others to his sons. I had five other rope ends that I passed out. Each was one piece of the giant kite.

This wasn't charity; this wasn't forgiveness. How could it be, after all that I had done, was still doing? I wanted to fling it in their faces, what they had lost. I wanted to see them hurt for that sky, sing for that lost planet. I wanted them to sing my own song and break open with it.

Then Tove led the eight of them forward, and they began running slowly with their curling legs. The kite, the sky over them as oppressive as my fear. All around me I heard gasps and yips, long protracted vowels, what they called their home planet in their own language. They moaned as the hang glider went up, that cathedral shard taking off above us, begging us all to rise.

What We Lost

We were losing parts of ourselves. A reporter discovered a trove of ears in a burlap sack, another found a church constructed of knee cartilage. Our leader said the papers were lying, but we weren't sure what was fake and what was fact. What happened to me, what happened to my neighbors— that wasn't enough proof of all we had lost.

It was easy enough, in the early days, to say, *Your hand? How strange. Are you sure you didn't misplace it somewhere?*

We know now about the field of hands, planted in the ground and waving like a crop of corn. The farmers who lost their collarbones and can't shoulder any weight. The fishermen who lost their rotator cuffs and can no longer pull their catch to shore.

I myself lost my nose, and now I can neither smell nor taste the poison in the water. My father lost his thumbs and can't hold his tools. He spends his evenings telling stories of the old days. My friend Salma lost her eyes. She lives near the leader's palace, and all in that district were blinded. She comes to my house, led by Milito, who cannot hear: his ears were at the bottom of the bag the reporter discovered. Another friend, Darciel, lost his feet, and when he visits me he claws himself up the hill, his body scraping on the sidewalk. After he says good-bye, he lets himself roll down the hill. Many women lost their kidneys, and their eyes and skin became yellow as gold. In the dialysis clinics they gossip as if they were in beauty parlors. And aren't they beautiful still?

Milito leads Salma up to my door. Darciel is not far behind, having just finished his scraping ascent up the hill. Salma smiles when I belt out my greeting.

In the afternoons, the four of us, plus my parents, still drink lemonade in the shade of my porch. It's not really lemonade, not with fresh water as rare as it is. I had found a lone scraggly grapevine in a ditch, and I crushed its grapes with lemons for the drink.

A bird trills in the trees. We haven't heard such a thing in months—most birds have lost their wings and their voices—and we pause in reverence, except for Milito, who cannot hear it. Salma tilts her head in the direction of the song.

How did all this happen? It started with the natu-ral world. First we lost the bugs that pollinated the crops, and then the aquifers ran out of water. Then the empty aquifers collapsed into sinkholes, which made several neighborhoods disappear. Then we lost the moon.

But we weren't concerned back then. We were tired. We closed our blinds. Back then, our leader promised to fix what was broken. He promised to make us a great nation no matter what the cost. It didn't matter to us then; he said the cost

would always be paid by others—other nations or the ene-
mies within.

My mother, who lost her teeth, creeps up behind
me as I am pouring. She mumbles a litany of praise for our
leader, how he has given us such delicious lemons. How great
it is that he has taken the seeds so we don't have to pick
them out.

I am tired of reminding her that without seeds we can't
grow lemon trees and have to beg for our fruit.

My father, sensing an argument about to ruin our afternoon, changes the subject and talks about how strong he
used to be, when he could still wield an ax. He waves his
hands as he talks: they look like paws without their thumbs.
Like my mother, he supported the leader because of all the
problems he promised to fix. Since my father only talks
about how he used to be, we all humor him.

I found the valley of noses myself, a few miles
north of the city. They trembled in the wind, inhaling the
smog. Was that my own nose calling to me from down in the
valley? To reclaim it, I would have to fight the police. If I
wanted to take back what was mine, I would have to start a
revolution. But I was alone, the smog cycloning around me.

The decrees read every week at the shopping mall say that
there is never any excuse for violence. Never mind how our
fights over rainwater give the police an excuse to beat us.
Never mind our missing organs, which disappeared so
slowly and silently we didn't even realize it was happening.

Everyone knows that what went missing can be found: in a burlap sack or a palace. But if you try to take back what is yours—the ear, the bone, the nose—the police will set upon you instantly, taking another part of you as punishment. You know when someone has tried, because suddenly their street is a sea of white police helmets.

You had to wonder about the police. They were people, too, people we knew well. One officer's wife said that there were chunks missing from her husband's back. So why were they so quick with the guns and the machetes? All of them, under their uniforms, had loss.

When Darciel first lost his left foot, he went hopping through the streets, looking for it. He thought he saw it in the gutter, but it floated away. He tracked it from a factory that used the feet to churn chemicals to a river trail of discarded waste. Finally, he found it in the water treatment plant. It was there along with thousands of other feet bobbing on the surface of the water, yellow and green with fungus. Maybe it was the feet that poisoned our drinking water. When he reached in with a net to try to fish his foot out, the police dragged him back and took his other one.

Darciel regales us with accounts of what he's seen as he's crawled through the streets: Boys with no fingers playing soccer in the suburbs. Publishing houses filled with historians who have no memories and write their books in the present tense. A neighborhood—the one closest to the water treatment plant—filled with people who have no brains. (It wasn't our leader that took those brains, though.

That was the poison in the water.) Farmers whose arms droop without collarbones, picking wild mulberries with their toes, the juice dripping from their feet. A district of girls with no voices, who are coveted by marriageable men. When they open the blinds in the morning, their mouths are cupped like Os. My mother says they're singing, but we know how some songs can be screams.

I hand Darciel a cup of lemonade.

My mother asks him if he's ever thought of walking on his hands. "It seems easy enough," she says.

"How easy it is," Darciel says, "to forget what's been done to us. No, I never want to forget."

"Traitor," my mother says, slamming the door on her way back into the house.

Milito fingers the guitar, playing a song that he still remembers from when he could hear. Sometimes the song is so off-key that we wince. Sometimes it's flawless and we want to dance. Today the song sounds like sparkling water.

"You know what I love about us?" Salma asks. "We're still mostly the same. Look at us, enjoying a drink on the porch."

I cover my face with my hand. I don't want to be looked at. I was beautiful once.

My father scoffs. Milito helps Salma to the bathroom. Now we have to ask each other for help to do everything. (Except for Darciel, who refuses to let me push him in a wheelbarrow.) Before, the ways in which we needed help were invisible to us.

Evening is falling. The sky is extinguishing.

Darciel says he passed by the palace and the windows from the ballroom gleamed with light. We wonder what the leader has lost. Some say he has lost nothing. Our leader has been known to wear us to state functions, our mouths strung in a necklace around his neck, our ears in a laurel crown. He has said to foreign diplomats that he is only the embodiment of the people, that he performs only our wishes. There are too many of us to blame.

My mother says he uses all of our missing parts for the good of the people. He is not to blame for everything that came before him. "You didn't need that nose," she says. She repeats the state-sponsored news about our soldier who was captured behind enemy lines: how he was being traded back one piece at a time. His kidney, one eye, and one hand were exchanged for the kidney, eye, and hand of one of our other citizens. "Maybe that eye was yours, Salma," my mother says. "You should be proud to help our soldiers come home."

Sometimes I wish my mother had lost her tongue instead of her teeth.

Now in the darkness of night, we hear in the neighborhood others losing parts, the sudden cry when the children realize that they are no longer whole, if they understand what is happening to them. Some never understand. Really, it's lucky that we lost the moon first. The darkness helps. At night when we go to sleep, we can't see which parts of us we're missing.

"I'm imagining the leader in his palace before we rush in with a revolution," Salma says.

In his bedroom, getting ready for the dinner feast, he is smiling. He has everything he's always wanted, organs to spare if he needs them. But why stop now? The hearts in the fruit bowl on the sideboard, don't they beat just for him?

Hasn't he made us, the world, beautiful with what we've lost? He is dancing, large belly on ancient legs. He is jumping on the mattress, laughing as his stomach drops. The moon rolls at the foot of his bed, its light straining against the windows.

When both my parents go inside, we make plans

in hushed voices and Milito reads our lips. A crawling man, a blind woman, a deaf man, and a woman without a nose—it will take all of us. And we try to shrug off our normalcy to have rage enough for twenty.

We will sneak into the palace and release the arms to fight the police. The hearts to beat the alarm we should have heard long ago. The legs to carry our messages. What is one leader compared to all of us who would come, led in chains of neighbor helping neighbor? The eyes will bear our witness. The throats will vibrate with our story.

The Rock Eaters

We were the first generation to leave our island country. We were the ones who developed a distinct float to our walk on the day we came of age. Soon enough we were hovering inches above the ground, then somersaulting with the clouds, finally discovering we could fly as far as we'd ever wanted. And so we left. Decades later, we brought our children back to see our home country. That year, we all decided we were ready to return.

We jackknifed through clouds and dodged large birds. We held our children tightly; they had not yet learned to fly. Behind us trailed roped-together lines of suitcases packed with gifts from abroad. We wondered who would remember us.

Our parents, those who were still alive, came out to greet us, hands on their brows like visors. Some were expecting us. Others were surprised, terrified at the spectacle of millions of their prodigals blotting the sky with our billowing skirts, our shirts starched for the arrival. We touched down on our parents' driveways, skidding to rough landings at their feet, denting cars, squashing flowers, rattling windows.

Our old friends and siblings, the ones we'd left behind, kept their doors locked. They peered through window blinds at the flattened flowerbeds, the suitcases that had burst and strewn packages all over the yards and streets, our youngest children squealing now that they'd been released, the peace we'd broken by returning. They didn't trust us, not after our betrayal decades ago, the whiff of money we'd earned or lost in other countries like a suspect stench. Our parents hugged their grandchildren and brought them inside to houses with no electricity, candles wavering like we were in a séance. "More brownouts," they told us. "We remember," we said, recoiling at how little the place fit us anymore. Those first nights we slept in our old beds, our feet hanging over the edges, the noises of the city and the country crowing and honking us awake, music from radios and guitars, celebrations we'd not been invited to.

We dragged our children along to knock on the doors of old friends and siblings, the ones who had never developed the ability to fly. They eventually, reluctantly, opened their doors. At first we sat stiffly on couches and inquired after their health and others we once knew. Then we got them to laugh with us about the time we pulled the nuns' skirts or put gum in the kink of a rival's hair, when we caught baby chicks in the village and raised them, or cracked open almonds on the malecón. Then their children came shyly out of their rooms and took ours by the hand. We smiled when we saw them climbing trees together in the patios, their children showing ours how to eat cajuilitos solimán and acerolas from the branch.

We introduced our children to everyone we used to know: at colmados, by the side of the road, at the baseball fields, at country clubs we had to beg to be let back into. We showed our children the flamboyán trees in the parks, blooms of coral red spilling in the dirt. We showed them the granite striated through the rock faces of mountains, the glimmering pebbles under waterfalls, the red dust that stained the seats of their best clothes. We walked past the stray dogs that growled and whined; the most ancient among them remembered us, wagging their tails when they saw us and running to sniff our offspring. We dunked our children into the rivers we'd once swum. We dug through the banks for the arrowheads that belonged to the Tainos, who'd been erased after the Spanish came, their remnants lost in the mud.

Lost, the children whispered in awe and fear, turning the black, glinting points in their palms, testing the hardness of flint between their teeth. Back in our foreign homes, we had never talked to them of history.

We remembered we'd been happy. "We loved this land," we said. We forget why we ever left.

Then the first child came of age. We weren't ex-pecting it. She seemed so young, skinny, her curly hair still in little girl's braids. Nevertheless, we saw the evidence: underwear buried in the trash, the unmistakable spots of blood. We saw her heels rise up, saw her walking on her toes like a careful ballerina. That was how it had started for us. We would soon no longer have to carry her and others strapped to our backs as we flew. We were excited for her, and sad.

We threw the first girl a party, everyone invited, but we didn't advertise why, hoping not to embarrass her or alienate our flightless old friends, who had been so welcoming, by rubbing her flight in their faces. The party brought us all together, all those children speaking the languages of the countries we'd adopted, the local children finding ours exotic and precious. They all screeched as they cannonballed into the pool.

The first girl raised her arms at the top of the diving board. We held our breath. She flipped off the board, spun like a starfish. She brought herself to an unnatural stop in the air just before hitting the skin of the pool. Then she let herself slip under without a splash. "Bravo!" we cheered.

We let the grandparents cut the cake. Their teeth glinted, their arms arced possessively around our children, showing them off to the parents of those who had stayed. The grandparents wore the fancy foreign clothes we had brought them, clothes we couldn't really afford and had put on credit cards or bought with pawned jewelry. But we had to show them we'd been right all this time to have flown away. After so many years of loneliness, and the futures we'd broken by disappearing from them, how proud they were that everyone had returned! But how long could we stay? We made no promises.

We searched for the first girl to give her a slice of cake, but when we saw her it was clear she did not want to be found. She was behind the bathroom sheds, floating in a squat near the dirt. We hid in the branches of the flamboyáns. We watched her gather fistfuls of red rocks from the dirt and place them on her tongue, sucking before she swallowed. This was nothing we'd ever done when we'd turned. After we let ourselves drift back to the party, we didn't speak of it. We thought perhaps it was the iron she needed, having lost her first blood.

A few days later another girl came of age, floating down her apartment stairs soundlessly. Her grandmother startled and dropped the pot of sancocho she was carrying. That night, the first girl and the second girl huddled together in the back of a colmado, the first girl showing the second how far up she could float, about the height of the counter. She spun gymnastics in the air. The second girl strained and bit her lip and rose half a foot. The boys (who would turn soon, too) surrounded them like a pack. They played jacks on the floor underneath the girls, but it was hard for the girls to play. If they didn't concentrate, they drifted up too high to reach the jacks. Eventually, the girls gave up, and the man who owned the colmado slid them both beers in plastic cups. They floated on their backs, hair hanging from the backs of their heads. The boys paced around them like magicians about to cut their lovely assistants in half.

When we put the younger children to bed that night, they would not be soothed with flying tricks or bedtime stories. When we told them their favorites, the ones about the children who flew off from home, never to return again, when we read them *Peter Pan*, when we told them about arriving in strange lands, they said they were afraid. "Will that happen to us?" they asked. "We don't want to ever leave," they said.

We underestimated the ways we were the same as our children: the drive to want what you didn't have. For us, it had been the blinding sky, distance, the promise of the unknown, forgetting our old lives, which seemed puny the farther we flew from them. For our children, it was the red ground, the summer sun, a feeling of belonging, a history that trailed back generations.

A few of the boys changed, sleepily stumbling out the door in the morning to converge in hovering packs by the rivers, parks, and alleyways. At first, they didn't even notice how their heels weren't striking when they ran out the front door. The ones who hadn't yet turned started compulsively checking the space under their feet for the slightest cushion of air.

More of the children turned. They came home later and

later every night. When sneaking back into the house, they had no need for tiptoeing. We turned on the lights. We asked them where they'd been. They smelled of beer and iron. They shrugged and said flippantly, "With our cousins." As they floated up the stairs, we saw burns from twisted rope on their ankles, beneath the hems of their jeans.

We spied on them from parked cars. Our old friends had to drive us, because the back alleyways and streams had changed courses since we'd moved away. We saw the local children, the sons and daughters of the people we'd left behind, hold out ropes made from palm leaves and point to the ground. The locals tied the ropes around our children's ankles, tied them to their own flightless ones.

"It's fine," our old friends said. "They're just playing."

Our siblings reminded us of our own coming-of-age: ropes tethered around our ankles in case we couldn't return, experimenting with how far up we could go while they watched from the ground. Our old friends dropped us back home, slamming car doors firmly behind us. Were they jealous, did they want us gone, were they hoping we would take them with us?

Already we could feel the itch in the arches of our feet that propelled us to fly over borders. We were relieved we would be leaving soon.

We didn't notice them at first, tied over the rope burns. Thin snippets of string, anklets threaded with pebbles. They reminded us of bell collars worn by errant cats. When we asked the children about it, they stayed silent. Among the parents, we called them friendship anklets to hide our uneasiness. Then the fad spread among those who hadn't even turned. From the balconies and patios where we drank coconut water and chinola juice with rum, we could hear their laughter as they wove their anklets. They spent the rest of their time playing tag in the canopies of the trees, leaping over roofs, splashing under waterfalls, and lounging with the stray dogs who put their heads in the children's laps and growled at us if we got too close.

We felt guilty that we would have to drag them back with us when we left, guilty for soon separating them from their new friends. But when they brought us puppies they'd watched a stray dog birth, still dripping with placenta, asking us if they could keep one, we told them no. "Everything belongs in its place," we said. We reminded them of the pets back in our other homes, the school friends, the painted bedrooms, all waiting for us to return. When we suggested how proud we would be when they flew home without our help, they froze and sank a little in their airspace.

They asked the grandparents to tell them stories of how we used to be when we were young. They couldn't believe that those versions of us had turned into our older selves. They hated us, we knew. It was inevitable, a phase.

The second girl who'd turned was always pushing herself to new heights, trying to outshine the first girl, who'd had a head start. One day the children came running to get us. "She's gone," they yelled. "She flew up in a race to touch a cloud. She won, but she couldn't stop." She kept going higher, shrinking in their sight. None of the children were able to go after her.

We sprung up from the ground, leapt off the balconies, searched for her in the atmosphere. Our old friends covered the ground in case she'd fallen. After days of searching, we still couldn't find her. Her parents kept looking. The rest of us thought maybe if we just waited, she'd find her way back.

The younger children had nightmares. When they played catch and balls sailed over their heads, they never jumped, for fear they'd leave the ground. They held hands and dug their fingers into the stray dogs' fur.

"What are you doing?" we asked.

"We don't want to fly," they said. "We want to stay."

The rocks tied around their ankles got heavier. The children no longer hovered. They were weighted down with the red stones of the mountains. The stones dragged on the floor and clattered as they walked. Even much younger children tied stones to their legs. A toddler tripped over hers and gashed her head. This was going too far, we agreed, and we cut them all off. That would end the matter, we thought. The summer was nearly over.

We watched the ones who had already turned sink lower and lower, even without ropes binding them. We conferred among ourselves. It's the locals, we thought, all those children of our former friends bringing them down, showing them how to stay rooted, doing terrible things in the dark. Look at how crime has tripled since we left, how the buildings crumble and rust, how horrible their clothes are. Who knows how this country has changed for the worse, we said. So we forbade them from seeing the other children, the flightless children.

Still, our children wouldn't fly. We couldn't explain it. We tried throwing them up into the air to give them a head start, but they came down hard. One girl broke her leg. Only then did we think it was cruel to keep lifting them up and dropping them, like mother birds pushing chicks from the nest. We noticed no more children turned. Perhaps no more were ready. Many of them were coming down with stomachaches, clutching their bellies, which we blamed on the awful sanitation of our old country. When the grandparents offered us ice with our water, we curled our noses in disgust.

On the hottest day of the year, we discovered the very first girl who had turned, crouched behind the concrete outhouse of the pool, dripping wet in her bathing suit, selecting rocks from the path that marked the edge of the civilized grass from the wild selva where rivers coursed through the mountains. She was eating them again. The confidence with which she selected them implied she'd done this often. She swallowed twenty of them while we watched, and then got up from her crouch. She hopped on one foot, landed awkwardly, heavily. Satisfied, she rejoined the others. Our hearts sank at her failure. Before, she'd flown as gracefully as a swan.

One by one, when they thought no one was looking, the children slipped behind the country club, into the woods of the farms, behind the fences, between the concrete hurricane-proof houses and wooden shacks where their grandparents still lived, and ate bellyfuls of rocks. Our children even offered stones to the hungry dogs, held pebbles out for the toucans and the parrots. They were generous with their weight.

The youngest, the ñoños who still listened to us, these we lifted, surprised and groaning with their new weight, and cradled them in our laps. Still sleepy with milk they confessed that they were still afraid, that they never wanted to leave, that they loved everything about our old country.

They wanted the ground more than they wanted to fly. "What was so great about flying?" they asked.

We shook the older children. They were responsible for all of this. We yanked them by their braids, dragged them by their collars, threatened them with belts or wooden spoons or chancletas like our parents had done, while our parents looked on. "They're too old for that," the grandparents said. "It never worked with you," they said. We yelled at them to stay out of it.

They wouldn't break. The children informed us they were staying here, holding in yelps of pain, whether we liked it or not. They would run away from us if they had to. They said that they ate rocks because if they did not, their bellies burned for them.

We knew it was time to go. It had been danger-ous, bringing our children back here, letting them fall in love with the history and with the people they could have been. We'd remembered all the things we had hated about our old country, but we'd forgotten our own rebelliousness.

We packed our suitcases, dressed our younger children warmly for the flight, said good-bye to our parents, who tried to cling to us as we rose into the air. Husbands and wives held hands in a circle around their struggling children, threading arms to lock in their incredible burdens: the children, with their bodies full of rocks, weighing them down immensely. Everyone groaned while the children kicked and screamed and bit and sobbed, boys and girls fighting us and pushing at our arms. The sky was like a battle between angels.

We jettisoned the smallest bags, the blankets for the cool air, the fruits for the journey—it all landed roughly in the red dirt. Our old friends watched the great struggle between us and our shameful kids, extending their hands to grab the items dropping to the ground. Then we cut loose the big luggage, the clothes we'd bought to impress everybody, all our precious things. But our children, we had to keep our children!

The oldest kids, the strongest kids, the ones with the biggest bellies full of the most rocks, they flew loose from our grasps. We tried to chase them midflight, but they were stronger than us. We would lose the younger children, too, if we kept after them. Some of them fell to their grandparents on the ground, where their hair was tucked back from their faces, their chins cupped, giant plates of food set out in front of them. Others, unmoored, had not eaten enough rocks, had a capacity for flight that overcame stone and flint and dirt. But they were young and did not have the skill we did to fly exactly where we wanted. We'd had decades to practice. We tried to catch them, but they kicked us away. They clumped in groups and fought us off. The last time we saw them, they were thousands of feet above the ground, grasping clumsily for each other, fingers stretching in terror through the thinnest of atmospheres.

The smallest ones, our babies, and the ones who didn't struggle, these we were able to save. We returned to our houses, our apartments, our ranches, the suburbs, the cities, the farmland. We returned to the lives we felt understood us.

But the taste for rocks never left their mouths.

Some of them we starved, forbidding them stones. They learned to fly. But they drifted, never quite in the direction we wanted, trajectories loose and winding. Some of them fasted by choice, growing into bags of bones before our eyes.

Lighter than ever, they floated away, sometimes in the middle of the night through open windows. We knew now, from our own parents' struggles, there was no bringing them back.

The ones we were left with, their bellies full of rocks, they hovered a few inches above the ground but no farther, never able to sink completely. They stayed in the homes of our new countries, always wanting to get back to that place where we all dreamed we were happy, but never able to return. These were the ones we could still embrace: our rock eaters, grit in their mouths, hearts too heavy, feet too light.

True Love Game

I n a basement, two girls play the true love game, guessing the boys and men they will love forever versus the ones they will marry. Ten years old and already they know these two things will not be the same. Half-broken junk teeters in giant piles, leaning against old pipes. The basement creaks and groans with ghosts. The ghosts feel neglected, so they taunt the girls with schoolyard rhymes. One of the ghosts sings, *Red rover, red rover,* and calls their names. *Gabriella, Gabriella, bring Rosario over.* The old ghost yell-sings, *Last one to squat's gonna hit the ground.*

Rosario draws lines on notebook paper and lists all the boys they know. Famous movie stars go on the list, too. Gaby adds the ice cream truck man. The girls are hungry. It is Gaby's basement, and her grandmother has not bought groceries for the third straight afternoon. Gaby's and Rosario's parents are working in the fields and won't be back until night. The girls found a stray box of saltines hidden in the basement, and these they eat doused in ketchup. The ghosts salivate. They have been cursed with wanting what they can't have and what they would hate if they actually got.

Rosario keeps one name from the list. She knows they will never marry, that she will tuck him like tobacco into her cheek, a secret to roll over her tongue. He's the reason why she keeps suggesting going to Gaby's house instead of wading into the mucked canals beside the road or drifting through the fields where their parents this year pull peanuts from roots. Gaby's oldest brother, Gustavo, the one always in trouble, the one that refuses to speak English even though he's lived in the States longer than in the village they came from. She always sees him across the schoolyard, in trouble again, waiting for the teacher to turn her back so he can reach into his pocket for his knife. He is an expert at flicking the blade across biceps, knuckles, and bellies, giving his opponents scars in places the teachers won't notice, scars that caterpillar and pucker as they heal, that sting rather than ache. The Anglo kids use bats and crowbars, crack ribs and skulls, set up fights in the ditches after school. Gustavo was furious the first time he went to school and a bat smashed him in the face in the schoolyard for not speaking English, and he vowed he would protect his brothers from the same. When Gustavo flicks, he feels himself cutting at the things trapping him in. Rosario mouths to him in Spanish, *Don't do it*, but he's never looking at her.

What the ghosts want most is to speak, but they

can only sing and chant schoolyard rhymes. The old ghost sings work hymns from the fields. All he wants is to rest, but instead he is doomed to clean up the same dust pile in the corner of the basement, over and over. Out of all the ghosts, he was the one that died of old age, well after his legs wanted to quit their walking, his hands their labor.

When the boy who drowned is not singing, he tries to tell Rosario his name. Instead, fish drop from his gurgling mouth, slapping their scales on the floor.

Gaby's ghost maternal grandparents, not the paternal ones still alive upstairs, died in a car accident on their way to church. They still feel silly for those few last seconds looking away from the truck in front of them to the farmer setting up watermelons for sale by the side of the road. They had planted watermelon one year on the farm they used to own in Mexico, before the northern prices and seed drove them out, and that vision of their old life had appeared in this new country like a mirage, the stands of watermelons glowing green in the road dust. Now, they try to look dignified in the corner. Gaby's grandfather gorges himself on a ghostly banquet of fish off the good Spanish china that survived this long only to languish in the basement. He is stuffed so full his stomach hits the table and he groans in pain. When alive, he hated those formal dishes. The ghost of his wife puts her head in her hands. Every time she tries to grab the dishes away, her favorite dishes, they break in her hands. This dish is the last one left. Gaby's grandfather thinks when the last one goes, they'll all be released from the basement, but his wife won't give him the satisfaction. He belches up a sulfurous smell, smears old radiator oil with his fingers over the last flower pattern. His wife tries to turn away but can't.

Gaby says, "I hope I get Michael." With a mouthful of stale saltines, she adds the school basketball star. There is only one cracker left, and the girls eye it with need. Gaby wraps the cracker back in the cellophane. It is her house, after all. "We shouldn't eat it," she says. "We'll also be hungry tomorrow."

Rosario bites her lip and looks away. She pencils the math that will add up to the boys they will never forget. The ghosts want the game to be over as quickly as possible. They want something less boring so at least they can spend their eternal lives entertained by games of make-believe in which they get to dress up in elaborate, ghostly costumes. Plus, they already know what will happen next, and so little of it is good. A ghost grips Rosario's hand steady while she tabulates. Another switches the names on the paper so Michael is in the right place. Of course, the pencil breaks.

The paper in Rosario's hand crackles with electricity as the ghosts crowd over her, trying to will her to sharpen her pencil faster. The drowned boy hovers closest to Rosario's side. She is his favorite. He drowned in the river at seven years old trying to save kittens in a sinking sack. Rosario was his age when her parents had first started coming in from Mexico every year on a dusty truck. Now, she is too old for the drowned boy, and he hates this. Before, his body could pass through hers and he could spend the afternoon curled inside her, the only times he ever felt warm after drowning in that icy river. Now, her body is strange and uncomfortable, and the heartaches she has gained in her extra years of crossings make lumps in her that stick into his back. He sings into her ear, *Red rover, red rover,* but she flinches like her ear has an itch.

She thinks she hears the front door slam and creaking footsteps on the old floor above them, Gaby's brothers coming home.

Earlier that day, Rosario was playing My Sweet Enemy with some of the Anglo girls, whacking their palms in a frenzy to distract themselves from the noose of midday heat. Gaby lingered by the line at the ice cream truck, hoping someone would drop change, or the man who give her a free one, and there she was in the best position to watch Michael pull layup after layup. Gustavo and the brothers were heckling. They had no respect for the gangly white kid who could roll a few balls into a net. Gaby was distracted for the moment, the ice cream man offering her a taste of a new flavor. Michael threw a basketball at Gustavo's head. Gustavo said, "Dále," and flicked open his knife. Michael laughed, "You're nothing without your knife." Rosario saw Gustavo fling his knife onto the court, where it skittered, and say, "Ni lo necesito." The boys across the playground tensed their knotted muscles and their fists. The basketball was still rolling toward the corner where the teachers were, and the teachers squinted their eyes at Gustavo, ignoring Michael.

Gustavo forced himself into an easy stance, taking their glares of hate, like he'd taken them even before he'd found his grandfather's pocketknife in his basement and polished it to a shine. The boys were quiet. Rosario was relieved and knocked her knuckles against the other girls' while they chanted. The game was getting faster, and now she had to concentrate on only the hands whizzing in front of her, the sharp smack of skin.

Then the head teacher rushed over to where a boy had fallen on his chin from the monkey bars. When Gustavo looked back at Michael, he could see the handle of his grandfather's knife in the other boy's hand. "See you tonight," Michael laughed. "Parking lot at eight."

The ghosts dance as the girls huddle over the notebook. They dance on top of piles of Gaby's and her brothers' old clothes that will be sent back to Mexico with Rosario's family. Then the brothers storm down the stairs. Their voices clatter, and they punch each other in the arm. The ghosts hide in the old clothing to avoid the brothers' recklessness.

Gaby yanks the notebook Rosario has been trying so

hard to resolve into pairs of names. She sits on it. She doesn't want the brothers to see a name and tease her forever with it. She picks up a doll to ward away her brothers, holds it between her and Rosario. The ghosts can smell hope steaming off the girls, but this is another thing that they can't have, no matter how hard they try.

Gustavo is saying, "Qué rabia. How dare that kid?" He was glad he threw his knife for the kid to pick up and fight with later. At home he also speaks English, because at least here the language doesn't taste like their spite.

"You'll show him," says one brother.

Rosario says, "You'll show him what? What will you show him?"

The other brother tells her to be quiet. Gustavo tosses junk around the basement.

Sticks and stones may break my bones, wails the old ghost from underneath his pile of patched and mended T-shirts.

"La cadena," Gustavo says. "Have you seen it?"

Gustavo wants a chain thick enough and sharp enough to do some damage, a chain heavy as the one he has felt his whole life choking him in the mornings before he can shake it off. One day, it will catch up to him, but he is pretty sure today is not the day. The other brothers tell him a chain is the only thing he should carry into the parking lot, to prove he can beat the other boy against his own knife.

Rosario remembers a fall morning last year, a few days before her family left on the trucks back to Mexico. The chain Gustavo wants was threaded between an iron hook and a hole in the front door where there had once been a doorknob. Locked out in the cold, Gaby and Rosario huddled together against the door, sitting on Gustavo's skateboard, and he'd caught them. Instead of yelling to leave his things alone, like he usually did, he took a deep breath of that dying-leaf air and felt the chain that plagued him drop off. He brought the skateboard out to the road to show them how to ride it. He held their hands so they could lean on him while he led them rolling toward the fields. The chill made their noses run and their hands like ice. As she rode, Rosario felt the wind that normally meant she was in the flatbed of a truck and leaving everything again, except now it was pulling her palm-to-palm with Gustavo. He laughed at their skinned knees.

The ghosts cross their arms where they are being jostled from their hiding places by the boys upchurning old clothes and children's toys. They climb out of the piles like kings of the mountain. Gaby's grandparents shake their heads in shame at the boys and make a wall with their transparent bodies to shield the girls. Rosario watches the light sliding off Gustavo's hair. A bottle of rum sloshes between the boys. They move under the stairs.

Gaby pulls the notebook out again from under her legs. "It's almost done," Gaby whispers, circling dark lead marks and tears into the paper. Then she sets the pencil down. She holds the paper up to the light, the ghosts crowding over her shoulder to take a look. The brothers feel brave and are boxing each other under the stairs.

The boy ghost holds Rosario's hand in dread. He tries again to tell Rosario his name, but the only thing that comes out of his mouth is murky water that spills down his chin and splats on the floor with fish.

Gaby's brow pinches in anger. Rosario has won Michael. Gaby won a boy who sits behind her in class. She doesn't want him, but the ghosts know he will kiss her in a few years and had put his name in the right place as a prophecy.

"How could you?" Gaby says. "I like him."

Rosario insists she doesn't know how Michael ended up

on her list; she wants nothing to do with him. The ghosts smirk in satisfaction.

"Esto és," yells Gustavo in triumph. The brothers surround him as he holds up a bicycle chain, dull and rusted, swaying in his hands like a captured snake.

"Please don't," says Rosario.

Gaby isn't speaking to her. Gaby rips up the true love tabulation notebook into ribbons. The pieces fall to the floor and the fish swim in the sea of paper.

"Quit it," Gustavo tells Gaby. He drops the chain into his backpack.

"Rosario is going to marry Michael," she says.

The brothers' lips curl, and Gustavo dismisses the little girls with his eyes.

"It's not true," Rosario says, but they've already turned away.

Upstairs, Gaby's living grandmother calls the brothers' names. Before going up, they stash the backpack under a stack of old clothing. Rosario savors the sight of Gustavo smoothing down his shirt with his palms, the same palms that caught her on that chilly fall day, steady on her waist, palms that felt, just for that moment, like a constant.

Gaby catches Rosario looking up the stairs. "You'll never have him," she says. "He will never want you."

The old ghost sings, *My friend, my enemy, my razor blade.*

The drowned boy lunges to knock Gaby down in Rosario's defense, but he passes right through her. Gaby's ghost grandparents are mortified. They came to this country to raise their family, to work across the border on the American farms that had gotten subsidies while their own farm withered. Not to end up like this: ungrateful grandchildren, themselves trapped in the basement with other ghosts who don't even belong there. They blame the country—the Americans with their bats and stares and land taken and treaties milking their old country dry—for their current situation, for how their family changed.

The drowned boy picks himself back up and tries to tell Rosario that she is loved. Catfish, bass, and piranhas roll in pirouettes from his lips. Rosario gathers the scraps of paper and fish from the floor. They wriggle out of her grasp. She starts to cry. She buries her face in the piles of old clothes, her nose hitting the hard lump of the chain inside Gustavo's book bag.

She uncovers the bag. She wants to discard the chain, prevent Gustavo from doing what he's about to do. She has a suspicion that Michael and Gustavo today will take it further than they ever have before in their fights, whatever was trapped and wanting release in them finally escaping.

The drowned boy knows her well from spending all those afternoons curled in her rib cage. Although his fingers pass through the tangible world, if he concentrates hard, he can move things just a tiny bit. Under his will, the chain snakes out from between the zipper. He gestures at Rosario.

Rosario sniffs up her sorrow. She fingers the cold metal of the links, passes her pinky through the spaces. This chain is the one thing of his she's ever touched besides his skateboard and his hands. She wants something of his. She wants him to stop because she thinks that staying good, staying silent, will save him.

Gaby isn't looking. She pulls from the closet another doll she's decided not to let Rosario play with.

Gaby's grandparents nod at Rosario and wave her on; they, too, want to put a stop to their grandson. The grandparents know what will happen to him without the chain, that he will be caught in an eternal struggle for everything and nothing that he wants. They've observed this is what it means to be American. They hope he will end up eternally in their basement.

An entire ocean pours out of the drowned boy's mouth with all the things he wants to say to Rosario. The old ghost scoops up water with his hands like a sieve, an eternal task.

There is a ruckus at the top of the stairs. In comes one brother, then another, then another. Gaby's ghostly grandmother reaches instinctively for her favorite dish to protect it, and it finally breaks in her hands. The grandparents look at each other with anticipation, but neither of them disappears. In despair, the grandfather starts eating fish whole from the rising spectral water sloshing around his ankles.

The drowned boy crams his mouth full of broken porcelain to stop the outpour. Suddenly he's heavier than he's been in eons, since dead, and his insides clink and clatter with the porcelain, sounding just like a chain. He nods to Rosario. He climbs in Gustavo's bag, zips it back up behind him, just as the brothers reach the bag. Gustavo won't notice the difference until he opens it, facing the other boy.

Red rover, red rover, send Gustavo right over, chants the boy ghost from inside the bag. He's finally going to escape the basement, even when what he most wants is to curl up inside Rosario.

Rosario is caught blushing and guilty. She hides the chain quickly underneath a T-shirt with holes.

"Don't go," Rosario tells Gustavo. She wants, for once, for love to be something that stays, that doesn't hurt, that she'll never have to drive away from.

The brother closest to their age pushes her aside, and then all the brothers clamor like a storm back up the stairs. Gaby, who this whole time has been pulling out the doll's hair, throws it at Rosario, runs upstairs to follow them, and locks her in the basement. No one will come looking for her for hours.

The ghosts dance around Rosario. She lies down in the pile of old clothes to wait, wrapping Gustavo's chain around her shoulders. She hugs herself with it, the cold metal links that feel at first like the surprising, freeing licks of a blade, then like cold, spectral fingers promising embrace.

The Touches

I've been touched exactly four times in real life. The first was when my mother gave birth to me. I picked up her bacteria as I slid out of her womb, the good stuff as well as the bad. My father caught me, and his hands—covered in everything that lives on our skins—made contact. His bacteria, the yeast, shed viruses, and anything else from under his fingernails spread to my newborn epidermis. That was the second touch.

I was gooey and crying, and they both held me for a moment before the robot assigned to me snipped my cord, took me up in its basket, and delivered me to the cubicle where I would live the rest of my life. There it hooked me into the virtual reality mind-set, the body-adapting and stimulating cradle station. Then Nan, what I eventually named my robot, turned on its caretaker mode and sent my mind into clean. Back in dirty, everything that came with me—the blanket my mother wrapped me in, the towel that wiped placenta from my face, the suction ball that pulled the goop from my nose and mouth, the basket—was incinerated. That was right after the first plague legislation, back when they were still allowing natural births and cohabitating marriage units.

I wish I remembered it. It wasn't the same, holding me in clean, my parents said. They'd tuck the blanket around me and sing me a song, and sometimes my mother would tell me what it felt like to actually touch me, to smell me. Then, my avatar still passed out back in my virtual reality bedroom, I'd pull out of clean and Nan would be above me, smiling with her LCD face screen, unhooking me from the wires and hugging me with her white plastic arms.

My parents are dead now. Their cubicle in dirty was incinerated. The only thing I have of the moment they held me is a video Nan recorded when she pulled me away from them and brought me here.

I've been thinking about them lately when Telo and I go to bed. I inherited the code for my parents' clean house, so the ephemera of their stuff is still there in the rooms, although I turned my childhood bedroom into the master bedroom and recoded the algorithm for how much space I could take up with the house. I've been thinking about which room would belong to the baby.

Since we elected to be assigned a baby, my avatar's belly has been growing. Most of the time I don't notice it, despite the code putting pressure feedback on my movement algorithms and my gait turning into a waddle. I'm getting stronger; that's what I mainly feel. But when I climb into bed, it's hard to get comfortable. Technically, Telo could have been the one to go through the pregnancy algorithm, since we don't believe in gender norming or any of those religious restrictions. He's the more nurturing of the two of us, and when I see him with his charges at the childcare center, surrounded by big-eyed, jumping kids that call him Mr. Telo, or more often with the younger ones, Mistelo, it melts me. But that's why I had to be the one to get pregnant. Supposedly going through all the algorithm motions of natural birth, even when you're getting the baby from a test tube, activates all those love centers and makes you feel more connected. I'm the one who needs the extra help.

Tonight, Telo pauses at the bedroom doorway, which tells me sex is on the horizon, and reaches for my hand. He scoops me up and I giggle at the rush upward. My face in his chest, he starts to rock me. It's the only thing that will turn me on. My therapist thinks I'm trying to get at whatever primal feeling would unleash in me if it were real touch. But since the pregnancy algorithm started showing, it's awkward and I don't fit right. He squeezes too hard on my belly and I can't lose myself like I used to. Telo can tell that I'm flinching. He sighs deeply, and then drops me on the bed.

"I'm sorry," I say. "Once the algorithm's run its course, things will get back to normal."

"It's not your fault," he says, and rolls over. "Good night, love."

And then we put our avatars to sleep, and I emerge into dirty.

There's Nan again, peering into my VR immersion ball. "Hi, sunshine," she says. She unhooks my headset, pulls me out of the ball so I don't start spinning it by getting up, and starts brightening lights slowly to get my eyes used to the idea that I'm in the real, dirty world again.

Not that I want to see much in dirty. Outside it's bald and diseased earth, trying to heal itself. All the superbugs—microbes and viruses that evolved immunity to antibiotics, that melted out of the polar ice caps and were released into the oceans, bugs we hadn't seen for a million years—they're all still out there, proliferating. Inside, the cubicle is a standard-issue sanitized room: only enough to feed yourself, hug your robot like you're supposed to, bathe when you need, and then plug right back in and sleep along with your avatar. Every crack is sealed, every intake and retake valve opened only once a vacuum is established in the rest of the system. Back before the toilets were vacuum sealed, they would spew all their bugs into the air, infecting everyone who used the same ventilation system, killing entire apartment complexes. It's revolting, knowing how even the bacteria we need is mutating on our very skins, inside us, just a roll of the dice before they turn into something deadly; knowing that if the seals around our doors were to give way, we'd probably be puking our guts out within the week, killed by any number of diseases, a bird flu or ancient mariner plague or limb-taking staph or airborne HIV. I'm itching to log back into clean where none of that matters.

"Time to eat," Nan announces brightly, a vacuum-sealed precooked meal arriving down the chute. "Beef chili."

It's chicken and potatoes—even blinking against the light, I can see that. Nan's glitches have been getting worse, but I haven't gotten around to ordering spare parts. I know it's important. Without our personal robotics assistants that function as our doctors, our caretakers, our alarm systems, we wouldn't have survived the first sweep of plagues. Without the drones and army of specialty robots meant to take our place in the outer, dirty world, farming and manufacturing and construction, we would have to expose ourselves.

Best I can tell, Nan's power supply is part of the problem. It's shorting and restarting her modules at different times, and the desynchronization makes her go buggy.

"Remind me tomorrow to order a new power supply," I say.

"Yes," she says, "babycakes."

"Telo?" Telo, a pro at logging into the caretaker units while at work, often logs into Nan. I hate when he does that. I feel naked in dirty, my real self less attractive than my avatar, my hair matted and greasy because no one can smell me alone in my cubicle.

"Surprise," he says with Nan's voice.

He hugs me with her white plastic arms, the way Nan is programmed to do every night. The hugs are supposed to be soothing, meant to combat the developmental disorders of a lifetime of not being touched, but it's awkward. Nan runs cold, and there's no part of her that gives. I've thought of wrapping her in memory foam, but that would block her panels. At least in dirty, I'm not pregnant. My stomach is flat and my range of motion intact, and I can hug him back good and hard.

He holds up the soap and makes Nan's face a goofy grin, and I laugh and jump in the shower.

But then Nan glitches again, and she just stands there frozen with the soap in midair. Ten minutes later when she starts up again, she's only Nan and Telo has logged out.

When I wake up in clean, morning light is slicing in through the blinds and the birdsong I've programmed is playing on a loop from the window. Telo is next to me in the bed, dead to the world. My hand passes through his shoulder; his avatar is empty and he hasn't logged back into it. His avatar has been sleeping later and later these mornings. I wonder what he's doing over there in dirty. Eating, voiding, getting ready for the morning? He's told me he looks almost the same as his avatar, except his dark hair is a lot curlier, and he lets it grow long. He has a scar on his shoulder where he fell on a sharp corner of his immersion rig when his robot wasn't looking, whereas his avatar's light skin is as smooth as glass.

"Remember to order a new power supply." I hear Nan's

voice barely in range of my perception, her whispering into my headset back in dirty. I disabled her direct clean log-in after the last time hearing her voice loud above me made me jump out of my skin. This way, she's soft and distant, the way I like the dirty world.

I groan, stretch, try to remember where I left my tablet before I logged out last time. If clean was unregulated, I could simply wish the tablet into my hands. I get annoyed that part of the legislation to create clean required that everything be tied to a physical representation as close to real life as possible—so we don't become alien to ourselves, supposedly, none of this living exclusively in our heads. They wanted to pretend the world was back the way they dreamed it. I get it—nostalgia. Even though none of us can eat in clean, my parents left the kitchen in the digital representation of the house they used to have in real life, and I didn't code it out when I inherited because it was always there in my childhood. I use it as my meditation room, where I try to imagine the smell of coffee.

I find the tablet in the kitchen, blinking on a stool.

Things have been tight since paying for our test-tube baby, so before I order the part, I check our bank account. But there's more money in there than there should be, by at least five hundred bitcoins.

Telo yawns loudly behind me, walking stiffly into the kitchen.

"What's this?" I say, and I show him the tablet screen.

"Oh, I took on a few extra kids."

"More than a few."

"We talked about this, right? Wasn't it what you wanted?"

"Just be careful. If anything went wrong with a few of them at the same time . . ."

"Nah. I've got all the luck. You shouldn't worry about it.

Off to work yet?" He leans against the doorframe, and I'm breathless, his avatar is that beautiful. His dirty self, of course, would look less perfect, less symmetrical, and his eyebrows droop downward. Still, the avatar is a cousin to him. Or at least that's what he says. I've never logged into his robot, and I don't want to. Even when he does it, it feels like he's looking into a secret self.

"Just as soon as I get this belly under control," I say, pulling on the dress I've recoded for maternity.

I ride the bus to the industry district. Avenue of the Giants features skyscrapers for the greatest minds in clean: the philosophers in the Commission for Digital Humanization, the engineers in the Commission for Stabilization, and the scientists in the Commission for Reentry, my building. There doesn't come a day when I'm not thankful that these are government task forces instead of corporate-run research, which would have guaranteed that only the rich would be able to reenter dirty once we figured out how to fight the diseases, with the rest of us remaining in tiny boxes. I flash my badge at the Reentry doors.

In the lab, Alicia is dancing behind the blood samples while they run. This lab is set up with a corresponding one over in dirty, manned by robots. Here, when Alicia puts in blood samples to run, robots put the real-life samples from humans or birds and set them spinning in the machine. It's seamless. It makes me wonder what would happen if clean were ever perfect, if we could eat and smell and taste here. Would we ever want to leave? Would we even care about that other world we ruined?

"Happy day, happy day," Alicia says.

I nod as Fermat walks in.

"How's reentry going?" Fermat says.

"Her robots have been breaking birds again," Alicia says brightly.

"Damn it." I turn around and something flutters in my corner of the lab, a reminder of the dirty world. Each TV screen on my wall is assigned to a drone feed or a robot following flocks of birds back in dirty. My tiny part of the reentry project is studying patterns of insect transmission of the avian flu. I'm working on a harmless version of the virus that spreads innocuously through mosquito transmission but prevents the worse one from taking hold in the host. We can't realistically vaccinate every bird on the planet, but if we inoculate a few and the harmless virus spreads . . . then we might gain traction. Of course, I'm always fighting with the research group on the top floor who thinks the answer is bringing mosquitoes to extinction altogether.

The bird flailing on the top right monitor has a broken wing. I can see the wavering outline of camouflaged robot hands holding it, one of my robots designed to sneak up on the birds and capture them for tagging, blood samples, and injections. Except some software glitch keeps making their hands too tight around the birds' bodies, killing my research subjects.

I log into the offending robot, bringing its tactile feed into my immersion ball back in dirty. In my hands is the bird. Every time I try to merely touch it, the plastic hands punch the bird's delicate body, jerking and missing its mark half the time.

Freeze, I instruct the robot. I log out and emerge back at the lab. I groan.

"Was that one of the incubators?" says Fermat.

The eighth bird in as many days, bringing my flock down to just the minimum for viral mutation conditions. I can't afford to send another robot and have the same thing happen. "I can't lose this grant," I say.

Alicia keeps pirouetting in front of the samples, her way of dealing with conflict. She must be having a bad day with her research, too.

Fermat, always the sensible one, glances down at my stomach, tabulates the cost against the pay of my grant. "You better get that sample some other way, then. I can't believe your data's almost wrecked."

Alicia stops her dancing, already knowing what I'm thinking. "No. You don't have to go out there."

I feel like a rock sinks through my torso. Leaving my container in dirty is one of my greatest nightmares. What if my bioball breaks? What if decontamination goes awry? At least I wouldn't be able to spread it to anyone else. "I think I have to," I say.

Fermat shudders. Alicia starts dancing again, taking one giant leap in the air. At the apex, she gets stuck and her avatar goes transparent, shimmering and splayed midjump. She's logged out of her avatar.

"We had work to do!" Fermat yells. He throws a lab notebook at her avatar, but the notebook goes right through her. For the rest of the day, with her avatar floating up there, we'll be distracted, waiting for her to drop from the air when she logs back in.

And that brings me to the third touch. An hour later back in dirty, I'm looking for my flock. I'm pushing the joystick, rolling my containment bioball forward near the waterfront, where both mosquitoes and birds are plentiful. I only see one other bioball out, likely another researcher since few people are approved for them. My bioball is clear plastic all around, and the bottom of it gives me a window through puddles and waste canals. It makes me gag, all that muck swirling around underneath me, filled with bugs that are compelled to feed off and destroy me. Inside, though, I'm safe.

The birds flutter around me as I roll down the old board-walk. I turn my camouflage mode on, and they stop seeing me. One of the rocks ripples, and I know that's my glitching robot, in camouflage mode, too. The bird is dead in its hands, although the robot's skin is reflecting the sky behind him, so it looks like an upside-down dead bird is stuck in the gray air. At times I think dirty is just as virtual as clean.

I push my hands through the sealed glove openings and unclench the robot's invisible hands. The bird spills into my gloves. A drone whirs overhead, delivering a sample kit. I pull out a needle from the kit and draw thick blood from the necrotizing bird. I pack the bird in a plastic bag and place it into the drone's trunk. Maybe something that can be used later to track how decomposing tissue spreads and nurtures the virus. "Name the sample Decomposing Subject 932," I say, looking at the code tag on the bird's ankle. The drone's light blinks once in affirmation.

I keep seeing ripples out of the corner of my eye back in-land, but I don't see any wildlife and the rest of my robots are dispatched to follow other control and experiment flocks. It must be vertigo from moving around in real life instead of the controlled movements of clean.

I carefully roll my ball into the flock, the starlings preen-ing and eating mites off each other. I pick them up gently for my samples, crooning their own birdsong at them through my speakers, holding their warm bodies in my hands—almost my hands, except separated by the rubber of the gloves. What would it feel like to run a bare fingertip along a feather?

I chose starlings for my research because of how invasive they are. Someone let them loose in New York's Central Park centuries ago out of nostalgia—they wanted to release all the birds from Shakespeare's plays—and within a hundred years they were all over the continent, taking over other birds' nests. If you wanted to track spread, what better species? Not much different from humans, in that respect. Germs were nature's population control, but we refuse to give up our freedom. We're another kind of germ, spreading unchecked.

I let the last bird go, dispatch the drone to our lab's twin in dirty. "Return to the lab for repairs," I tell the robot, but it appears to be glitching, frozen. "Reboot," I say.

Nothing.

Fine. I roll back down the boardwalk, cross past the barricade holding back the rising sea. The ripples in the air start up again, this time accelerating down the street toward me. A camouflage's slight delay. It's on a collision course.

I pull the joystick hard left, and whatever it is glances off my ball, throwing me. I smash into the closest wall, my seat belt throttling my chest, and I plunge into darkness.

My ball's emergency lights flash in my face. There's a hissing air leak somewhere. The lights show me I'm inside the wreckage of what used to be an ancient restaurant, one of those places where people in dirty used to congregate and infect each other. My chest throbs against the seat harness, but other than that, I'm not hurt. The air smells like rotten fish and mold. I want to cry; if I can smell dirty that means it's in here with me. I roll the ball out of the crunching mess and emerge into the gray light.

"Are you okay?" I hear a female voice over crackling speakers.

I want to scream at her for not seeing me, but then I realize I left my camouflage mode on, too. We couldn't see each other. "The ball's breached," I say. Center left, where the air is hissing out. I hold my hand up to the hole, trying to plug the air.

"Mine, too," she says. She drops the camouflage. She's holding her arm. Her hair is everywhere, come loose from the crash. She looks like Alicia, almost, except her eyes are black instead of violet, her nose more hooked.

"Alicia?"

She grimaces.

"What are you doing out here?"

"I was trying to help," she says. "We have to get back to filtered air."

Panic surges up in me. I turn my bioball, message Nan to prepare a decontamination entry.

"Wait!" Alicia says. She pushes her ball up to mine, lining up our breaches.

"Do you have a patch?" I say. "What are you doing?"

She puts a finger through, her fingertip suddenly on my palm.

At first, I'm revolted. All the microbes from her hands, from everything she's ever touched, cultured underneath her fingernails and attaching to me. Then the soft rub, the heat of her fingertip, the prickle of the virgin sensation. It feels like joy and pain at once, everything forbidden.

Mosquitoes hover around us. Are they my mosquitoes, harmless? Or wild ones, carrying death?

"I have to go," I say, yanking my ball away, rushing back to decontamination with my palm pressed against the breach.

My hand burns the whole way back, and I keep telling myself it's not flesh-eating bacteria, it's not a mosquito bite, it's just touch. My third touch. The only one I remember.

Nan gasses me, burns the ball, and opens the inner door back into my cubicle with a roar. "You are now class five contaminated. Your permit to leave your cubicle is rescinded," she says cheerily.

"It was just my hand." But I know that's a lie. I know how bugs spread and cross-contaminate, and even the breeze of my breath can push bugs farther than the initial contact area.

"Permit rescinded," Nan says, and leans in to hug me, wrapping me in cold plastic. Then she freezes around me, glitching.

In a week or two, all that infected me should manifest itself, and if it kills me, Nan will be incinerated along with my body. I want to smash her into pieces already, this broken world along with her. Shouldn't we just bury it all? Instead, I hold her hand, mold it around mine where it burns. Her hand cools mine. I breathe deeply, the plastic smell of her.

"Everything will be okay, Nan. Reboot."

"Welcome home, sunshine," she says, as she reactivates and releases me.

When I get back to clean, Alicia is still hanging up by the ceiling. Fermat is coding DNA and squinting his eyes. I drop heavily into my chair and start composing a message to Telo about what happened. My eyes keep glancing up to Alicia's hovering form, her translucent hands, the whorls of her fingertips. I want to talk to her about what just hap-

THE TOUCHES

pened. We touched. I touched her real skin, traded micro-biomes, contaminated myself. Surely, I'm infected. I take deep breaths and try to calm down.

Trembling, I message Telo from my console. *Something happened to me. I had to go into dirty. Video me?* But I get his logged-out autoresponse. I realize he's in dirty. All of us are, but I'm used to thinking of everyone as somewhere else, *out there*, or nonexistent until they log into clean. But Telo could live in the dirty cubicle right next to me. I could have passed feet from his body. I could have touched him instead of Alicia.

I wrench myself from that line of thinking. It's forbidden for good reason, dangerous even without the superbugs out there, each of our microbiomes completely unused to the other's. Microbiome shock alone could kill. Would I inflict that on someone I loved, just to feel their skin in real life? Before today, I would have said no.

When I was in high school, I saw someone who was infected. She didn't catch it from anywhere; it was her own bacteria that had mutated. It wasn't killing her, exactly, but it was eating her slowly. Her avatar was unaffected and perfect: clothes ironed, black hair sleek, eyes bright. But she kept closing them and putting her head on the desk, and her breaths sounded like she was gasping for air. None of us wanted to be around her, and come lunchtime we scattered away from her. We knew, logically, we couldn't catch anything in clean, but that didn't stop our instincts from kicking in, the part of us that wanted to burn her up in her cubicle so that whatever she had went down with her. Even the teachers asked her to stay at her home in clean from then on.

I get a message from Telo. *Sorry, trouble at work. One of the kids had a problem and then her robot wouldn't respond to me. I'm heading home now. Tell me all about it when I see you?*

Above me, Alicia's avatar turns solid and the gravity algorithm kicks in, her hair flying up around her until she lands on the floor. She catches my eye, and her leg taps to a rhythm. Her dancing means her heart is racing as much as mine. Her avatar's long hair is flat and sleek, but I know back in dirty, her hair is wild as a halo. Back in dirty, has she been infected?

"Salipa." She calls my name, holding out her hand from behind the lab equipment.

I see Fermat, hunched over his screen. "Not here," I say.

I lead her outside into the hallway. Down the elevator, where we stand next to each other. She slips her hand into mine. It's the same hand she touched before, and I don't pull back. She's nearly dancing again as we go out the glass doors to the fountain at the center of the Avenue of the Giants. The fountain trickles in a rhythmic, programmed loop. The water smells like nothing. Completely clean. Children are playing in the arcs of water, but back in dirty, they aren't actually wet. They don't have to worry about water being a petri dish full of killer bugs.

Alicia's hand slides up my arm. But it doesn't feel like it did earlier, our hands finally naked atop each other. It feels dull, muted, her small hands feathers that have been covered in wax.

I move away, breaking contact. "Are you okay?"

She shrugs. "It might be a few weeks before we would get symptoms, Sal."

"What were you doing out there, anyway?" I walk toward the children, a little girl perching atop a ledge. Nothing here can hurt her. Be careful, I want to warn anyway. We've already lost so much.

"I go outside sometimes, and I didn't want you to be alone. Plus, I'm a scientist. I was curious."

"You knew I was out there. Why weren't you more careful?"

"Please," she says, touching me with that dull hand again, resting it on the hump of my stomach. She leans in, looking at my eyes, and then grabs me and kisses me. I don't pull away. She feels just like Telo, the same algorithm.

"Wait," I say, gasping.

She's going to cry as she pulls back. Then she logs out, her hands frozen still reaching for me.

When I get home, Telo has programmed our living room the way I like, the light frozen in the fierce orange of sunset, the sound of waves hitting shore somewhere nearby, a double Brazilian hammock strung up in the center of the room underneath the chandeliers. He's glowing in the light.

"Bad day at work?" he asks.

I shed all my clothes. I'm naked and I need him, so I jump into the hammock, ignoring the pressure of my giant belly, and wave him in. Once he's wrapped around me, I tell him what happened in dirty. I don't tell him that it was like nothing I'd ever felt before, because the comparison would mean that I'd never felt it with him. I don't tell him about Alicia's kiss.

"So now we just wait for the incubation period to end," he says. "Maybe you get lucky."

"Lucky?" I say. "Everything around our cubicles in clean is devastated."

"Lots of people get lucky. Let's hope for the best and cross that bridge when we come to it."

His response makes no sense. Lots of people? "You're so calm about this," I say.

He shrugs into me. "Nothing else to do."

Something kicks me in the stomach hard. I gasp.

He freezes like he's the one that's done something. "What?"

"Just the baby." The simulated kicks punch me a few times in the stomach, then they're gone. I know that to increase bonding when they finally assign us the child, I should stop thinking of it as a simulation and start thinking of it as our child. I wish I had Telo's gift, but I see how it runs him ragged, trying to fulfill everyone, all those children crying, hungry, not yet able to find the words for what they need. But then I imagine Telo smiling above a baby startled with wonder, both of them without me. I can't help but wonder, "If I got infected and you lose me, would you keep the baby?"

"Stop," Telo says. "Trust me, you'll be fine."

"Even if I'm not infected, I'm not fine. If I can't pick up robot slack, I might lose my research. But now I'm quarantined and I can't go out again."

"I could go for you." He puts his face in my neck, and he's tangled around me. Back in my immersion ball in dirty, tiny electrical impulses prick my nerves, simulating his weight on my skin. Just like Alicia.

"Telo, no. Look what happened to me. That's just a hypothetical permission you have. *If* one of your kids is in danger and *if* their robot fails or glitches too bad for you to log in. And that hasn't happened yet. I would never ask you to risk yourself. Forget it; it's just data. I can start again when the robots stop glitching."

"And redo two years of work? Lose your grant? Could we still afford the baby? I guess . . . I'll have to take on more kids."

"Telo," I say, now the strong one, and I put my finger crosswise against his lips, shushing him. It's the hand with the palm that has felt another person. The waves soundtrack washes over us. I close my eyes and wish with all my being that it felt the same, that the same electricity would flow through me as when Alicia's fingertip jolted me awake.

"Don't you want more from life?" I ask, even though everything around us is designed as a paradise: the waves, the light of sunset licking our skin, the hammocks and the slow rocking sensation.

"Every single day I want more," he says, and he grips me hard, like a secret is being dragged out of him, like he's struggling to breathe.

I awake from Nan shaking me. "Hello, sunshine," she says. "Time for food and voiding."

"Excellent," I say.

My arm has pinprick marks nestled in the crook. She's been taking samples. I look toward the door, the decontamination chamber that lies just beyond. The lock screen is activated with a new code that says PERMANENT. What she does while I'm in clean.

"My new power supply has arrived," she says.

It's unpackaged, carefully placed on the floor by my immersion ball. "That's great, Nan. Want to bend over so I can install it?"

"Yes," she says, and complies.

I open up her back, pull out the old supply. I can hear it sparking. I click in the new one.

"Reboot," I tell Nan. But nothing. She stays bent over like that. When I ran her debug, it didn't throw up any other hardware flags. Could the problem be something else? Are Nan's glitches connected with the other robots' errors?

She looks broken in half. Suddenly my ten-by-ten cubicle in dirty feels empty and crushing. I wolf down my meal, log back into clean.

In clean, I'm still in the hammock, Telo asleep and logged out next to me. I can't tell what time it is because the blinds are still programmed to leak out sunset.

If there is ever a time to log into his robot, it's now. He gave me the passcode when I gave him the digital key to my house, and never once had I been tempted to use it. But is he okay? Do I need to warn him about the robot glitches? Do I need to see him in real life even if I'd be embodied in a plastic humanoid? Do I need to tell him about the kiss, about my numbness, about my hunger?

I say his cubicle number into the air, then the passcode.

"Accept log-in?" I hear.

"Accept."

His cubicle looks exactly like mine, but his robot seems to be working fine. My hands, the robot's hands, aim and squeeze correctly.

"Telo?" I say, and the bright robot voice saying my words startles me.

He's probably asleep in his immersion ball, but when I open the padded door, he's not in there. He's not anywhere in his cubicle. He's gone out into the dirty world. I open and close my robot hands, grasping air.

In the morning, the news has figured it all out, about the glitching robots having all contracted a code virus. Usually the sick ones are robots that have been repeatedly logged into. They're working on a fix.

Telo still hasn't come back by the time I leave for work.

At work, Alicia is there, but she is translucent with her head on her desk, the polite way to log out.

"She said she was feeling sick," Fermat says.

"Feeling sick?" I ask.

He shrugs. "I don't need her for this part anyway."

If she's sick, is it something I contracted?

And of course, on the monitors, I see my robot gathering samples is still frozen in place. It's like dirty is infecting clean, spiraling out of control.

Telo, are you okay?

Yeah, just at work. I slept in this morning.

Late night?

The usual.

When Fermat logs out to use the bathroom back in dirty, something comes over me and I hug Alicia, of course falling through her empty avatar, landing headfirst on her desk inside her. Through her translucent form, I see that she's written something on a notebook. My name, over and over. Then at the end, a phone number.

I pick up the notebook through the haze of her empty avatar. I call the contact, one trembling number at a time.

"Have you used us before?" says the person who picks up.

"Who is this?" I ask.

The woman sighs. "Okay, new customer." A moment's pause. "Alright, I have your details and your account. Ten p.m. tonight. Just be sure that your robot is disabled and that your cubicle door can be accessed from the outside."

"In dirty?" I say, terrified.

"Are you kidding me?" she says, and she hangs up.

For the rest of the day, I watch my flocks on the drone monitors. The robots with useful digits are all glitching, not to be trusted near the test subjects. But not even I am to be trusted, apparently—not in dirty, not in clean.

When I think about the phone call, my heart skips a beat. I try to call the number back, cancel what I might have just signed up for, but the number is now disconnected. The baby kicks again, and I grip the lab desk until it passes.

What was coming for me at my cubicle? A delivery? A replacement robot? A person? And despite myself, despite knowing what it would cost them, me being class five contaminated, I want it to be a person. I'm willing to ruin them.

When I get home, Telo is waiting for me. No ham-mocks this time, or sunset. Just the regular couches and afternoon light. He's left the waves programming, which he usually does before he brings up something sure to cause an argument, meant to calm me in advance. His avatar doesn't register any of the visible effects of tiredness; he looks as perfect and unruffled as ever. But he yawns.

My anger eclipses everything else. "Where were you last night?"

"What do you mean?"

"You weren't in your cubicle."

"You logged into my robot?"

"You hypocrite. You log into mine all the time."

"I mean, I don't mind, it's just you never have before. Of course you can log in. But why last night?"

I shrug. "Why aren't you answering the question?"

"Just the kids, obviously. With the robots down I had to help with some of the babies. What is wrong with you?"

"You weren't trying to help me with my research, were you?"

"No, I was definitely not trying to help you." He's amused, smirking.

I snort. I don't know why I'm so angry. "I'm sorry," I say. "It's just—I needed you and you weren't there. It's a glitch, I know. But anything could have happened to you." I don't mention my own guilt.

"I'm here now."

He hugs me. I let myself be swept up, but I can barely feel it. The projection clock on the mantel says nine o'clock.

He yawns again. "Maybe we should go to sleep early tonight," he says, draping me over the bed. "Since we were both up late."

I shrug, trying to remain calm. "If you're tired."

"You know *you* are, babycakes," he says, nestling himself behind me. He spoons me, and we both close our eyes before we log out, our avatars back in clean locked together and shimmering.

In dirty, Nan is stuck folded over and motionless.

Just in case, I point her camera toward the corner. My cubicle still says that it's permanently locked, but it's always been accessible from the outside, in case the government, scientists, or caretaker robots need to come in beyond the delivery chute. Some people are so paranoid about the bugs outside that they smash the screen, blowtorch the entrance shut. The occasion anyone would have to use it is so rare as to be ridiculous, but once, a cubicle row caught on fire and the drones couldn't put it out. The people who had sealed themselves in burned in there, everyone else rolling their bioballs toward their new cubicle row. All of these people rolling through the smog-filled, devastated world with their own frail, impoverished selves, and now they could see each other: uglier, greasier, weaker than their avatars.

I feel nauseous and hold my head over the toilet just in case. A symptom of a disease? Nerves? Then it passes.

Still an hour to go. It's been a few days since I showered, and I can smell myself. I pull the curtains in the corner opposite Nan around myself, turn on the vacuum-sealed drain. I soap myself carefully. If I slip and fall, no one will come running. Not even Nan can save me now. As I pass the soap over my skin, I tremble. Here, my stomach is flat. In a month, if I'm not dead from superbugs, a baby will be placed into my arms. Which version is the lie? I think of Alicia, her fingertip, my palm, and let the water touch me clean.

At ten o'clock, nothing happens. My door stays shut, and I am alone. I want to confess to Telo right away, nudge him awake and tell him what I hoped for, how much this world is not enough, how this cubicle that I might never leave feels like a trap and all I am able to do is run in the fields of the virtual world. Would he be enough? Would the baby be enough? Would all of our research for reentry be enough?

The decontamination chamber outer door opens. A man rolls in, then steps out of his bioball and lifts his arms to be scrubbed by gas. The door to my cubicle opens.

He moves quickly to wedge the inner door open with one of Nan's arms. He freezes when he looks up, as if he's as surprised to see me as I am him. Then he relaxes and grins.

"Hi," he says. "We have ten minutes."

I don't say anything. My hair is dripping down my back, moisture immediately absorbed by the floor's dehumidifier. I keep glancing toward the door that should be shut, that should be the second barrier protecting me.

"Here I am," he says.

"I'm contaminated," I warn. "Class five."

"I guess that's the risk," he says, like he's not surprised. He's much shorter than Telo, balding even though he's about my age, skinny like all of us in real life, much darker skin, green eyes to Telo's startling black eyes. He has a scar on his shoulder. His palms are stretched out to me.

"Here I am," I say, but I don't move.

When he walks toward me, I flinch. He surrounds me with his arms. I can smell him, his underarms, my breath on his skin. I drown in the tidal wave of him. I put my arms around his neck, and his squeeze lifts me to my tiptoes. I am floating on someone else's skin. In a few weeks, we could both be gone, dead from infection, nothing left of us—not our cubicles or robots, incinerated; not our ephemera, wiped from clean.

"Babycakes." He breathes into my hair. He is crying.

I realize. The extra money, the late nights, his nonchalance about the risks of touch. Telo has touched many people before me. I'll be angry later, confess my own, but there's no time for that now.

"You look nothing like your avatar," I say, but I don't let go. Telo is alien, uncanny, the resemblance only slight. Who are we? How can we raise a human child and teach it who we are without lying, without shame?

"That's what you have to say to me?" He grabs my hair, puts his other arm underneath my legs, and lifts. He trembles with the weight of me, something he doesn't do in clean. How little we are, for how much we can ruin.

"Take me," I say.

"Take you where?" he asks. "This is how we live."

We're snotting in each other's necks, licking the salt from our wet faces, smelling each other down to the feet. I run my fingers in the curves of his ear. If we hurry, this touch could last a lifetime.

And this is what we can tell the baby assigned to us, if we survive: We can pass on our ruin through love. This box that you wake up in is evidence of how dangerous you are with need. We will give you what we can. We will offer up the world to your hunger.

The Man I Could Be

My dad tried to give me the jacket the army awarded him for serving in Korea. It looked like a varsity letterman jacket, soft blue felt, pale arms. On the back it said, I KNOW I'M GOING TO HEAVEN BECAUSE I'VE BEEN TO HELL. I was fifteen, and I thought a lot of my dad, where he'd been, how he'd built each of my family's three houses with his bare hands and a hammer, how he'd held up during my mother's death. And there he was, trying to give me the jacket that stood for all of that. "Son," he said, "you have it."

I was a greedy little shit. I took it.

As soon as I brought it to my room, a man grew inside the jacket. He had my red hair, my freckles, my short legs and big shoulders. But he was older. He looked upstanding and clean-cut. He wore fancy shoes and his hair swept to the side in just the perfect way I'd never been able to finesse.

"Son," he said, "I'm the man you could be." He saluted me.

I was horrified. I shoved him and the jacket into the closet, scaffolded on a hanger.

The next day, getting ready for school, the sleeve of that jacket whacked me in the face. The man kept grinning at me. I had goose bumps. It was a cold fall morning. I looked at the stupid skull T-shirt I'd grabbed and then at the jacket. I saw the hole in the armpit of the T-shirt, how it was stained yellow on the neck. I gave in. I slung the jacket over my shoulders and walked to catch the bus.

The man I could be was still in the jacket, and I wore him like a cyborg suit. I let him do all the talking and moving, and the me that was still a kid shriveled inside of him. He picked up a girl's books when someone sent them flying to the floor. He did not spit on the senior that tried to slam his head into the lockers, like I usually did. He just held up his hands and crouched low to the ground like a coiled snake about to spring. The senior didn't know what to do except stare. The man told the hottest girl in school that she was beautiful, and he brushed her arm in the hallway. Her pupils dilated and everything. He signed me up for JROTC, when I'd never even made a ten-minute mile. Before, I had lost every game in gym because I was always staring at the clouds, finding the shapes of girls who could never love me. By lunchtime, when I walked down the hallway, everyone gave me a wide berth. The principal called my name over the PA speakers.

The man I could be marched me into the office. He saluted the principal and sat down in the chairs in front of the desk. He leaned back, legs crossed so easily, like a resting predator.

"What do you think I've done wrong?" I said.

The principal said, "So, your daddy's been to hell, has he?"

"I respect my father," I said. "So should you."

I could tell how afraid he was of me. His lip quivered when I stood up, and he shrank in his chair.

"You're suspended today," the principal said.

"That's exactly what I wanted," I said to him in Russian, his parents' language, one I didn't even know how to speak.

I went home and waited for my dad to finish work at the lumber mill, where he'd already lost two fingers. I hid in the closet with the man I could be, both of us cross-legged on the floor. I was terrified. I was impressed. "What else can you do?" I asked.

"I know how to make love to a woman," he said. "I've been on every continent. I've killed a man. This is what you could be."

Dread climbed up my spine like a monkey on my back. Would I have to wear the jacket for the rest of my life to be this man? When I took it off, would I be skinny and atrophied, worse than I had been? Would I be a passenger in my own life? The truth was, I didn't deserve to say I had been to hell until I had. It had felt miraculous that day, but also shameful, lying to everyone. I wanted to *earn* the jacket. I wanted to be that man, not wear him.

I hung the jacket up for safekeeping in the rickety shed behind our house, alongside my dad's old army gear, canteens, boots, flashlights.

"You're making a mistake," the man said, arms out on the hanger like I had crucified him.

I locked him in the shed with a double padlock.

Girls all looked my way when I showed up on the school lawn the next day, but one by one their faces fell. I was skinny, ragged, my hair going every which way. My teeth were crooked. I was not what they'd dreamed about the previous night. They blushed and looked away, hoping no one else had caught them making eyes at such a boy. When I entered the front door, the principal stood behind a policeman who fingered his Taser. The officer wanded me with a metal detector and told me to lift my shirt. I showed my puny ribs, and the principal squirmed, feeling silly that he had ever been afraid of me.

The senior who liked to bash my head into the lockers was waiting in the hall with a group of his basketball buddies. "Where's your fancy jacket?" he asked, knuckling a baseball bat.

I wanted to spit on him. But I thought about the man I could be, and what he would do. I thought about what my dad had survived. So I invited hell. I spread my arms out wide. I could feel my stomach draining out through my legs. I smiled. "Go ahead," I said.

His fist exploded in my face, and I saw galaxies. I fell down, frozen with pain, adrenaline commanding me to stand up again. His buddies held me down on the floor while he kicked my ribs. I could hear my body breaking. I thought this was what war must be like. I thought I was going to die.

A sweet voice trickled down the hallway through my pain. "You're all so small," the voice said.

They let me go and left, and I heard light sneakers running toward me. One of my eyes still hadn't swollen shut. A girl stood over me. Renata, the girl whose books I had picked up yesterday. She didn't yet see that I was not the same person. But I wanted to be.

I went to the hospital several times that year, before the seniors graduated. The principal and the police officer did nothing.

I kissed Renata behind the fence of the grade school playground. I didn't tell her about the jacket or the man inside it, but she didn't even seem to notice I was less than. I kept her away from the padlocked shed across the meadow, although sometimes at night I swore I heard the man singing. Renata often had dinner with my dad and me. He liked her, and that meant a lot to me. I was fifteen and stupid, and I thought I would marry her. We hadn't yet had sex because I thought waiting was the honorable thing to do.

One day, Renata was out sick from school. I came home to strange noises from the shed, like hands clapping. I sprinted across the meadow, blackberry vines snagging me the whole way. The chains swung loosely. The windows rattled with noise. I burst through the door.

Renata had let the man off his hanger, and he was hunched over her. She lay naked in a pile of old sleeping bags on the floor. His face was buried in her hair, and he was telling her that he loved her, words I hadn't yet been able to say. I wanted to puke.

"What are you doing?" I yelled.

"He's you," Renata said. "Almost."

I lunged. While she scrambled up from the floor and grabbed her clothes, he got in front of her like he was protecting her. But I wasn't going for her.

He flipped me over, and the breath drained from my chest. I lunged again and spat at him. I fell flat on my face, cold dirt busting my mouth.

I waited for the finishing blow I had felt so many times in that high school hallway, the one that sent me into the stars, that blacked out who I was.

"I don't need to hit a boy while he's down," the man said.

"It isn't really cheating," Renata said from the shed doorway.

"I will always remember you," he told Renata. "But you better not see him in this state."

He sent her away, and she left, as compliant as a lamb to his wishes. Then the man squatted down on his heels to watch me recover, snot and shameful tears mashing with the dirt on my face.

"You can still be me," he said. "You can still wear this jacket."

When I finally got up, I wrapped chains around his arms. I dug a hole in the dirt floor of that shed, and I buried him up to his stomach. I didn't go any further because I respected the jacket too much to sling dirt all over it. Meanwhile, he just sat there, taking all of it, looking like a saint in full martyrdom. He watched me with pity. With pity! My rage boiled over. I added five padlocks, all with different keys and codes. I blacked out the windows. I camouflaged the shed in green paint and laced it with barbed wire.

Renata never spoke to me again. I kept the girlfriends that came after away from my house for as long as I could. When they finally insisted, everything would be fine at first, and then, inevitably as clockwork, they'd get this distant look in their eyes. They'd gaze longingly in the direction of the shed. How could they possibly know what was in there? Maybe they could hear him still singing. They'd sigh and push their spaghetti around on their plate, and then eventually they would leave me.

I sped out of that town when I graduated high school, waving good-bye in the rearview to my father, who'd gotten slow, too many disappointments hunching him down. He lifted a three-fingered hand in tired salute. I slammed the gas pedal, old T-shirts and jeans in a cardboard box in the passenger seat, waves of hot air rising over the asphalt. I left the state for college. I studied meteorology. Something about the way women would sigh and look up at the clouds in thought just before they left me made me want to figure out what they saw there. I started a career. I appeared every morning at seven, eight, and nine on the local TV station. I forgot about the man I could be.

Years later, my father died. I went home to bury him, clear out our old things, sell the house. My girlfriend, Clara, drove down with me. We tagged the furniture and stuff into what we would take with us, what we would sell, what we would bring out to the curb in boxes. She picked through my old toys, pictures of my mother. My mother had died before I could make many memories of her, and this only made Clara more curious. I gave her a box of old photographs to pack. When we were done, we sat on the porch and watched ducks ease into the pond. I could smell her sweat from the day's effort, like bread and lemonade, plain and good, sharp yet comforting. I felt like I should tell her something about the little I remembered of my mother, about all the hopes my father had for us, but my tongue felt heavy with dust.

"What's that?" she said, pointing across the meadow.

Then I remembered what I'd been avoiding all this time. I said, "It's nothing. It's an old shed with nothing in it."

"Hmm," she said. She turned her face toward the pond. She took in the meadow where my mother's ghost picked white flowers for my father's grave.

Later, while Clara was inside gathering her things from the bathroom, I ran across the meadow.

Sections of the shed's roof had caved in. The razor wire had fallen loose into the grass. I could hear soft little thuds in the dirt. When I pulled the door, the whole frame came off in my hands. The man was in there, still buried to his hips. He was spinning coins around his knuckles and dropping them into the dirt. He'd lost a few teeth. Mud and bird shit had dripped into the shed from the giant holes. The jacket I once told myself I would earn had rotted in tatters and bloomed mold on the shoulders. It was so shameful. Someone should have taken better care of that jacket.

The man winked at me. "Have you come back for me?" he said. "Have you finally given in?"

"I came back because my father died," I said.

"And who are you now without him? You need me."

"I'm a weatherman," I said. "I can tell when it will storm."

"Son," he says. "I can skin a bear. I can kill any man or predator unarmed. I can speak languages no one even remembers. You see storms. You *see* storms? I can feel a storm in my very soul. I *am* a storm. I could have let myself out. You think I've been waiting here all this while because I couldn't get out?"

He rose out of the pit effortlessly and hunched like a tiger. I backed away.

He whipped me in the face. He stuck his hands out a hole in the wood and shook the rusted, crumbling chains dangling uselessly from the discarded door. "Let me out," he said, taunting me. "What are you so afraid of?"

"I know how you get," I said.

He hit me again. I spit out a tooth.

"You don't trust her?" he said. "Why not let her decide?"

He started singing this deep crooning song, so beautiful I almost cried.

"Please," I said. "Don't make me. I love her."

"I'm not asking for your permission," he said.

I knew I would never escape him. So I called her name

from the shed, wailing for her. Dread hung on me in giant folds.

When Clara appeared in the broken doorway of the shed, the light glinted behind her in sharp spears.

She saw the man. She squinted at me. She put her hands on her hips.

Everything I had ever done wrong to her loomed in my memory. She had been with another man when I decided I wanted her. We were in a movie neither of our partners wanted to see, and I put my hand on her leg. "Don't," she'd said, but I left my hand there. "I'm happy with him," she said, but she kissed me back. Years later when we were living together, she told me about her past lovers while we walked around a lake, and that once, I called her names because I was never okay with all the people she had loved, how I could imagine her happy with them, without me. She was a writer, always so curious about other lives, following them to their natural conclusions, leaving me behind. That day, she cried. She had every right to leave me. I had enacted countless other sins against her. She made me sleep in the backyard. I begged for forgiveness for months from a shelter I'd erected in the grass, a pitiful imitation of what my dad had taught me about bugging out. "Grow up," she said. And I tried. I changed. She let me back into the house. I hadn't yet asked her to marry me because I was afraid of what she'd say.

Seeing her eyes flit between me and the man I could be, I burned with shame. I was filled with fire. I pulled at the seams of my ordinary life. I could see, just behind her, my mother's ghost flitting in and out of the meadow and through rooms of the house.

"You vindictive brute," Clara said, pointing at my crooked nose, broken from all those years of fighting.

She said, "You blind toad, always looking up at the clouds instead of at what's in front of you." Even now, I was watching the sky through the hole in the rotted roof.

"You're so afraid," she said. "You were going to let me leave you behind."

She knew me so well. She ran her fingertips over the spray of acne scars across my cheeks, my crooked nose. She kissed me on the neck so softly her breath was like feathers. Chills jolted me. To steady myself, I put my hand down on a stack of boxes of my mother's old clothes.

"Will we ever be enough?" she asked.

Clara took the moldy jacket off that toothless man I could have been. She pinned onto my chest every award that had rusted and fallen to the dirt.

The man shook his head. He crushed the padlocks in his fist and left. He walked naked across the field.

I slipped my mother's moth-eaten white dress over Clara's shoulders, kissed the freckles on her collarbone, the chicken pox scar by her nose, the pinky that had grown bent after breaking. I would love her better.

We stepped out into the meadow. Grass poked through the gaps in our toes. The sky was wide open and turning orange. A storm brewed low on the horizon. We walked into it.

Catarina

I n the bedroom, Rely cups my chin and kisses me. I pull back a little because his wife, Catarina, is in the living room throwing her therapy Legos, whole handfuls of them that slam against our wall and skitter on the floor. It's hard to lose myself in his lips while the avalanche of tiny bricks is going on, but these are the terms of our relationship, and I know that I'll take him on any terms. Sometimes I feel like she's doing it on purpose, but I know better. Her actions are just random neurological sequences, the aftershocks of her old self.

I knew Catarina, before the accident. I would give anything for us to have been friends, or maybe for me to have not known her at all. Some nights I lie awake next to Rely trying to hammer my memories into different shapes so I can imagine her as a good person. But what I remember always turns out the same way.

She was one of those people who only did something nice because she wanted you to see and she needed you to like her. At our accounting firm, she once gave everyone in our hallway dollar-store picture frames so flimsy they were already falling apart at the staples. Every time she walked by she made a big deal about how she'd given us a gift. This was a week before she asked for a raise. Once a year, around Christmas bonus time, she would clean out the paper shredder for the secretary and remind the rest of us how much more work she was doing than everyone else. Otherwise, she was a notoriously messy and scattered person, expecting the rest of us to tidy up the office, the accounts, the paperwork in her wake. Much later, Rely told me they had once gotten into a fight because he felt alone and overwhelmed, doing all of the cooking and the chores despite his own demanding job as the manager of a call center. So she told him that he was situationally depressed and he should get on antidepressants. Not *I'm sorry*, not *I'll do better*, but *Take a pill for that*. And you know what? He did, he was that kind of person. According to her, she'd never done anything wrong. Or she would wail and cry until you were the one comforting her for her having said something awful to you. She was that kind of person.

I went to a few of their dinner parties. She had decorated their house in glitz and glam; chandeliers and bedazzled things, the stage for a star. He was mostly silent, the chef on those nights, and she wouldn't let anyone get a word in edgewise. We were forced to listen to her boring stories about something she thought would make you like her, like how she'd met a famous actress and snubbed her, how she'd won some spelling bee when she was eight years old, or how she had impressed some client, and always she'd be snippy by the end of dinner if she didn't hear applause in your response. Once, I was excited about something she said about her family, added "Me, too!" while she took in a breath, and she looked me in the face and said, "This wasn't about you." Meanwhile, Rely encouraged her and nodded. You could tell they loved each other. It was baffling to me. I was willing to bear a lot for the people I loved, but where was the joy in keeping *her* company? At the time I just thought, they can have each other but I don't have to suffer for it, and I stopped going.

I shouldn't speak ill of the dead, even when her body hasn't quit yet. But this is how I spend my nights, remembering her, hoping to find some clue that makes changing her diaper something I would gladly do for her, hoping there is a happy ending to all this. And I know I have flaws, too. I end my nights with a litany of every cutting word I've ever said to Rely, to anyone, any moment I've broken down, trying to show myself how Catarina and I are the same. Were the same.

Another memory I turn over: the one evening, while I still graced their dinner parties, when she stopped talking about herself for a minute and told a story that was about him. "He has a talent for reading dreams." At the time, I wanted to snort at the new-agey-ness, but at least this was interesting. "We were giving a friend of ours a ride to her new apartment. She was moving away from an abusive boyfriend she had finally managed to extricate herself from, and she told us about a dream where tiny birds followed her everywhere she went. First they attacked her, but then she went searching for them and couldn't find them.

"Rely looked away from the road for a second to ask, 'Tell me something. What do little birds mean to you?'

"And then next thing you know, our friend was sobbing, saying, 'That's what he always called me, Little Bird. *Where are you, Little Bird?* is what he'd say.'"

Rely grimaced at the attention and shrugged. She smiled at him, big and beaming, like he was a god on earth. And I was inexplicably jealous. Something gripped me deep within my chest and wanted to be known, wanted to be revealed like that with merely the right question from him. Then Catarina waved her dessert fork and started in on herself again, and the moment was gone. She was talking about the time she went to Spain, but we'd already heard all the details. The other two guests and I called it a night shortly after that. Still, I barely thought of Rely after the moment passed. He was someone else's husband. But every once in a while, I would remember the jolt that had come unbidden.

I went over there with a casserole when I heard what had happened to her, the car crash and the coma. I remembered their love, and it moved me. The casserole was a mess, and I knew he could make something twenty times better, but I brought it anyway, because how do you even put an egg in a pan during grief? Only once had I been close to breaking, and it had been after my father's death.

Rely opened the door, took the dish from my hands in silence.

"It's a mangú casserole," I said.

"Thank you," he said. He looked at it, and I could tell he did not want me to bring another. Then he shut the door. It didn't matter what I thought of him. When he did something, it was because he cared and for no other reason. I admired that.

I didn't see him again for years. I heard from coworkers at the accounting firm about the experimental operation where they connected the body to the subconscious part of the brain, bypassing anything conscious that was dead. They hoped the brain would adapt, rewire the conscious part on its own, and all these coma patients would wake up. There were about a dozen people getting the procedure done. Afterward, I moved firms—to get bigger clients, more work, always moving up, doing longer hours, bags under my eyes—and stopped hearing about them.

Six years later, I saw him at a grocery store. He was back to his culinary ways: ricotta, pears, and a French baguette in his cart, selecting lemons beside an old lady commenting on their brightness.

"How are you?" I asked. "How's Catarina?"

He whirled around. "Oh," he said, his momentary smile collapsing. "So, you've heard?"

"About what?" I knew I had said the wrong thing.

His eyes narrowed. "That the experiment failed. That anything she does is just random."

"I'm sorry," I said.

Something about the way that his mouth parted open, his tall frame hunched forward—he wanted to say more, he wanted someone to *see* him the way he'd seen little birds in that woman. Maybe it was that he'd been so quiet since I'd met him, how he seemed to have sacrificed so much of himself for her, but I wanted him, for once, to have what he needed. I said, "What is it like, for you?"

Later I would learn that he was utterly alone, that all their friends who used to go to their dinner parties (the ones left who had been willing to put up with or were oblivious to Catarina's self-centeredness) had cut ties, not wanting to deal with Catarina's body, disturbed by the experiment and not having been great friends to begin with. That he had started the habit of cooking again, making her favorite meals in hopes it would serve as some kind of memory therapy to recover her. But at that moment in the grocery store, he looked hard at a lemon and said, "I keep cooking for two . . . Would you like to come over?"

It was an accident, falling in love. At the beginning, I just listened to him. It was the most words I'd ever heard him speak; it was like he was blooming in front of me. And in return, he got to the core of me, a memory from when I was sixteen or so, still an athlete. My family had visited relatives back on the island who took us out to a sandbar on their boat. We waded out, swam for a bit. After a few hours, I was the first to try to get back to the boat. Turned out, the tide had come in, and a riptide between my family and the boat dragged me out. When I realized what was happening, how far I had gone past the boat, I was almost certain I would drown. For a second, I considered screaming for help. But then I weighed my family: a cousin who was barely four still in a life jacket, my dad and some out-of-shape uncles with beer bellies, my mom and some aunts I'd never seen run a day in their lives. I was a runner and a tennis player, and I knew that if I couldn't make it, none of them could save me. I knew if I yelled, they'd be pulled under, too. So I kept quiet. I swam harder than I'd ever thought possible, choking, muscles burning. Eventually, I reached the boat. I drove it up to them like nothing had happened. After I told him that, Rely said, "And you're still swimming, aren't you?" I sobbed.

At first, we just held hands, hiding them under the table or a blanket when Catarina's body was in the room. We were shy. The company was meant as a balm to soothe other wounds. For me, a terrible ex who would put me down and spend hours at the mirror telling himself how handsome he was—it felt like he was dating himself. And Rely's wife—it had been five years since the surgery and everyone was sure by then that she would never wake up from brain death. He didn't have a wife, not really. He had a grave he could visit, except the grave was her breathing body and it lived in his house.

Now it's just a few days before the Cada legisla-
tion goes into effect. No new coma zombies, but the anti-
brain-modification wording of the statute also means no
undoing the ones who've already had it done. So if Rely
thinks he's made a mistake, he has to undo it soon.

Do I mention it, when I come up behind him as he's adding cream to hominy and humming to himself, the steam
fogging up his glasses? Of course not. I hug him. I try to lose
myself in the dream of him, the scent of him—garlic and
lemons, his hands smelling like that even under the pillows
at night, the mark of a chef. Our relationship rests on secrets.
I know people always say that the only good relationships
are honest ones, and really, that sounds wonderful and great
for them, but we don't get to choose the ones we love, the
paths needed to reach them. So I don't tell him that I hated
her before, that I wish her gone, that I resent her ultimate
selfishness even more now that I have to take care of her
husk, that I'm fine with disconnecting her—the remnants of
her, I mean. I'm sure he can read it in me. But that kind of
thing hurts once you say it out loud. It has consequences. He
knows her brain's random firings mean nothing, just old
subroutines flickering on but with no force to guide them.
But more than once when she says a word, I've seen him
move closer to her, try to interpret her as if she's a code. He
can't help but open himself to it.

I have dreams. Some of them I tell him. I tell him that the
three of us are all together on a vacation and she's our child
in the back seat. I tell him about the one where we have a dog
except it turns rabid and eats me alive, but I don't elaborate
that the dog had been Catarina moments before. I don't tell
him about the one where she's stitching my lips shut, or the
one where she takes the shovel and buries me while she kills

him in a game of Russian roulette. Or the one where he and I are driving home and we know she's waiting for us back at the house, and I wake up clawing the bed because it's a nightmare. How much can he see? All my nightmares are about her. Even though now—while he's cooking and I'm nuzzling his back, my arms around his stomach, and I take the spoon from his hands and stir the pot as if I'm another set of his hands—she's just lying on her special anti-bedsore bed, zombie-like, her brain emitting white noise. How could I be afraid of something so sad?

"Madame," he says, bowing playfully, spattering sauce as he moves the spoon through the air. "How was your day?" He puts the spoon down and looks me in the eye. He's watching and listening for what I don't say as much as what I do, that's how much he sees through me. Still we dance around what I don't say. *Disconnect her.*

"She ate fine today. I was able to do a little work while she was lying down." The other silence: how much work I'm not doing. How I got fired from my firm because taking care of Catarina took its toll, and I'd been having to find clients on my own; except I've been losing even those because they need their numbers quarterly and I struggle to keep up. Before, I'd always been known as dependable, the rising star of the firm, the person who could always get the job done. But there is so much more I would give up for him, and I won't leave him alone with this burden. He was so grateful there was someone to help, and he needed me. I knew it from the first moment I stepped into his house after the accident, the chandeliers and Hollywood lights pulled down, everything broken, in disarray on the floor except in Catarina's room, bare but for a hospital bed so she couldn't hurt herself.

"Thank you," he says, like he's read my burden. He puts a finger wet with sauce on my lips, and I open my mouth.

Cinnamon filling out the softness of cream, the hominy a solid base. It tastes like a mix of clouds and earth.

"You haven't made that before," I say.

"It's . . . just something I used to make."

It must have been a favorite dish of hers, from the hesitation. A last meal before death row? A meal so central to the core of her that she might wake up?

I hug him close, my face in his chest, not looking him in the eyes so he doesn't have to betray himself to me.

When Catarina's family visits her body, they expect me not to be there. They want the house to be the way she left it, the same photographs featuring herself, Rely behind the camera, all over the walls. I don't exactly mind. I know how it looks to them, and if I didn't before, the news special about Catarina and the others who had the operation, featuring interviews with her family and Rely, certainly made it clear. They kept saying that she could wake up any day now—ignoring all the science and the doctor who invented the procedure. To them, Rely is still married to someone who's sick, temporarily, a nice white woman. I am an affair, the person with everything to gain if Catarina loses, a Latina besides. And who, in the public eye, is more worthy of love?

This time, they're coming to plead with Rely not to undo her. They'll ask, we're sure, if he'll give her over to them. But this is the kind of person he is, and it softens me to Catarina, too, sometimes—her father molested her when she was young, and Rely won't give even her vacated body into their care. The TV news specials don't know that; he's still keeping her secrets. And sometimes I think it's not even Catarina's fault, who she was as a person. It was her environment that shaped the software of her brain. There's so much we can't choose, and even choice itself is part of the software. And love—we can't force it to come even when we've forgiven someone.

Before leaving, I make sure her diaper is clean and she's dressed in fresh clothes while Rely picks up the house. She's pretty limp, reclining against the couch while I pull her arms through a clean shirt. I knead her hands open so they don't get cramped and stuck as fists festering fungus and bacteria in the folds. Suddenly, her hands rip out of my grasp and she's punching at nonexistent targets in front of her, one blow catching my eye. I gasp. It wouldn't be my first shiner from her, and I try not to make any more noise from the pain so Rely doesn't come running.

You're gone, I whisper to her. *You're not even here.*

She goes limp again. Her eyes are closed.

I prop her up, grab a cold pack from the freezer, and call good luck to Rely. I breathe a sigh of relief when I roll the garage door up and see the bright sun, the palm trees waving at the foot of the lawn. My relief is what love should feel like when it's easy, but who needs easy? Part of me wants to run back inside, stand my ground, and defend Rely from Catarina's family. It's times like this I understand his love for her, his burden, why every day for the first five years he guided her hands around the therapy Legos, repeated commands and her own stories back to her, hoping.

I should work, bring my laptop with me while I'm out, but I know it won't be any use. I need to rest, most of all, to spend a day without thinking of the caretaking. It's like having a kid without the good moments, without the hope that they might grow up to be an awesome human being one day. So instead I go to the Welcome Home store.

The Welcome Home store is my refuge. I enter a fairy-tale life, dreams made of interior design. People browse the aisles, sorting through the patio items at the front. There are a few younger girls with their boyfriends, and they seem to be choosing their new lives together, the dishes and the recliners. The bargain prices make us all feel like we've gotten something we don't deserve.

I know what kind of person would buy the pineapple dish, the flamingo flatware caddy, what they hope to say about themselves. I can enter their lives, love them, briefly. This hand-turned rustic dish says, *I am made of earth, I am a deer, at any moment I may escape you even though I have stood here in this grass since before the suburbs flooded in.* The melamine orange flower bowl says, *We are fun and nothing that we do is permanent, though we will always be filled with light. We are the kind of people who serve mojitos to watch the sunset by the man-made lake and are content with that.* If I had a dream place, though, it would be blue as the sea. Teals and soft cerulean, seeded glass bowls and acrylic furniture that reflect light in mottled waves. I would love freely and let Rely flow equally between his love and his mourning.

For all of us in Welcome Home, it's about containers and coverings and daily tools. What we contain, what we reveal, all bodies and their extensions and the frames of our hope. It makes sense that the doctor thought he could re-create a person from the outside in, using the house to conjure the inhabitant.

The girl behind register number two has spacers in her ears, unshaven legs, and curly hair. I can guess what she loves in the store: she buys smooth wood trays, terra-cotta jars, olive oil soap in dark brown glass bottles. In her dreams, her body is her own and molds to her simply. When the manager leaves the front, the girl watches a video on her phone as she checks me out. I heard her get in trouble for being on her phone a few months ago, except that time she was talking on the phone to her lover, laughing easily, blushing. "Just unthaw the chicken, okay? No biggie," she said just as the manager stormed over.

I don't buy anything except a plum and wisteria candle. For one, I can't change anything in the house, because of when Catarina's family visits. For two, I like imagining I haven't committed to anything yet. Like the store, I could give everyone the happiness they need; love everyone who walks through my doors. Like Rely, I can hold on to dreams of other lives.

When I get home, Catarina's sister's van is still in the driveway, so I park across the street and eat a granola bar. When they leave, her sister's mascara runs down her face. I'm not unsympathetic. I can't imagine what it would be like, losing someone but believing every time you visited her grave that you could bring her back to life.

Sometimes, I pretend that I'm Rely. I pretend that I love her, that every day I hope against all rational hope that she might return to me. I think of the only good memory of her I have, when my father died and I called in sick to work, and the next day she stopped by my office. I had been working myself to death, always working more hours, pushing up against collapse. And the moment I feared, the moment I'd finally break down, it came that day after my father's funeral when I had carried his casket and wanted to throw it into the air, bust it open, as if strength alone could bring him back. I had my head on my desk. Catarina stepped in, rubbed my back. "That's so hard," she said, and her hand on my back made me feel like I could hold it all in. In that moment, I was ready to forgive her anything. I was ready to see why someone would love her. I wanted to break bread with her again.

"My dad," I began, "was a complicated person."

"Sure, yeah, but listen, my dad was probably more complicated. My therapist says that the reason I should cut my mother out of my life . . ." and then she was off to the races about herself again. I wanted to sob in my hands. I had almost been ready to share the load of this grief, and I could feel that dam in me, so carefully built up, cracking. I was collapsing. I remembered why we weren't friends. I had to take the week off before I could recover.

Now, I try really hard not to conjure up that part. Just the brief moment when she put her hand on my shoulders, like there was something we could share. Usually, I do this when I turn off the light right after checking on her. In the darkness I can picture her sitting up, uttering full sentences like *Where am I? What day is it? How long have I been out?* But then I think about what would happen next. Would I answer her? Would I run away, lock myself in the bathroom to hide, hope it was only momentary? And Rely—would he choose? Would he weigh each of our faults against the other's? Could he have us both? But there would be no happy ending for us. It's not that he loves someone else. If I loved her, too, I would welcome her with open arms; we could talk all night and share him, understand what each of us meant to him; we could be another missing piece of each other's puzzle. There would only be more love. And Rely happy. But we couldn't live together, she and I. I don't blame her for the car accident, the way she is now; but I do for how she was before, the choices she made. How do you bring someone you resent into your family? How could we share a meal with the three of us, more of her undying attention to herself? Right now is bad enough.

I wipe drool from her mouth. Rely places the sauce he has prepared on the tip of her tongue. Not with his finger on her lips like he does for me, but with an eyedropper, so she won't choke. She swallows, and we wait a moment before we insert the tube down her throat to feed her.

While the machine's going, I eat quickly, and the food is so good it doesn't last long on my plate. I squeeze Rely's hand across the table. Meanwhile, Catarina's hands have begun hovering. When she does this, it looks like she is a sloth dancing the slowest dance on earth, the tension beautiful and hard to bear.

After dinner, we pull the tube out. A smell wafts from her that means she's had a bowel movement and her diaper needs to be changed. Rely wheels her back to her room to take care of it. I clean the dishes, scrape the white sauce stuck to the pans.

From the other room, I hear her say *please*. I cringe. Sometimes she says things like *money* or *fuck*. When she says *please* is the worst. She's looking at you sometimes, or other times her eyes are closed, and it almost sounds like she's pleading. But what would she be asking for? The doctors say this is alphabetizing. There's no consciousness there; it's just a random word, like letting the dictionary fall open to any page, her verbal center throwing off a random spark. I can hear her repeating it. When the dishes are done, I go in to help.

Rely is at her feet. He's sat her in the shower stool and is using the detachable shower head to wash her. "Please," he's saying, sobbing.

"Please," she says, her eyes closed.

"Please," he cries.

"Please," she says.

When he sees me at the doorway, he wipes his eyes and is quiet. He keeps washing her feet.

"I didn't want to interrupt," I say. I help him wash the other foot. I know this is only half of him.

We're getting ready for bed, Catarina safely tucked

away in her room. We're brushing our teeth, dancing around each other to get room at the sink. When he spits out the last of the paste, he sags. "I can't believe how long we've been doing this."

I nod, my mouth still filled with toothpaste foam. Eleven years for Rely since Catarina's coma. Four years since I moved in with them.

"Should I undo it?" he asks.

He's asked when I can't answer, my mouth full, that's how badly he doesn't want to know what I would say. We're both looking in the mirror.

He holds me, then crumples down, kneeling. He's so tall that this brings him almost to my shoulders. I squeeze him, trying not to drip foam into his hair, but loving the sudden warmth, the way his limbs feel around me. He's in pain.

"Little Bird," I croon to him around the toothbrush in my mouth. I told him the story about that night, about wanting him then, and the name stuck. It's also a name she never called him, to keep the memory of us straight in his mind.

"I'll be okay," he says.

It's a lie. Neither of us is okay. I lean over, spit, and rinse. He guides me to sitting on the bench in front of the sink. Now we are face-to-face. He pulls out a basin, fills it with hot water. He starts washing my feet. I gasp from the feeling, tickling in a slow, calm wave.

CATARINA

We are so attendant to each other's bodies, these grand receptacles of our selves. Before Rely, I never felt passion like this, electric and without thinking, equal through sorrow and joy. He says he never did either, not even with Catarina. With her, it was a calculus. She was allergic to lube, she moved awkwardly, she was only to be touched in certain ways on the lower back, but never on the legs. He was happy to do it, of course; he loved her. But the love between him and me, it's like breathing.

I kiss him as he passes soap over my feet, and now he's washing by touch alone. His eyes are closed, our lips seeking refuge. I feel almost like a body without a mind, like I'm dreaming. But that's what Catarina is now. What is a body to the mind? A vessel to hold it? An alembic, a transformation? Hardware for flash memory? A messaging device? If I were delivering a message in this moment it would say *I love you I love you I love you*. But that, I know, would sound too much like her, alphabetizing.

And then Catarina jumps into the bathroom, arms flailing. I scream, and Rely pulls back, the washbasin overturning. Both of us stare silently for a while, entranced. She is jumping and spinning without rhythm or pattern. She looks like she's about to fall, tipping over too far, but then her autonomic nervous system kicks in and rights her. It's beautiful, that empty, wasted body. Then he steers her to bed, and I mop up the water, and this time he locks our door.

On the way to the hospital, he drives. At nearly every stoplight, when the red light turns green, he pauses for too long. Twice, he is honked at by people in traffic. I almost think he's going to turn around. I stay still; it's his decision. I squeeze his shoulders. Catarina is in the back, humming one note.

When we park in front of the hospital and he lowers her into her wheelchair, I say I have to use the restroom. I want to give him a chance to say good-bye. The nurses, however, recognize me from the news. "Here they are," one says to the other. I can't tell if I'm the demon to them that I am on the TV special. The girlfriend who wants to get rid of the wife. Some of it, of course, is true. But the wife is not there anymore. Her body is merely a shield for the self, and the self has vacated. How many second wives would like the first wife's undead body moving like a ghost through their rooms? But I have never pushed him on this, have always taken care of her body. I am not his wife.

Dr. Feltic comes out to shake my hand. "Where're Rely and Catarina?"

"Still getting out of the car."

"Ah," he says, heaving a great sigh, loving the attention. "It's too bad the experiment failed."

"It would have been a great breakthrough, for you," I say, knowing what that would have meant for me.

He turns red. At that moment, Catarina's family rushes through the automatic doors. They've brought picketers from their church, outside chanting, "She's a-live! She's a-live!" That much, of course, is true.

Cameras catch Rely rolling Catarina in. I don't know why we didn't expect this spectacle, the politicizing of one man's sorrow.

Catarina's mother locks eyes with me. "She shouldn't be here," she screams.

Rely closes his eyes tight against her. The security guards keep the cameras out as Rely pushes Catarina through.

I'm not family. I'm only the person dedicated to feeding her, carrying her from day to day, making sure her body doesn't get hurt. I am, to them, insult to injury. "I was just leaving," I say.

"I need you," Rely says.

I don't want my presence to push him into something he will inevitably regret in his darkest moments. I want him to be able to change his mind even as the scalpel hovers over her fragile body. So I say the hardest thing, a truth that feels like a lie, like we are on either side of a riptide. "You don't need me. You are so strong. I'll be home waiting for you." And what will we be, after?

I walk quickly through the doors, not looking back so Rely won't see my tears, and none of the picketers recognize me until the last moment, as I am ducking into the driver's seat. Then they rush my car. Women press themselves up to the back bumper, chanting. I look at them in the rearview. They don't look back. They want so badly to do good in the world, and they want that good to be loud. They want to wear justice. I want love and to give myself to it. I am selfish, I know. If she had woken up, how easily would I have given him up to her? I back up slowly to avoid hitting the picketers, and it takes me twenty minutes to inch out of the lot.

I should go home. I should pack up all of her things. I should repaint. I should stop resenting her because she's about to be finally, truly gone. But I drive past the Welcome Home and I'm already in that lane, so I wind up in the parking lot.

At the entrance, there is a batch of pillows, mugs, and bowls with love messages, overstock from months-ago Valentine's. In gold lowercase cursive, the items say things like *You're the only one for me* and *Love at first sight* and *My other half*. I know better. I did not love him at first sight. I know you can love two people at once, even if one is a memory. If she woke up, I know he would instantly forgive her everything I saw in her, the same way he forgives me for when I'm too rough with him, teasing, for how much I judge others' weaknesses. There can be more than one person you love completely and deeply. I know true, deep, selfless love can hurt so much. We don't have the words for this. All we have are little kitschy phrases, embroidered on pillows lest we forget even that much. But the best I can come up with to replace them is just a deep, resounding *You* that feels like a current.

I sit at the velvet dining sets, the seats soft and plush. I push my cart through the mattress section, collapse on the memory foam beds, imagine what it will be like to hold Rely through each night after this one. The fluorescent lights hum like a lullaby. I close my eyes and dream the future. Tonight, Rely will come home. "I did it," he'll say. And I'll open my arms, surrounding him while he sobs, his body shaking mine to the core, my own tears safely exhausted earlier in the afternoon. I'll do what I have always done; how do you hold the man you love through his sorrow over someone else?

The glassware aisle is full of a family selecting cups, so I skip to the bowls. I could buy something this time, replace all of Catarina's pictures. Breathe in deep relief at a home of my own making. But maybe I'll start with a bowl. To me, a bowl feels like *please*. It feels like *fill me* and supplicant hands cupped around it and *I'll hold you*. I surprise myself; the one I pick up isn't blue glass, it's olive wood, the inside enameled in coral. A bowl that can be two things, that can split itself while remaining unbroken. I put it in my cart.

The girl with the spacers is at my register again, watching the news on her phone. She gasps softly when she catches my eyes. "You're the girlfriend," she says. Everything is on her face. I know what it looks like: while they're unhooking her in the hospital, I am shopping. She looks at my mom pants, wonders how someone like Rely can love me enough to let go of Catarina. To her, the news is a soap opera of fictional characters. Love is as simple and fitting as a story. She can try to guess what happens next in the plot. I remember her on the phone months ago, blushing, so full of hope. I don't want to break her.

"Don't worry," I say. "He'll always have loved her first."

I don't let go of the bowl when she tugs on it. I want to drown in it. Her eyes are panicked. She wants me gone.

"Please," she says.

How long can we bear it, these burdens, before the moment of breaking? Finally, I release it.

She rings up my bowl quickly, and I hug it to myself on the way out. The heat slams me but the bowl is cool. I could break myself in it and still not fill it.

The Dreamers

n my ten p.m. class, I keep my eyes on the streetlamps outside, their buzzing lights over Bayview. I'll never sleep, not for years, not for decades if I can help it. When I'm at my worst, eyes bloodshot, thoughts racing, I'll excuse myself to the bathroom, slap my face, and pinch the insides of my arms. Sometimes when I'm studying I even tape my eyelids open. At the beach, I let the salt burn my eyes.

Prom is tonight, all of us soon to be twerking on the dance floor in dresses and tuxes. I'm running over the plan in my head: how I'm going to break my boyfriend, Joaquin, out of his glass sleeper coffin so he can come with me to prom.

At the desk in front of me, a girl from the track team bobs her head—not those small twitches all of us do, but a really slow descent, and then she jerks herself up. It looks like a dance move. Beside me another girl rolls a quarter between her fingers too fast to see, a blur of silver. A boy pulls his hair in frustration. My ex–best friend, Karina, sitting at the front of the classroom, is the only one relaxed, leaning back with her arm over her chair; she's also the only one of us who's ever slept. Sister Olivera drones on about quadratic equations at the blackboard. I look back to the streetlamps, the dark of the bay just beyond the basketball court. My heart pulses so fast I could dance to it.

But then my eyes skip back to the track girl, nodding her head lower. Right in front of me, *BAM!* Her head hits the desk and doesn't rise again. She is facedown in her own drool.

I don't know what to do. What just happened? Sister Olivera doesn't even notice. It's Karina who sends the nun into hysterics and signs of the cross by raising her hand and saying, "Sister, she's fallen asleep."

The nuns are followers of Santa Acostara the

Sleepless, the first person able to stay awake for her whole life. After forty-four years of wakefulness, she fell into a coma for twenty-two years. There was a vigil for every day of those sleeping years, everyone thinking she would wake up again, but in the end she just died in her sleep. They sainted her, celebrated her four decades of wakefulness, taught the importance of her example: sleep is weakness, and weakness is sin. Her following grew. But then other nuns and people outside the convent, people godless and unbelieving, started being able to stay awake for decades, live their whole lives before their final sleeps. Now, almost all of us do it, desperate to live every second of our youth. Still, the nuns—they cling to wakefulness like it's a sacrament. *Guard against the heavy eyelids,* they say. *It's a sin to choose sleep before your time. You teens are especially vulnerable. We must pray for the sleepers' souls.*

And yet, some people—heretics, sinners, people from other religions or godless—still choose to go to sleep before their time.

Sister Olivera phones the office, and an announce-
ment shudders over the speaker system. Grief counseling, by
which they mean sin shaming, will be held in the chapel during next period.

We crowd into the chapel, and by some ill luck, I'm pushed
into line behind Karina. When our elbows touch, my eyelids
droop and I feel tired, so tired. I pinch the inside of my upper
arm as I walk behind her. We're told sleep is something we
naturally resist in this day and age (except for teens, who,
during puberty, start to feel both manic and drowsy). But if
I've never fallen asleep, how do I know when I'm doing it
until it's already too late? Of course, the nuns can't tell us
anything, because they've never done it either, and they
think keeping us in the dark is the best way to make sure we
don't try it. Which is why Karina, the traitor, is so popular
now; she's one of the only people our age who went to sleep
early by choice and woke up in time to tell us about it.

Humans sleep about a third of their lives, but since Santa
Acostara it's almost always at the end, all in one go before we
die. We live our youth and sleep away our old age. If we try,
we can fall asleep early, but that sleep is still a third of our
life span, and then we wake up and live out the time we have
left. Like Karina. She fell asleep when she was ten and woke
up when she was sixteen. The doctors say she has until she's
eighteen before her body craps out on her—not that they
know what's wrong yet; they've just done the math. It gives
her an air of the doomed. But her sleep also made her popular. When she woke up, everyone flocked around her and
wanted to know what dreaming was like. They crowded her
in the halls and showed up at her house. They left invitations
in her locker and candy on her desk. Never mind that I was

the one who had defended her, and she'd closed her eyes because of them.

Before she slept, these same girls had teased Karina because of her hair, which poofed out in a half-mast afro. Girls in our class kept pulling it straight, asking, "How long is it really?" or getting their fists caught in it, yanking her head around. Boys called her Puffhead. One day in gym class, girls held her down on the basketball courts while boys patted her hair and stepped on it. I threw basketballs at them until they let her go, but the damage was done. She sobbed and wouldn't come out of the locker room until everyone but me had left. We missed the bell.

She had asked her father if she could switch schools, to move farther from the beach and the mean kids, but he just kept telling her to tough it out. He's the town's dreamcatcher, and he'd leave newspaper clippings on the table for her, sob stories about kids he'd picked up in his dreamcatcher van who'd let themselves fall asleep young. "When things get hard, you face them. You don't run away," he said when she told him about the basketball court. He was white, and Karina often told me how he didn't understand her. Her mother, Afro–Puerto Rican, tried to console her: "Things may get better in a few years. Just wait until high school." But then she got quiet and said, "I don't know. Sometimes things get worse."

I found Karina the day after, asleep. Tripped over her, actually, when I was running down the beach looking for her. The dunes rose up around her, and the cattails and grasses waved over her head. She had tucked herself into an old turtle's nest. She was swaddled in sand, her halo of curly hair glittered with grit. Her smooth cheeks puffed in and out. She was dreaming, gasping and letting out whispering little breaths.

We were used to coming upon people sleeping in the dunes, a sleeper or the dreaming dead. Sometimes a bum curled up in a meadow, usually naked, their clothing and shoes stolen by the wakeful. They were rounded up by dreamcatchers, then claimed by loved ones or unclaimed and sent to a state facility. This was back when my parents were still together, and I made my dad call Karina's to tell him where to find her. I never imagined it was her I'd have to give up.

Six years later, Karina walked into our two a.m. biology class like she hadn't been gone a minute. I barely recognized her: her hair heavy and wavy, boobs bigger than mine, taller than anyone in our class. When I did realize who it was, I was so angry. She had abandoned me, and I thought she wouldn't wake up until after I'd graduated college and gotten married and my kids were the age she'd been when she went down. I had already mourned her. And if she was awake now, it meant she was dying soon and I would have to mourn her again.

It was Joaquin who said, "Easy. The last thing she remembers is fourth grade." He knew how much we'd meant to each other. He was the one who patted the desk next to mine. He was always going against what everyone expected of him, surprising me in the hallway with shells when he should have been in class, finding weird kitsch on eBay that I loved, laughing when I thought he was going to shout in frustration, saying the most random things that had us cracking up for days.

Soon Karina and I were having sleepovers again, Joaquin climbing in through the window after basketball practice. We showed her high school algebra, the bands and TV shows she'd missed, how to smoke, told her what things were expected of us now that we were older. I taught her how to flake on plans and how to ghost and how to drift away from someone without causing a fight. She still had the sad innocence of a child, hadn't yet learned the defense mechanisms that we high schoolers had for dealing with grief and hurt. She was so earnest. Every time we showed her something new, she'd jump up and down and laugh. She squealed when we ordered our usual combination of coffee and fries at the diner. Joaquin and I took turns teaching her how to kiss, and she'd gasp every time, dig her fingers into our arms. I'd lie down on the floor holding her, with my fingers tangled in her hair, the ceiling spinning until it was time to go to school. It was like we were kids again, had gotten a do-over to promise everything, even better than before. We swore we would never believe in a god who would condemn us for how we loved or when we slept.

The three of us were inseparable. I wasn't angry anymore that she'd left me; I was just happy she was back. I was as in love with her as with Joaquin. Out of the three of us, I was the protector, the one who would pull someone by the shirt if they cut in line, who would glare anyone down who made a crack about our threesome, who would keep her old bullies away. "It ended up true," she said, "that sometimes you give things time and they get even better." But there was the shadow of her short life. She told me she was afraid. Not of death, which she thought would be like dreaming, being pulled apart and into a new form; but of pain. The doctors couldn't say what would kill her, not yet anyway. It could be a tumor or a lightning strike or a murder.

Then, Joaquin fell asleep a few months later, leaving us to figure out anew what we meant to each other. At first, Karina and I spent all our days and nights in the Denny's that his parents owned, just to be near him where he slept in his glass coffin. When his mother brought in a prayer group to chant novenas for his great sin, surrounding him behind the hostess station on their knees, Karina and I talked loudly to drown them out in case their words would infect his dreams. Karina held my hand under the table, and just before daybreak we lay on the beach where she'd first gone to sleep, watching the turtles shamble out to the sea. I wept and I railed. Karina was quiet, but she opened her arms for me to curl against her in the sand. When we made each other come then, we were tender and quiet.

At first, I recounted memories about him like it was his funeral, things even Karina didn't know. But the whispers at school about his sin were getting to me. Joaquin would have shrugged, or danced in front of them and given them a bow. But without him, it was up to me to make them treat him like a person.

When I told Karina my plan to break him out for prom, wheel him in, and let everyone remember him, she lost it. She slammed down her coffee mug. She was sitting next to me because Joaquin always used to sit across from us. Coffee sloshed onto my lap. "You're as bad as his parents, making him into a doll against his will. Parading him around. He's sleeping."

"What?" I said, grabbing napkins. "I'm defending him."

"Don't defend him," she said. "Love him." She pressed the napkins into my shorts, soaking up the coffee.

I wrung my hands. "He wanted us to come with him."

"You know I can't anymore. I've done all my sleep."

I knew. How to choose between the two of them? One awake, one asleep. Joaquin got to have dream-versions of the two of us until he would come back and find Karina gone. "Well, he might wake up early, like you."

"Oh, so you're wishing him an early death?" She had learned to be whip-quick at pulling out truth from where it was hidden away.

"That's not what I said." I scooted away from her down the booth, but she caught my belt loops and pulled me back.

"You're going to change so much in the decades it takes for him to wake up. You'll go to college, have a career, go to my funeral. You won't know what each other has been through. You don't know what either of you are going to want." She tucked my hair behind my ear, moved my chin with her fingertips so I would face her. "You were so different when I saw you again."

I shrugged her off. Then it occurred to me. "He was always asking you about what it was like. Did you tell him it was a good idea?"

She shrugged. "He made his choice, and you have to let him lie. Don't be selfish."

"*I'm* selfish?" I couldn't believe her. I had thought we were a team. "Maybe I *should* join him."

I could feel her studying me from the side, like when she was learning something new about the world. "Maybe you should," she said. "Maybe then you'd understand."

I waited in silence while she piled all the brown-wet napkins on our plate of fries.

She put a five on the table and walked out, brushing her fingertips against Joaquin's glass on the way.

I stayed in that booth for hours, but she didn't come back. At school, she sat in a new desk on the other side of the classroom, joined a cafeteria table full of the girls who'd bullied her and gave them her earnest smile, ignored me even when I blocked her path in the hallway. She stepped around me. She stopped returning my phone calls, started fucking other boys and girls from the basketball teams, ghosted me. The very things I had taught her how to do. I felt ten years old again. She was so good at it—betrayal.

We fidget in the pews, our shoes squeaking against the tile floors. A fever flushes over me. Is it wrong that my body still aches for Karina, even during a chapel assembly?

"Sleep," the nuns begin in unison, "is letting go of what is beautiful about this hard world, shrugging off our burdens for the easy temptation of slumber. Staying awake is shaping your burden into a life, into a righteous form that God can be proud of. The sleepers hear no one's voice but their own, not even God's. They've given up. They didn't choose the path God showed them."

I can feel Karina tense next to me, her hands in fists.

At home, I grab my prom dress from the closet, its aquamarine tulle skirt like the ocean foaming against the shore. My mother is rushing around the living room in her scrubs. In the old days, when we still needed daily sleep, doctors were always messing up hours-long surgeries from lack of rest, but now doctors keep going on nearly seventy-two-hour shifts. It's Mami's one-hour break to change clothes, shower, and say hi to me and check in on abuela Selena, who sleeps in a pretty frosted glass capsule behind the couch. Mami offers to paint my nails and asks me how school went, but when I open my mouth to answer, she's already talking about some patient and then saying she hopes I have a lovely time. Like she doesn't even get the fact that I'm going alone, no Joaquin, no Karina. She doesn't even notice that, underneath abuela Selena's sleeping capsule, I've stowed a wheelchair I snagged from the hospital the last time I visited her at work.

The phone rings while I'm doing my hair. Because it's

Papi, and Mami refuses to speak to him, she yells at me to pick it up. I bring the cordless into the bathroom.

"Hey, sweetheart," he says, which is always a bad sign.

"What time are you coming to see me off?" I ask. Then I hear the ocean behind him, his silence. "Oh. You're not coming, are you?"

"I miss you guys," he says, "I just . . . I just need to take a walk." Which means he's going to the beach where they got married, reliving memories of when my mom still loved him. He once told me that he often thinks of when he proposed to her between two palm trees while she was still a resident, luring her outside with the idea of shell collecting. That he retraces their life since that moment and thinks about all the other choices he could have made that would have let her keep loving him.

"Papi, stop going by the cove. It's a teen hangout now, and you being there is creepy. And have you forgotten it's prom night? Be an adult, will you? You know I'm still here, right? While you're feeling sorry for yourself?"

He takes a deep breath. "How's your mother doing?"

I hang up. My mother is gone by the time I come out of the bathroom.

At the Denny's, Joaquin looks peaceful in his glass coffin behind the hostess station. He used to look deathly underneath the fluorescents, but a few weeks ago I threaded a string of chili pepper lights through the hinges and handles of the coffin, and now his skin is lit up in splotches of red and green. His face has the bright, dewed hope of the dreaming. His black hair has grown long around his ears, but his mother wets his hair into this ridiculous comb-over. Now that he's asleep, his parents take advantage of how unconsciousness has defeated his attitude. His parents attend to his every need in between running the restaurant, but they've made him into a toy, the model son. He's already wearing a tux.

Every so often, his eyes flicker behind his lids, and sometimes he rolls over. It always stops my heart when he does that. I think he's waking up.

The traitor, Karina, is in a booth across the restaurant, surrounded by her newfound admirers and their cooing parents taking pictures. They don't even look my way. Instead, they're gossiping.

"Did you see that track girl go down?"

"What a face-plant."

"And right before prom."

I keep my eyes on my fries. I'm waiting for the right moment to break Joaquin out. I pull my greasy fingers away from my prom dress, the turquoise fluff of my skirt, though the fabric sticks to the booth and to my skin, damp from the ocean a few streets away. I feel awake from adrenaline, the night stars bright and piercing. Joaquin's parents haven't retreated to the back room for the day's accounting, and it's not time for the three a.m. dance yet.

"She didn't even warn anyone," a girl says to their table. "Just, bam, snoozing."

"Maybe it wasn't by choice," Karina says. Everyone at Karina's table gets quiet, not wanting to mention Karina's own choice.

Sure, it happens; kids fall asleep young because they'll die early, usually from some sickness, cancer or something that'll grow as they sleep. But this girl, she had a smile on her face the whole day, like she was planning it. Beatific or wicked, depending on whom you asked.

Karina's dad is giving the boy who is taking her to prom

"the talk." He keeps a selfie-drone camera rolling to capture the moment. How his tune has changed, sobered and softened by the fact that he's only got a few more years with his daughter. This is the same guy who used to shout and clap in our faces to be sure we weren't feeling drowsy.

Karina and I catch eyes for a moment, but I look down and slurp my coffee.

Karina glows. She's lost all the innocence I loved, her strapless dress a sultry red satin that forms a V from underneath her armpits down to her inner thigh before splaying out into a full mermaid skirt, a line Joaquin and I had traced with our tongues until she moaned and promised to never let us go. Now, her hair coils in ornate braids around a tiara. Her dark cheeks shine with bronze blush. Her eyes beam the way they used to only when she was surprised—by a striated shell, the last scene of our favorite anime, an ice cube on her neck. Her red lipstick swells her lips into a perfect, lying heart.

Suddenly, I can feel my body droop, my eyelids start to fall, and I dig my fingernails into my arms hard enough to make myself inhale sharply.

Joaquin's mother, Mrs. Velasquez, drops a carafe of coffee on my table without looking at me, not even warning me "Ten cuidado, it's hot" or telling me to have a nice time at the dance. She hates me, I know. Joaquin wrote a note before he went under saying, *Cariño, ven conmigo,* and so they thought it was *my* fault, that I somehow knew something, or we'd had some kind of plan together. Now they hate how I hang around Denny's, watching over his trussed-up coffin. The one exception to their iciness was when they let me put up the string lights on his birthday.

Karina and her friends peel themselves out of their booths, their parents fawning. They're heading over to the dance. Karina holds hands with a boy from the basketball team, the guy who took over the power forward position from Joaquin.

Finally, the Velasquezes retreat to the back room. I hitch up my dress and hustle behind the hostess station. I unlatch the top of the coffin, which hisses open with air. Joaquin's all deadweight, limp as jelly. I drag him to the wheelchair I stashed behind the bushes outside. The last thing I see is the one remaining customer, mouth agape, watching me stagger out. I wonder if I'm the one who's dreaming.

We're flying down the hill, Joaquin strapped into the wheelchair, my feet on the back bar so we can roll un-hampered. The ocean roars beyond the parking lot at the bottom of the hill, and for just a moment, things are how they used to be, when Joaquin and I would steal grocery carts and race them down this same street, wind whipping our hair, our love blind and seeing at the same time, crashing together at the bottom in a tangle of metal and limbs and aliveness. But then I blink, and Joaquin is asleep in the wheelchair, and I'm alone again.

At the dance, there's a pair of nuns at the door, checking dress code and searching pockets for flasks. Karina's dad paces back and forth by the line, whispering into his pocket radio. All the softness from earlier is gone. And, just like that, my plan disintegrates. The nuns would have been enough; they would have turned Joaquin away as a sinner, not allowed into their sacred kingdom. But Karina's dad strutting around like he's on a case, hunting some sleeper gone astray, means that Joaquin's parents have already dis-covered he's missing and they'll be looking for me. A limo purrs behind me, and I yank Joaquin back into the bushes alongside the gym.

I sit on Joaquin's lap and pull his arms around me while I think. The sea breeze and his even breath on my back give me goose bumps. It's almost like he's really here. I know he'd tell me the whole thing is silly anyway. He would have worn running shoes instead of dress shoes. No, if he'd been awake, we wouldn't even have gone. We would have had an anti-prom on the beach, blazed up a bonfire for ourselves and for all those lost, dreaming souls not allowed into heaven.

Then I hear Karina's dad's radio coming up the street on the other side of the bushes, and I make a break for the mangroves, the wheelchair dragging through patches of sand.

Moonlight glints off the sea, through the trees, and I'm pushing Joaquin over dunes and mangrove roots. He's sliding around between the headrest and the chair's arms until I reach the cove. I catch my breath. Waves push more ocean trash to the side of the inlet: the familiar used condoms, plastic bags, broken bottles stroked into sea glass. I spot the head of a bum resting on rough mangrove roots. When we were little, Karina and I would go over and throw sand at bums' faces to see if they were sleeping, until the first time one of them wasn't—he rose, furious and spitting grit from his face. After that, we left them alone.

The cove and the sandbar across the water from it only appeared last summer, when the hurricane recarved the coast. Before that, this was a long beach where people liked to get married. Even my parents promised themselves to each other forever here—in sickness, in health, in wakeful-ness, in sleep—except that now they couldn't be in the same room with each other, and when I stayed at Dad's apartment my mother wouldn't even drop me off outside because she didn't want to see him wave.

The night before Joaquin fell asleep, we came to the cove. There was a party, the basketball team celebrating a big win with a bonfire. We left Karina on the beach with the others, and Joaquin and I swam to the sandbar a thousand feet out. At its edge, the strobing waves rushed and roared at our feet. The universe broke into stars above us. After the hurricane had swept through, we'd told each other that even if the rain blew one of us away, we'd never stop loving each other.

We lay down and watched the stars. My toes poked up out of the surf, and the pulsing water cooled our backs.

"I don't know why anyone would sleep," I said, "and give up all of this."

"What, you scared of getting old and being awake for it?"

I pulled on my cheeks, made them sag, and laughed.

Joaquin was silent for a minute. "Close your eyes," he said.

I blinked, the dark of night and the dark behind my eyelids barely different.

"No," he said, "keep them closed."

He kissed me on my neck, licked the salt from my ears. The surf crashed around us, and my body floated in his arms. Suddenly I felt like I was falling down, tumbling, drowning.

I gasped and jerked up. *Was that falling asleep?*

And then his smile, bright as the crescent moon, always surprising me. "Why are we so scared of sleeping anyway? Why this life? Why not any other life? You're beautiful with my eyes open, my eyes closed. You'd be beautiful old. You'll be there in my dreams, too."

"You don't know that. Dreaming's random. You could be lost in a maze. You could be chased by monsters. It's the pain of your life as well as the joy, that's what Karina says."

"So what if you're my pain and my joy? I would choose you both again."

"When you wake up? Karina would be gone by then. All the decades between, you'd be turning away."

"Don't tell me you still believe in God."

"No," I said. I clung to him and rolled him over, our sandy chests pressed together, my body held out of the water by him. I ran my fingernails down his arms slowly. I kept my eyes open, toward the dark eating at the shore. *Awake, awake, we had to stay awake.* Dawn was coming, the candle flame burning at the other end of the world.

Eventually, we swam back. On the beach, cicadas burst from their shells and water moccasins slid all around us.

The next day, Joaquin fell asleep.

Voices climb up over the rush of water—probably

people leaving prom early to make out somewhere the nuns can't see, or people looking for me and Joaquin, picking their way into the cove. I drag Joaquin's wheelchair through the sand toward the bum, where I know the others won't go. But then I trip over a root and the wheelchair pitches forward, spilling Joaquin into the sand. I end up on my knees. I see into the bum's face and realize who it is.

I kick my father in the ribs, sharp and quick, sand flying into my face and his. He won't wake up again until I'm old and my mother's already sleeping-dead.

I drag Joaquin away from the mangrove roots hiding my father.

My breath shudders, and I fall back into Joaquin's lap. Last year, he would have held me tight, kissed me. Now I blink against my wavering sight, trying not to collapse into sleep.

I slap Joaquin. I slap him and I punch him in the chest and

I shake him, his head falling back and his mouth hanging slack. I put his hands on my breasts, but they fall as soon as I let go.

"Wake up!" I yell into his face, wet with my tears.

I kiss him; in all the stories of lovers liberated from sleep and glass coffins, it's the kiss that wakes. He tastes like the ocean, deep and desperate in his dreams. Or is that me? I'm sobbing salty tears into his open mouth. His eyes trace mazes behind his lids, and his breath stays even. Laughter and shrieks approach through the trees, but I don't care.

Love me, I want to yell, but instead I unzip his pants to reveal the hard-on that grows automatically to touch, the real Joaquin not even noticing.

"What are you doing?" I hear behind me. I'd know Karina's voice anywhere.

I keep unbuttoning his shirt. I've lost so much.

"Wake up," I whisper.

Karina's hands grab mine, pull me off of him.

"Leave me alone," I yell.

"I'm saving you from yourself," she says, her face inches away from mine, her hair frizzing out of her prom braids. Her tiara has been discarded. "You'd regret it, later."

I twist my wrists so she can't hold on. "I don't need you," I say, rubbing the salty snot from where it's run onto my lip. I say, "Go back to sleep," like I'm telling her to go back to hell.

"He's not awake, and you can't keep pretending that he is," she says. "He made a choice. I made a choice. That's what we took for ourselves."

I lie down in the sand between roots, my dress gritty and wet. "Please just go away." My eyelids sag, and this time I let them.

"Oh, so you're going to sleep?" she says. "You're going to join him after all?"

"That's not being together," I say with my eyes still closed. "That's just dreaming side by side."

"That's what we're always doing, Delia. Always."

I say nothing, images fracturing behind my eyelids. Why not come back twenty years from now, when my father and Joaquin will be up, when Karina will be gone? When the whole world will be different, more giving, the coastline shattered and remade into its newest, glowing form?

"Fine," Karina says. I feel the heat of her bloom next to me as she lies down.

My fingers dig into the cool sand. I'm determined: if a dream comes to me, I'm going to hold it down and ride it so hard, wherever it goes.

"I heard they used to sing people to sleep in the old days," she says. She starts humming, and the melody reminds me of something she said after she woke up, when she told me she was afraid of pain and talked about what dreams were like. *Sometimes they're sharp as a needle, sometimes frantic with love. They could hurt like drowning or roll you softly like tumbling into waves.*

Karina's fingers unearth from the sand and lie on mine. Brief flashes of images frantic and sharp, drowning and soft: The kids who pant in Karina's tragic wake, starting a bonfire on the shore. Lighters and magnesium shavings and dryer lint someone had saved for kindling. How she looked when I first found her in the turtle's nest. I feel like I'm falling down a rabbit hole, deep and dark and long.

Suddenly I'm afraid. I start up like I'm leaping out of an abyss, open my eyes.

Her hand is still on mine, and I'm throbbing with the effort of not gripping hers back. How long can we hold on to things that change? The bonfire flares up, lashes the sky with need.

"Still here," I say.

She stops humming. "So *be* here."

I roll over. She pulls me into her lap, brushes the hair and sand and wet from my face. There she is: black eyes like Joaquin's, broad shoulders, her dark hair limned with moonlight.

I bring my lips to hers and she kisses me back, tenderly biting in a way she's never done before; she must have learned it from someone else. I start crying again, but this time we both laugh, too.

"I'll call my dad to pick them up," she says.

I nod. I keep my eyes open toward the flames. Behind them, the dawn is birthing green like an old bruise.

We're dancing and laughing around the bonfire. Someone has stolen the track team girl's textbooks, notebooks, and pencils out of her desk, her posters and secret notes out of her locker. Karina's ripping out pages from the journal and passing them to me, and I deliver them fluttering into the fire. We're letting her go, page by page. I'm screaming over the sounds of everyone else.

Behind me, Joaquin and my father dream, and I let the ghosts of their dreams dance with me. Joaquin's, of the nights we could have lived together, the cicadas that sleep for decades before bursting from the ground, his defiance against the world even as it spins underneath him; my father's, of his pain, his memory of my mother collecting shells and tossing them back at him, my disappointment in him fading to a dull throb—all of these dreams tumbling into smooth sea glass. In front of me: the fire of this life, the heat pressing on my face. Aren't we all beautiful here, the dreamers behind me in the mangroves and the ones awake at the fire with bloodshot eyes, unable to turn away from what we see and feel? The warmth of the blaze and the soft calm of the dark, the day opening up like a door and the night still blooming in the corners of our eyes.

We Work in Miraculous Cages

was one of millions of college graduates try-ing to pay off student loans and credit card debt on minimum wage. I worked as a receptionist at a hair salon from nine to five and a veterinary emergency hospital on nights and weekends. I had a boyfriend, but he kept wanting to take my clothes off during the few hours I had for sleep. At the vet, I ran around catching cats who'd escaped their carri-ers, weighing the dogs, sorting through mountains of paper-work. Sometimes you turned around and a dog had hacked up an organ, or a cat came in on the Fourth of July with a firecracker through its head, or a police dog was being rushed in from a shooting, or a ferret had escaped its cage and vomited green all over the hospital.

No one wants to hear about our anger, I know. We haven't earned it yet. And yet, I was so angry—at myself, at the cli-ents. At the salon, angry at the superficial rich; at the vet's, angry at the salt of the earth, the farmers who brought in their potbellied pigs, the welfare poor's shaking hands as they handed over their animals. These were most of the peo-ple we saw at the emergency vet. People with money, with time, they shuttled their animals to their regular vets as soon as they sensed something amiss. Everyone else tried to wait it out, only brought us the animals when they were near death. At first, I told the hysterical owners clutching their dying pets, "It will be okay." But after a few months and enough dogs and cats dying, my own life like molecules that would not bind, like the electricity of a heart that fades and will not restart, I knew it would not be okay.

Then I started to say, "We'll try everything we can."

But that was even worse, because everything we could try cost money that less and less people seemed to have, and we had all seen where trying had gotten us.

At the hair salon, I checked people in and out of their appointments, answered the phones, counted cash. I had to stand behind the counter. The owner had thrown away the stools because he thought sitting made us look lazy, less ready to serve. I also doubled as an office manager since they couldn't afford to hire a second person. It was a high-end salon, so actually it wasn't that they couldn't. They wouldn't. I got a few extra dollars an hour, but it wasn't enough to make a dent, not when I was paying twice my rent in credit card and student loan repayments.

They would call me into the back to shampoo someone's head or massage hands if they were in a pinch. These people I shampooed, they were fake breasts and balloon lips, the stretched faces of age artificially preserved, all those people who could afford to spend money just to have their hair washed or get their eyebrows arched in the perfect way. I did not want to hear about their lives. When the person was young, I didn't mind. They thought they had their whole life ahead of them, and while I massaged their hands, I wished this for them. With the older women, it was different. I thought about how they had spent not just their lives, but our lives, too, gobbled up or snorted up or injected into their faces all that good fortune of the eighties and the dot-com boom, them laying their heads back into the shampoo bowl and me wasting all my understanding about the world—fluid dynamics, the great monologues of literature, the construction of engines, the physics of flight—on rubbing their skin over their bones.

At the vet hospital, a woman brought in a python

in a cardboard box, bleeding heavily, chunks missing from his body.

"Triage to the front," I breathed into the speakerphone.

"How can I help you?" I said.

A tech appeared and took the box away from her into the back.

"It's a long story," she said. "I feed it live rats, because that's better for them, you know? I send one wriggling down into the tank, and my python eats it. Well, this week it wasn't hungry, so I left the rat in there, thinking when he finally got up the hunger he'd pounce."

I shoved the paperwork at her.

She said, "The rat started chewing on my python instead."

"The rat ate the python?" I repeated.

A sobbing girl ran into the hospital, yelling, "Someone please tell me if my dog is alive."

"Triage to the front," I breathed into the speakerphone, and triage came and stretchered the dog, a Saint Bernard, into the hospital. *Alive*, the tech mouthed as he headed to the back.

So I made this girl and her father who walked in afterward

fill out the paperwork. She was skinny, her eyebrows tweezed to slivers.

Then a man came in with a cat that hadn't peed in days, which meant its bladder would probably rupture. Then a couple walked in with a dog, a big one, seizing and twitching in their arms.

"Triage to the front. Triage to the front." I wanted to sit, because my feet hurt, but then I needed to stand because my back hurt, and I wanted to sleep, and for a moment, I wanted to cut my brain out of my head, like throwing baggage overboard from a sinking ship. I was the python, eaten by a thing I was told should be mine.

My boyfriend brought me dinner. He felt apologetic for an argument we'd had the night before. My boyfriend had found a real job at a bank, but we all knew his position was precarious. He was one of the lucky ones. When I mentioned this, he'd huff and argue. He would cover the rent for me when I was a few days late, until the next paycheck came, but he was trying to pay off debt, too. "It's not like I'm hoarding it," he'd said. He believed he'd gotten everything entirely of his own merit. But there was not a one of us without merit, so said the certificates mailed to us by the merit-scholarship-this and the merit-scholarship-that we'd had thrown at us during college. We had been the valedictorians from our high schools, the straitlaced, work-hard kind of students, and our teachers had told us we were brilliant, we were going places. None of that was enough.

Mostly we had argued about my "laziness." I was never home, so I didn't cook, I didn't clean, and still I could barely pay rent. I was driving my car around uninsured.

The night before, I discovered he'd put one of my dirty dishes on my side of the bed, nestled in my pillow like it was cradling my failure. "I'm not your maid," was what he said in defense. "Clean up after yourself."

I had spent hours cleaning up animal defecation and other undetermined ooze at the vet's office, plus bowls of chemical ammonia and gunk and slime from hair products that had crusted the walls and fixtures at the hair salon. When I came home, I had six hours and counting until I had to be awake again. "The very thing I don't want to do," I told him, "is to clean up after myself, the one thing I have control over in this new life."

"Look at me," he said. "I have time to cook for myself and clean and run to keep myself in shape." He even spun around for me to admire his perfect shape, his biceps and calves threaded with muscle.

"So you think I'm gaining weight?" I said. I knew I was. "You're the one with all the free time. Would it kill you to clean a dish?"

"It's never one dish," he said.

"My life is on hold," I said.

He reminded me of my complicity in all that, how I'd spent thousands on credit cards, banking on promises that I would pay it off later with a career. He said, "You put yourself in this position. When you live like a king in a time of debt, you invite the ransomer to come collecting."

"What are you, Shakespeare?" I yelled.

He liked to lunge suddenly toward an expensive lamp I'd bought using student loans, or the antique chair from Craigslist, or the designer clothes that sat on my hangers, as if to smash, break, or tear.

"I'm taking everything you own to Goodwill," he said.

"And that's the sad part; you wouldn't even notice they were gone."

"Please don't," I begged, cradling the last things of value I had.

The truth was I didn't remember the last time I had turned that lamp on or had sat in that antique chair. I was too busy wearing a uniform emblazoned with a company logo to wear my expensive clothes. The veterinarian's was embroidered with the EKG line of a perfect, healthy heartbeat. The hair salon's logo was a rising kite made of a hair braid. Underneath, the logo said *Reach for your perfect self.*

He wasn't a bad guy, my boyfriend. I knew he wanted love as much as I did. But I had no time to give him the kind of love we were both convinced we deserved. Picnics or long walks in the park, talking until late into the night. The night before, when I had come home and seen the desperation on his face, I saw a tick mark adding one more to-do on the list I drowned in. When I smiled at him, it felt like chucking sand down an unfillable sinkhole. Then that's when I found the dish crusted with spaghetti sauce on my side of the bed. My situation was only temporary, we promised each other when we made up.

Now, he was apologetic. So that's why he was bringing me dinner at the vet. Often, he brought these elaborate meals with five courses that he had cooked, which I would have to shovel down in cold mouthfuls when my bosses' backs were turned. I wanted to be more appreciative. I knew it was a gift I could never repay, the time to cook a five-course meal, package it, bring it to him. This time, I could see hurt on his face when I barely had a second to say hi, grab the food, go back to work.

After he left, I calmed down the couple with the seizing dog. I had to pee and I'd been holding it since my shift at the salon. I threw the remaining paperwork at one of the vet techs and went to the bathroom. I called my friend Gemma from the toilet, the only way I got to talk to her anymore. She was one of these blond Hispanics who looked so American, you wouldn't even know she was born in another country, hadn't gotten her citizenship yet. Smartest one out of all of us. She'd done everything that had ever been asked of her. We'd barely seen each other since graduation.

"How are you?" I asked, my bladder emptying with relief. From outside the bathroom, I could hear another person hysterical about their animal walk into the hospital. I locked the door.

"If I tell you," Gemma said, "I'm going to cry."

So we caught up quickly on other friends instead. We were all hitting our heads on ceilings erected after graduation overnight. The more we worked our minimum-wage jobs, the less likely we were to get a real job, the ones we coveted, with health insurance and a salary and paid sick days and holidays when we could rest. But it wasn't factory work, like some of our grandparents had done; it wasn't coal mining, like so many of our ancestors thought their descendants would be doing for all of eternity. It was not macheteing sugarcane in scorching fields like some of our parents had come here to avoid. We were not being hunted down by the government. So how could we complain?

The couple with the seizing dog elected to eutha-nize. That's how I'd been told to say it: "election," as if everything we'd come to we had chosen, as if we always had options. They were told that treating the epilepsy would cost them thousands upon thousands. Sure, afterward the dog could have a close to normal life. He was already out of the seizure and kept trying to climb into their laps. But the couple had kids and a mortgage and were running thin on savings. So they decided to put him down. "It's just like falling asleep," the woman kept repeating. Then, when they were checking out, the woman had one of those moments when you realize what you've done. She laid her head down on the counter. It was already too late. Their dog was dead.

"I know you think I'm terrible," she sobbed. "God forbid anyone would ever make that decision for me, to put me down because of money."

"We do what we do," I said, which was not a consolation.

The skinny girl and her father were another matter. They'd been told they could save their dog, which had been attacked by a bigger dog from a neighboring farm. That, too, would cost thousands. IV bags, catheters, antibiotics, surgery with lasers to graft skin and sew together muscles.

"Yes, do it all," she said, "but I don't have any money."

"Credit cards," I had been trained to suggest.

"I have none," she said, "but do it all. Save my dog."

"Or we can have you fill out an application for credit," I said. "Or you can call friends and we can take their payment over the phone."

Then she was hysterical. "You don't understand," she said. "I can try all those, but even if someone would lend me the money—which they won't—eventually I have to pay them back, and I. Have. No. Money."

Her father looked on silently. There wasn't anything to do. She didn't have any money and I didn't have any money and we didn't have any money, and the dog was going to die and I hated the both of us for it. She was crying over the dog that she couldn't save, and then she was laughing at herself because what else could she do?

A few weeks later, a girl came into the hair salon with hair she described as thinning. She told me while I squeezed shampoo onto her head that she was feeling run-down. Her husband had lost his job and she was working overtime to make up the difference. She was barely older than me, maybe late twenties. She said she passed the salon every day on her way to work and finally decided to treat herself.

As I shampooed, her hair fell from her head in giant clumps and tangled around my fingers. I was preoccupied in horror and fascination as the hairs slithered down the drain, when she asked me if I'd gone to school to be a hairstylist.

"Oh, no," I said, "I'm not a stylist. I'm an engineer. I'm just doing this in between."

Hairstylists at the other shampoo bowls glared at me and my snobbery.

"I will not be here forever!" I wanted to yell in defiance. Meanwhile I lifted my hands up from the bowl with a web of this girl's hair netting between my fingers.

The other stylists shook their heads side to side in threatening ways.

"Sell her the hair-thickening shampoo," one of them whispered.

But I couldn't help myself. "You should be going to a doctor," I said, "and not the hair salon."

The next day, I got called into the salon on a day I wasn't working, yet another meeting I wasn't getting paid for. I thought they were going to fire me.

"We think you have an attitude problem," said the owner.

I couldn't deny it.

"Stop telling people that you do other things," they said. "This is now your real job. They're paying for some degree of servitude. It makes them uncomfortable to imagine their college professor massaging their scalp."

"Must my mind be a slave?" I asked.

"That's the point. Your mind has nothing to do with it."

In bed that night, my boyfriend said, "You've always been tough. You can wait this out. We'll get through this."

He was massaging my back. I closed my eyes.

"What if there is no end to this darkness?" I said.

He switched off the light.

On my one day off a week, I slept. If I had an interview, I'd sacrifice my day off and don a suit and try my best to convince someone to give me a salary. I had a degree in astronautics and I could tell you how in your very own body the molecules methylated, I could build a motor that would take you to Jupiter, I could tell you what love was in the most scientific terms, and none of that meant anything to anyone. The year I graduated was when the space shuttle program was dismantled. Not that it mattered. Even most of my friends in fields that hadn't died were searching for jobs.

I ironed a collared shirt and the suit I had bought on credit, when I should have been sleeping, when I should have been cleaning or keeping house or eating.

I was called to interview with a stereo company, for a job involving engineering speakers and sound waves. I interviewed twice with an oil company, once as a project manager, once as an engineer. With a technology audit firm, with a cell phone company in R&D, with another company that it turned out wasn't really hiring. They just wanted to feel out the applicant pool, apparently. In the cell phone company's interview, a panel of three men and one woman in their fifties interrogated me from behind clipboards.

When they asked me about my greatest weakness, I said I worked too hard and overextended myself.

"Design an evacuation plan for San Francisco," an interviewer said. "Go."

"How many traffic lights are there in all of Manhattan? Go."

"How many quarters would it take to reach the moon?"

"Okay," I said. I estimated the quarters, the distance to the moon divided by the width of a quarter, factoring in the latitude position on earth and the time of the month and the time of day for deviation. "Figuring all that," I said, "you would need approximately fifteen billion quarters to reach the moon."

They nodded. One of them closed her eyes. Another put his feet on the conference table.

"However," I continued, "that would be about four billion dollars. It might take fewer quarters if you used them to buy a space shuttle from the now-defunct space shuttle program, plus staff and research, and used that to reach the moon."

They grunted in approval. An awkward silence slithered between us. The interview ended. They all shook my hand.

"We're really excited about you," they said. "You seem like exactly what we're looking for. Out-of-the-box thinking. We'll be making our decision very, very soon."

"How'd it go?" my boyfriend asked.

"I think this one's the one," I said.

"You'll get through this," he said, and I noticed he didn't say we.

A few of the interviewers were nice enough to put me out of my misery and tell me that another qualified candidate was selected for the job. Most of them never called, despite emails I sent politely asking when they would come to their decision. They would all but throw the job into my lap, the interview bloated with promises. I'd be in hoping agony for weeks. Then one day I would wake up realizing they weren't going to call. I would trudge into the hair salon or the veterinarian's with the knowledge that I would never be anything but a receptionist. I felt like a gerbil in an exercise wheel, fooled into thinking I was climbing a ladder of quarters to reach the moon, and the wheel goes and goes and goes and the moon never gets any bigger.

Months passed, and I couldn't even tell you what
I had done besides work. I marked the time in terms of friends that had moved away, looking for jobs in the bigger cities where everyone was crowding or moving back in with parents who still had space. I drove from the hair salon to the veterinarian's across town, back home, on repeat. The only way I ever saw anyone I knew, unless they walked into my work, was driving past them. I saw some old friends and we honked and waved, and then sped off again because we were late and every second counted.

I had to be careful because I'd already been pulled over for speeding and being uninsured. "Please," I told the cop, "I can't afford the ticket."

He was one of those cops with a smirk. "The law is the law," he said.

I put that ticket on a credit card. I sped even faster from work to work to clock in earlier so I could pay off the charge.

One night, I got home and my boyfriend was already asleep.

I showered, put on a silk shirt and soft leggings, the clothes I could no longer wear during the day and I had paid for so dearly. My feet throbbed. I slipped between the covers smelling like lavender, and for just a moment I was not about to burst into sobs.

He stirred. His hand reached for my stomach and he said, "Mmm," because it was covered in silk.

"Not tonight," I said.

His eyes opened. "When?" he said.

"On my day off," I said.

"We need to talk," he said.

Now we were both awake and listening to the cars outside, their drones and thrumming like spaceships taking off.

"Please," I said, "can't it wait until tomorrow? I have a job interview on my lunch break. I have to sleep."

"What if you never get the job? How can we live like this?"

"So we're going to do this now?" I said.

"I keep waiting," he said. "I keep waiting for the person you used to be, who was wonderful, who was loving." He tugged on my shirt, the silk bunched in his soft hands.

"I am that person," I said. "This is not me."

He said, "There is no such thing as who you are. Only what you do. Over and over. Like bringing you dinner at the vet. Love is a verb."

"I love you," I said.

"Prove it," he said. He kept tugging.

"I appreciate everything you do for me," I said, too tired to cry.

He yanked, and all the buttons flew up into the air. For a moment I thought they would stay up there, buttons frozen and floating above us. They looked like coins, spinning and glittering in moonlight. But then they came back down and skittered everywhere.

I got out of the bed. I got down on hands and knees to collect all the buttons on the floor. I said, "Could you even tell me how many millions of these buttons it would take to reach the sun?"

"Why are we together?" he asked. "What are we doing except subsisting and waiting?"

I held my hands out, palms open. I had nothing to offer. I wanted to fight, I wanted to love, I wanted to sleep. I remembered going on a picnic with him on the university green, studying together, designing a space shuttle capsule to his measurements for my thesis, both of us standing on the dorm roof ready to take the landscape underneath us by storm.

He must have felt guilty. He got out of bed and tried to hold me with my shirt flapping open.

I pushed him away. I said, "I have to sleep. I can interview to be your girlfriend soon, but not tonight."

"I've been meaning to tell you," he said, grabbing at his head with his hands. "I'm no longer hiring for the position."

I threw a handful of buttons at his chest. I poured the rest into a drawer and collapsed into bed. I closed my eyes.

He began to pack his bags.

I couldn't afford the apartment, and he knew it. Behind my eyelids, I called triage to the front. I climbed quarters to the moon. Somewhere in the craters, if I kept searching, I'd find a man at rest.

The next day, I crammed what I could in my trunk and threw a sleeping bag in the back seat. I left a note telling my now ex-boyfriend he could take everything to Goodwill. I drove to the salon wound so tightly with expectation that had I been flicked with a finger, I would have snapped.

Gemma walked into the salon. She slapped a ten on the counter. "This is all I have," she said, "so give me what you can."

"I'm so glad you're here," I said, "but why are you here?"

"I heard you broke up," she said.

I hadn't had the time to tell her. "I can't talk about it," I said, "or I won't be able to get through today."

I brought her to the back to give her a hand massage, intending to pocket the cash and give it back to her. I rubbed her palms with my thumbs. For the first time in so long, I wasn't angry about where I was or what I was doing.

"I have something to tell you," she announced. "I'm moving back to Venezuela."

"My god," I said. "You don't even remember that country. You can't even speak proper Spanish anymore."

"My mom says I have a great-aunt who will take me in."

"Stay," I said. "I'll play hooky, and we'll have lunch."

She laughed softly. "I hear there are jobs there," she said.

I knew it was a lie. These bodies were our cages. I wished so hard to be just the cage, this miraculous cage of atoms, with nothing but the wind inside. I wanted *Flowers for Algernon* but in reverse: the part of me that expected so much more, dying and withering into a seed. I wanted to bloom into someone who lived the life of work like in it there was sustenance.

"You're shaking," she said. "Just tell me what happened."

I rubbed lotion over Gemma's palms slowly, its smell of

lavender flowers engulfing me. I closed my eyes. I could feel myself emptying. Then I felt her heartbeat with my fingertips holding her wrist steady, more than just iron and oxygen and cells. I held her hand. A feeling flooded me I'd forgotten how to name.

That night at the vet's, a lizard lost its eye, and one of the interviewers emailed to say they'd hired another candidate for the position. I called triage to the front, and I tried not to think about the future, spending the night in my car. I muzzled the dogs that curled their lips around their teeth with fear in their eyes. It was like they could smell how expendable they were, despite all the love in the world, despite how many times they sat and fetched and played dead and spun around in a circle. One dog kept standing up then sitting, over and over, and the owner kept saying, "That's a good girl. Good girl. Good girl."

A tech called me to the back operating room. The vet and three techs huddled over a Dalmatian with her stomach flapped open. They pulled little wriggling gelatinous balls from the hole—an emergency C-section.

"Grab a puppy," yelled the vet. "Too many puppies and not enough techs."

She handed me one of these hot, gelatinous blobs. Inside the brown mess was a furry creature with its eyes closed. I followed the techs' lead, using the suction wand to pull the placenta from its eyes and nose and mouth.

"Wake it up," the vet told me over her face mask.

"How?" I asked, almost choking. One more impossible thing.

"Beat it up. It's what the mother does, swings it around

in her teeth and bats it with her paws until it starts crying, except this mother is knocked out from the anesthetic."

So we flung our puppies up and down, we rolled them out like fingers of dough on the operating table, we danced with them. The doctor brought out another brown ball from the stomach, set it down on the table. The doctor said, "Leave it. There aren't enough of us."

But I thought it wasn't fair that something came into this world in which there just wasn't enough. So I sucked the placenta from the puppy's face as best I could with one hand, while shaking the first puppy with the other. I rolled both next to each other on the table, hoping to keep the second puppy warm and that any shaking of the first would reverberate into the second. Behind me, the doctor announced she'd lost the mother's heartbeat, and she was starting defibrillation. We kept with the puppies. My body, this miraculous cage, its electric atoms, danced. I waltzed with them toward the moon. I shook them. I wanted them to wail for milk they would never get. I beat them up until they cried.

The Radioactives

We read the government ad in the newspaper. Wanted: technicians and a driver for a
high-tech gift from the United States, a super-
truck that could pull up alongside any other
vehicle and scan it for drugs. We applied, even though Jesús's
wife, Estela's parents, Marco's seven siblings, and Héctor's
girls who danced with him at the club, hoping to marry, all
said the same thing: Don't get involved in that business of
foreign gifts from unknown motives; don't get between
Chávez and his advisers, between the narcotraficantes and
their money. You only have two eyes, not enough to watch
your back from all sides. But Jesús was paying for med
school, and all of us were supporting families. The money,
paid in dollars and not in the bolivars (whose value slipped
through our fingers while we slept), was too good.

The truck arrived on the docks like a present, a big red
ribbon around the shipping container. The bulletproof
armor bulked like it was on steroids, white and gleaming,
too crisp to believe. And there was the long arm that could
extend its X-ray scanner around another vehicle, showing us
what was inside. The arm folded up on the truck's roof when
not in use. The truck was surrounded by American military

specialists who squinted at us with distrust. Even Chávez was there, tight-lipped and tense, shaking the hand of the head specialist, someone high up in the CIA, and cutting the ribbon with giant golden scissors. We cheered. We begged to crack a champagne bottle on the hull, but they told us it was a million-dollar piece of technology. Then we wanted to test the two-ton strength of the arm by swinging on it. We were too excited for suspicion.

"Chamos," Chávez said as he handed us the key, "if it breaks, I will arrest your families."

One of the specialists pointed toward the X-ray arm folded up against the back of the truck, where the radioactive source was hidden in a little box. "Be careful," he said. "You'll see things you'll wish were still hidden."

We knew how X-rays worked. The radioactive source was protected in a box of lead. It was only when the lens opened in the act of taking pictures that the radioactive source was exposed and glaring on our black film.

Estela revved the truck. It rolled out like a tank. We rode it back to the highway garage where we would park it when not on patrol. We inspected it, the arm that would hug the other vehicle, send images back toward us, and show us everything hidden in false bottoms and false ceilings.

We celebrated by getting drunk in the cabin and riding out into the jungle to scan the animals. Héctor, who controlled the arm with a joystick, danced in the dark of the truck, a ridículo chicken dance. Estela, the driver, ordered everyone to listen to her stories. Jesús, the one studying to be a doctor, the main X-ray technician, drunk-dialed his wife and his daughter and told them he loved them from the aluminum floor of the truck. Marco, the photographer who controlled the truck's camera, set up shots in the jungle: the little white animal skeletons in a sea of black. The next morning we would still have the X-ray images burned in our memories: a monkey holding out a plastic bottle, an escaped llama bowing to the weeds, a family of four sitting down to dinner in their house.

The next day we watched a truck shimmer down
the road like a mirage, and we said, "Vamos."

It was a Daihatsu, an ice cream company logo painted on its side. A mustache twitched on the driver's lips. Estela pulled a ski mask over her face as she hit the gas, so the driver, if he was a narco, if those ice cream cones held more than ice cream, wouldn't be able to identify her later. The rest of us hid in the back with the equipment. Jesús stood in front of the X-ray displayer. Héctor sat in his chair with his hand on the arm's joystick. Marco sat at the controls for the radioactive camera. Estela pulled up next to the other truck. We watched through our screens and displays.

The driver sped up to pass us, yelling into his radio. Héctor manipulated the joystick for the robotic arm. *Whhzzzr—* we heard the arm extending. Marco took the shot. On the deep black landscape of the X-ray panel, the ice cream sat in neat little stacks, and at the bottom of the cones: little balls of intense white.

"We have a winner," Jesús yelled. Estela radioed the police, stationed farther up the highway with machine guns, and we repositioned ourselves on the road.

We took down another narco, a truck delivering dolls with heads that popped off, revealing little plastic bags inside. Then another, a furniture truck with a false bottom. They were betting on nobody wanting to move the heavy furniture to investigate underneath. But we didn't have to move anything.

We whooped and we celebrated at the end of that day.

We knew who the enemy was, and for once in our lives we were beating them.

Over the months, as we caught more and more drug runners, we started to notice strange things. We could all swear Marco was glowing. He was just brighter somehow, and when you looked away from him, his dark shadow of an afterimage still burned in your retina. You saw his form every way you looked, until it wore off after a while. It was like a film with multiple exposures. And the afterimages stayed longer and longer.

Héctor kept accusing us of sitting in his seat and readjusting it. It was too far forward, he claimed. "Who keeps sitting in my seat?" he asked. "My arms are all crammed up against my chest."

We looked at his arms, which did look rather cramped. But none of us had sat there. The girls he danced with said he had developed his own move; they called it the Héctor Narco, his arms spread out like wings, craning back and forth at the elbow and wrist, mimicking the motion of the truck arm.

Estela always came to work tired. When she stared at those little white dashes on the road, she zoned out, and we thought she'd fallen asleep at the wheel. She insisted that she got enough sleep at home, but we worried. We dreamed we got on a boat that would never come home, that we caught a fish too big to swallow. "That's so strange," said Estela, "because just last week I caught a fish and choked on too big a mouthful." But she hadn't told any of us about that.

Jesús's wife, when she brought us lunch, told us it was just our imaginations acting up.

Jesús—who while learning to be a doctor had also learned

to be a hypochondriac—insisted that his heart was beating too fast, that it was doing double time; perhaps he had developed an arrhythmia. Jesús told us how he lay in bed one night with his wife watching Globovisión, his daughter asleep at the foot of the bed, her dark curls tickling his toes, the TV light washing over them in waves of gray, and he could actually feel his heart breaking. He could feel himself ripped in two, like this happiness was something he wouldn't have for long. "But why would that be?" he asked. "My family was right there next to me, and they were beautiful and alive."

What *was* there to be sad about? Over months, we confiscated so many bags of cocaine that inside the evidence locker the walls were lined in white bricks. When we walked through the police station to log our paperwork, the police officers, even the dirty ones, cheered. A sour-looking official came by with a medal we could pin up in our garage.

Of course our streak of good luck would have to break. There was the one time we picked up someone we knew, yes. A van full of women on their way to the airport. The X-rays had been unclear. Either they were leaning against the bags in the walls or they had eaten them. When the police rounded up the women out of the back, and Marco held the X-rays up to the light to pinpoint where the bags would be, the rest of us stood beside him, nervous to be exposed. "Hurry up," Héctor said. One of the women—the one who wasn't crying—said, "Héctor?"

He was too smart to react and give himself away behind the ski mask, so he looked off at the horizon. But later, when the police interrogated the women and the driver, he stood behind the door and listened. He had once stayed up all night with the woman at an arepa stand, talking about their families; a few years earlier they had embraced for too long during a dance. She said in the interrogation room as an excuse: "They were paying us dollars."

Same as us. But no, we weren't the same. We were doing good, of course.

Marco spent hours in his darkroom after our shifts, his face locked in concentration inches away from the slick papers bathing in chemicals. He wanted the images to be perfect like they were in his head. But every time he pulled the photo out, the light was different or overdeveloped; the children he'd photographed kicking a ball in the street were flat and without shadow, like he had flashes coming at them from all sides. His many sisters begged him to come out and eat something.

At the clubs where Héctor danced, the women he knew started disappearing, the bright flashing lights strobing empty spaces. At first their friends wouldn't tell him where they'd gone. "Narco Héctor," they called him, mocking now. Finally, one who kissed him on the dance floor confessed. Their fathers' farmlands were all dying from NAFTA prices or engineered seed, and the narcos needed more mules. "The Americans want more," she said. "And you keep confiscating. Their appetites are inexhaustible."

Half a year after we first got the truck, American inspectors in black jeeps arrived at our little hangar. Chávez rode in another car behind them. They pounded on the garage door. They all had clipboards. "Get out," they yelled.

When Estela, looking like she'd just woken up, lifted the door, two men in hazmat suits ran scanners and miniature satellite dishes over the arm of the truck. Their scanners beeped rapidly.

"What's going on?" we said.

"Be patient," said an inspector. "The experts are working."

Héctor reached with his long arms and grabbed the clipboard out of the American inspector's hands. "Lee-ahk ciento por ciento," he tried to read in English.

"What's leaking?" asked Jesús.

"We thought this might be the case," said the inspector, apparently satisfied. "Radiation. The source isn't closing properly. Software glitch."

Jesús went pale; he imagined his daughter growing up without a father, or his skin melting off until she couldn't recognize him.

"Tell me what this means," said Estela, leading the inspector away from Jesús.

We couldn't hear what they were saying, but suddenly we had images in our heads of humans with three heads, of girls sprouting reptilian skin, of people's necks with thyroid glands as big as grapefruits.

"Go home," the inspector said. "Pack your bags. You will all need to be checked by the specialists. You were exposed to as much radiation as people on the outskirts of Hiroshima."

We looked at each other. Dark images of Marco hovered around the inspector. Héctor's arms dragged almost to the floor.

Chávez asked, "How did this happen?"

"You'll have to speak to our superiors," said the inspector.

"I'll do that," Chávez said, jamming his fingers into the inspector's chest. He left black oil fingerprints on the inspector's shirt. "Take the men," he said. "I'll keep the truck and the source."

They flew us to London without our families, to what they called neutral territory. We barely got the chance to look up at the iron sky before being ushered into a hospital. They took samples out of our bodies. They spun magnets around us in MRIs, but stopped when it made Estela scream. They measured Héctor's arms, which had grown so long they would drag behind him on the floor when he walked; he took to folding them up like wings and holding them to his chest. He hugged himself in the London cold, his hands in his armpits. Jesús, the doctors informed us, had grown a second heart on the right side of his chest, and both were incredibly strong. You could see his chest lifting in alternation, like fists boxing inside him. Marco's afterimages lingered longer, and the copies of him started playing tricks on the doctors, pulling pens out of their pockets when they weren't looking, writing funny and nonsensical things in Spanish on their charts. Marco found that if he concentrated hard enough, he could control them, and they would cluster around him in a dark crowd. Estela could make everyone dream her dreams. She dreamed of a road with lanes marked off in lines of white. Dashes of white, which grew into little blocks of bread that shoved themselves down our throats and drowned us. She dreamed of a green sea, at the bottom of which lay doctors and news commentators from Globovisión judging us on our perfect pirouettes as we struggled to the ocean floor. We dreamed that all the white in the hospital was the mantle of a woman who invited us into her nose and down her throat until she choked.

At first it was just the four of us that Estela could make

dream her dreams, but eventually it was the doctors, and then the whole hospital was caught in a collective nightmare.

"Will we die?" we asked the doctors.

"Let's focus, most importantly," they said, "on stopping all of this."

They put us in our own separate room in the hospital, our four skinny beds lining the gray wall. Quarantined. Otherwise, Marco would multiply among them; their dreams would no longer be their own.

Chávez called us at the hospital.

"You are nothing," he said. "Remember that. You must be martyrs. If you die, we can start a war with this gift of the Americans. I will give your families millions. You will become national heroes."

"Millions?" Marco said, wise to the illusion of multiplying zeros. "Of bolivars? Tomorrow they will be worth nothing."

"Dollars," Chávez said.

Estela said, "President-Dictator, what is your most secret dream?"

Chávez got quiet; we could hear him harrumph on the phone. We saw inside of him a ravenous worm, slimy and cold.

He hung up. We were all in awe of Estela's power. She had discovered she could pull the dreams out of people's heads even from thousands of miles away.

They had to move Héctor out into the hall. His arms at this point were the length of the whole hospital. The doctors gave him antigrowth hormones. They tried breaking his arms. They tried deadening the nerves so the arms would shrivel, but none of these things worked.

"Your options," they said, "are dwindling. We could try amputating. It would mean living without arms, but what else is there?"

The doctors were so focused on us as things to fix, problems to study. We were made from American mistakes and our own desires. We were different and therefore something to be feared. "I'll keep my arms," Héctor insisted.

Jesús's two hearts were tearing him apart. When he tried to walk straight, you could see their struggle. He jerked one way, then the other, with every step. Forget about running, when both hearts would beat so rapidly that it looked as if he were having a seizure on the treadmill. When the doctors discovered this, they made him run longer and faster and harder, fascinated by his malady. A third heart started to grow in the pit of his stomach.

Estela could no longer tell the difference between dream and reality. She said to Jesús, "You spoke to your daughter yesterday, and she asked you if you were a hero."

Jesús shook his head. His hearts jumped furiously. "You dreamed that," he said. "My wife called me to ask for a divorce."

Marco was divided by his multitudinous self. Everything you asked him, he would give you a thousand answers. You would call him by his name—"Marco!"—and around the hospital you would hear a chorus of a thousand yell, "Polo!" And somewhere, the real Marco, who was as dim as his other images now, would say, "There is no Marco."

One night, while we were all dreaming Estela's dreams, the doctors wrapped their heads in lead and tinfoil to escape her and snuck into Héctor's hallway. They amputated his arms. We dreamed of Héctor's pain, of tearing off the wings of a dragonfly. They shipped the amputated appendages to Switzerland, CERN's mile-long tunnels, and were busy bombarding them with atoms to figure out the load those arms could take, to test the weight of atoms they could bear. But when we woke up in the morning, his arms had grown back.

Were we heroes? We were super. We were more than we used to be. Who were we meant to save?

We told the doctors we wanted to go. "It's clear," we said, "that you can't help us. Send us back to our country."

But they said there were more tests, there was always hope, there were political ramifications to think of. Estela dreamed the truth: they were afraid of us.

In the comics we'd read as kids, people like us smashed out of prisons. One night, we hid in Héctor's giant fists as he popped the walls out with a punch, and we dragged him out behind us. The alarms blared. Finally we had escaped, a few Marcos left behind in the struggle.

We chartered a boat from a Venezuelan on the London docks by telling him we were out to assassinate Chávez. "Con suerte," he said, and loaded us into the biggest ship he had. He didn't even charge us.

Back in Venezuela, we hid in the caves of Pico Bolívar. Chávez was after us. He dreamed he was a mule for a bag of money and we pulled it out of his throat by a string, and that as soon as we did that, his presidential palace crumbled. We told Estela to stop tormenting him; we didn't want to endanger our families.

We dreamed the same things; we spoke the same fear and secrets. We were no longer Héctor and Marco and Estela and Jesús. We were a unit, waiting in those mountains. Marco multiplied, all of us fortified in the shadows, getting ready.

Héctor's arms grew as long as a village. The rest of us could hide, but those arms were impossible. In the mountains, the people who saw the fleshy line of Héctor's arm followed it back to its origin. Even though some loved Chávez, they loved us more. We could tell them the secrets within them. We could reach across villages and bring them news of those who had left. When buildings were toppling in mudslides down the mountain, Marco lined up a hundred of his selves as sandbags, Héctor's arms functioned as a crane, and Jesús, with his many hearts pumping his legs, ran marathons pulling children out of the collapsing buildings. "National heroes," people called us. More and more people came to visit our cave on a pilgrimage. We heard whispers in people's dreams of the Radioactive Four.

We wanted to kill Chávez, who had started by wanting to alleviate suffering but now only dreamed of power, but we knew he was just the tail of the lizard. We knew he would send out soldiers with machine guns to search the jungles and mountains. But most of all, Chávez was afraid of martyring us. So he couldn't kill us, but he could steal everything most precious to us.

One night, the drivers of one of the cargo trucks we'd scanned snuck into our cave and tranquilized us. Chávez and his second-in-command cut off Héctor's arms with a blunt machete. They carved Jesús's third heart out of him and sewed him back up. They stole the original Marco away but left his army of afterimages.

When we woke up, it was almost like nothing had changed. Héctor's arms had grown back. We could see Marcos everywhere around us. "I didn't even want that third heart," said Jesús.

"But I did," said Estela, weeping in the dark of the cave. "It was the one that dreamed."

And then Jesús's cell phone rang. It was his wife, a voice he hadn't heard in months, telling him that his daughter had been disappeared.

"Mi amor," he said, his voice rasping, his remaining hearts pounding.

We heard that Chávez had sent our treasures to the United States as a threat of war. The bloody stumps of Héctor's arms, the original Marco raging in one of Héctor's tightly closed fists, Jesús's daughter asleep in the other, a tiny heart strung around her neck. Then we heard they were being kept in a vault in Texas.

The villagers that visited brought us news and wept with us. Chávez was on the brink of violence. And despite everything, the Americans were now using the same scanner trucks on the streets of New York City. This time, they weren't just scanning vehicles; they were pointing their rays at people on the street who looked suspicious, which meant people that looked like us or darker. "They might be anywhere," the American commentators said, "those radioactives. They can multiply. They're coming for our jobs."

We laughed. Those jobs, those little dinky things? "Chamos," we said, "we want what has been taken from us and no less."

So we began our march toward the border between the United States and Mexico. Héctor swung us over rivers and borders, over crops of coca, poppy, and corn, over roads that channeled drug runners south to north. Millions of ghosts, people who had been disappeared over politics enabled by American guns, followed us. Bands of women walked next to us but always stayed out of the reach of Héctor's arms. Farmers who had lost their farms after NAFTA put them out of business joined our procession. They were going to pick fruit across the border at the farms that had stolen their trade. We could see the pattern, the gifts that had reduced us to begging for scraps.

"Who are you trying to save?" they asked.

We shook our heads. "We want what has been stolen from us, no less," we repeated.

We followed the coyotes' trail across the desert, the dust littered with bodies of those who had not made it across. The Rio Grande glittered in front of us, both shores of which used to belong to Mexico. Across the border of the Rio Grande, we saw a wall had been erected on the stolen land, snipers at every turret.

But Héctor's arms could reach across any border. They spread out in front of us like an advance guard of cavalry, his forearms and biceps shielding us. They approached as if on tiptoe, giant fingers walking them forward so Héctor would not have to hold them up. Jesús, our navigator, swayed from side to side as his chest leapt and yanked one way and then another, one a compass to the riches we were soon to rob back, the other pulling him home.

We were an army thousands strong, shadows that multiplied when you looked away. We knew that soon, other radioactives would be joining our march from the other side, made super by the scanning trucks on the Americans' own streets. And we said, "Venímos. We are coming for what has always been ours, we will storm a wall that will never be high enough, and you will dream our dreams, too." Estela, who knew how beautiful all our dreams were, would be, chanted to lull the snipers to sleep: "Do not be afraid—we are reborn from your own gift. We are not monsters. We are heroes."

Acknowledgments

I am bursting with gratitude for the wonderful people who gave this book flight. All my thanks to three brilliant women: Margaux Weisman, a superhero who saw the core of every story with X-ray vision and has electrified these stories; Michelle Brower, who believed in the stories and my voice and fought for them; and Danya Kukafka, who gave me insightful feedback.

To my mentors: Michael Griffith, who taught me about risk-taking; Leah Stewart, who taught me about plot and genre; Adrienne Harun, who taught me about piercing the veil of the magical; Chris Bachelder, who took each story on its own terms; Julianna Baggott, who taught me to value process; Mark Winegardner, who taught me so much about structure in stories; Robert Olen Butler, who taught me about character; Virgil Suárez, who championed Latinx writing in all its forms; Jennine Capo-Crucet, who taught me about theme; and Bob Shacochis and Diane Roberts, whose lessons on telling the essential truth in nonfiction translated perfectly to fiction. And my first writing teachers: Junot Díaz, Marilyn Sides, Margaret Cezair-Thompson, who encouraged me when I was just an overeager and stubborn piojita. To my teachers who pushed me to think harder: Jennifer Glaser, Phillip Tsang, Lynn Turbak, Takis Metaxas, Lisa Rodensky, Mark Goldman, Kenneth Winkler, Adrien Piper,

Scott Anderson. Without you all, I never would have been able to get it together.

To the editors who championed my stories for their magazines: Emily Nemens, Sy Safranski, Ann VanderMeer, Elizabeth Taylor, Stephen Corey, Jenny Gropp, John Joseph Adams, David Lynn, Caitlin Horrocks, Beth Staples, Celia Johnson, Michael Koch, Kim Winterheimer, Sadye Teiser, Jedediah Berry, Emily Louise Smith, Anna Lena Phillips Bell, Ann Hood, Carmen Johnson, Atom Atkinson, Sara Eliza Johnson, Claire Wahmanholm, Jodee Stanley, Phong Nguyen, Jonathan Freedman, Laura Furman, and Maggie Su; and to everyone else at *The Georgia Review*, *The Southern Review*, *Kenyon Review Online*, *The Masters Review*, *The Chicago Tribune Printers Row Journal*, *The Sun*, Tor.com, *Epoch*, *Ecotone*, *Hunger Mountain*, *Slice*, *Ninth Letter*, *Quarterly West*, and *Day One* who helped bring my stories into the world. Also, to Adeena Reitberger at *American Short Fiction* and Adina Talve-Goodman at *One Story*, who sent the most encouraging messages about these stories.

To my workshop classmates at the University of Cincinnati, Florida State University, and Sewanee that saw these stories, grappled with them, cheered them even in their malformed, first-draft shapes, especially: Katie Knoll, Dan Paul, Gwen Kirby, Julialicia Case, Bess Winter, Woody Skinner, A'dora Phillips, Eric Van Hoose, Molly Reid, Ryan Smith, Dario Sulzman, Marian Crotty, Jake Wolff, Katie Cortese, Laura Smith, John Wang, Michael Yoon, Kent Wascom, Leslee Chan, Sophie Rosenblum, Lisa Nikolidakis, Lindsey Drager, Rita Bullwinkel, Raul Palmas, Samuel Snoek-Brown, Jason Skipper, Kelly Luce, and Jesse Goolsby. To everyone else there who supported my writing: Misha Rai, Emily Rose Cole, Ondrej Pazdirek, Dustin Atkinson, Anna Claire Hodge, Jill Koopman, David Moody, John Beardsley,

Melinda Wilson, Lindsay Sproul, Dyan Neary, Anne Valente, Rochelle Hurt, Nicole Dennis-Benn, Mikayla Ávila Vilá, Brandi George, Michael Barach, Joy Allen, Sujata Shekar, Liz Ziemska, Kristina Gorcheva-Newberry, Renée Zuckerbrot, and R. L. Maizes.

Several grants and awards have supported the writing of this book, including the US Student Fulbright Grant to the Dominican Republic, a year during which I wrote several of these stories, the Taft Travel Fellowship from the University of Cincinnati, two fellowships from the Vermont Studio Center, a Sangam House residency, and a fellowship to the Sewanee Writers Conference. To Erika Martinez, for all her help with applying to the Fulbright. And to the people who made those long months away feel like being refueled with light, especially V. V. Ganeshananthan, Josh Aiken, Katie Hayes, Jennifer Thorpe, Mo Davies, Ilana Masad, Sonya Larson, Judith Hertog, Chekwube Danladi, Danielle Harms, Sarah Stolar, Caylin Capra-Thomas, Amina Gautier, Giles Hazelgrove, Hubert Giraud, Arshia Sattar, Bom Kim, Saubhik De Sarkar, and Zahid Rafiq.

To Tracy Wisneski, who taught me about truth and writing at an early age, and Lisa Lawson, Christian Sandoval, Samuel Harr, Kayce Morton, Nick Lucero (and Alia, Ginger, and Ron), Celisse Arcuri, Joanie Williams, N. Bryant Kirkland, and John "Jack" Bryan Jr., who encouraged me more than they might have realized.

To my Wellesley siblings who were there for me during all my vacillations, especially Erin Krizay, Jessica Urban, Jessica Milan, Courtney Klaips, Emily Y. Wu, Molly Trezise-Martin, Liz McEnulty, Mala Sarkar, Gowun Kim Koh, Mfoniso Udofia, Ashley Lauren Ortiz, Joy Wu, Justina Wang, Emily Siedell, Chiara Georgiadis, Michelle Iandoli, Nicole Kwoh, Sarah Crichton, Nooshin Hosseini, Erin Usmen, and Sarah

Hope Lincoln. And to my friends in Beta, you know who you are.

To my University of Central Florida community not already mentioned: Jamie Poissant, Terry Ann Thaxton, Chrissy Kolaya, Farrah Cato, Laurie Uttich, Cecilia Milanés, and all my students who make a life teaching and thinking about writing worth it.

To my family: Esteban Peynado, Celia Peynado, Bianca Peynado, Daniel Peynado, Sonia Sanchez, Miguelina Sanchez, Rachel Cordero, and Josefina Peynado. I learned how to tell stories from listening to you. For teaching me to be strongheaded. To all of the Peynado, Cott, Sanchez, Cordero, Fernandez, Leschhörn, and Bonnelly clans, who gave me adventures to write about and tolerated me reading books and writing notes during them.

Most importantly, to Micah Dean Hicks, my first reader, whose enthusiasm, creativity, and challenges keep the fire burning even during the darkest days. Without you, I would not have even begun so many of these stories.

And to so many more who were not named here who paved the way.